BLACKSTONE AND THE BALLOON OF DEATH

Recent Titles by Sally Spencer from Severn House

THE BUTCHER BEYOND
THE DARK LADY
DEAD ON CUE
DEATH OF A CAVE DWELLER
DEATH OF AN INNOCENT
A DEATH LEFT HANGING
DYING IN THE DARK
THE ENEMY WITHIN
GOLDEN MILE TO MURDER
A LONG TIME DEAD
MURDER AT SWANN'S LAKE
THE PARADISE JOB
THE RED HERRING
THE SALTON KILLINGS
STONE KILLER
THE WITCH MAKER

Writing as Alan Rustage

RENDEZVOUS WITH DEATH
BLACKSTONE AND THE TIGER
BLACKSTONE AND THE GOLDEN EGG
BLACKSTONE AND THE FIRE BUG

BLACKSTONE AND THE BALLOON OF DEATH

Sally Spencer

writing as

Alan Rustage

severn House

This first world edition published in Great Britain 2006 by
SEVERN HOUSE PUBLISHERS LTD of
9–15 High Street, Sutton, Surrey SM1 1DF.
This first world edition published in the USA 2006 by
SEVERN HOUSE PUBLISHERS INC of
595 Madison Avenue, New York, N.Y. 10022.

British Library Cataloguing in Publication Data

Rustage, Alan
   Blackstone and the balloon of death
   1.   Blackstone, Sam (Fictitious character) - Fiction
   2.   Police - England - London - Fiction
   3.   London (England) - Social life and customs - 19th century - Fiction
   4.   Detective and mystery stories
   I.   Title II. Spencer, Sally
   823.9'14 [F]

   ISBN-13: 978-0-7278-6405-5
   ISBN-10: 0-7278-6405-X

All Severn House titles are printed on acid-free paper.

Typeset by Palimpsest Book Production Ltd.,
Polmont, Stirlingshire, Scotland.
Printed and bound in Great Britain by
MPG Books Ltd., Bodmin, Cornwall.

For Barry and Brenda
Wonderful friends and dog-sitters *extraordinaires*

One

Lady Eustacia Wilton looked down at the letter she was holding in her trembling hands, and read through it once more.

There had been no mistake, the expression on her face said, when she raised her head: the news that the letter contained was truly as dreadful as she'd first taken it to be.

'We are completely ruined,' she moaned, looking out from the centre stage into the darkened auditorium.

'Ruined?' asked a voice at her side.

'Completely!' Lady Wilton answered.

She turned to face the other woman, but it was only a calculated half-turn, so that the audience did not lose sight of her handsome profile.

'Thanks to the ruthless machinations of Mr Septimus Pittstock,' she continued, 'the family estate will have to be sold—'

'But that is so terrible!'

'—your poor father will be imprisoned for the rest of his natural life, our faithful servants must be turned out on to the street, and you, my dear, darling Elizabeth – my pretty little angel of a daughter – will now never be able to marry the man of your dreams.'

'Oh, Mamma!' the girl sobbed. 'Is there *nothing* we can do to prevent this horrible disaster?'

Lady Wilton laid her hand gently on her daughter's shoulder. 'Nothing,' she said mournfully.

'Then I will kill myself,' the daughter said.

'You will do no such thing,' her mother told her severely. 'Our family has worn the name of Wilton as a badge of honour for five hundred years, and whatever the loathsome, lowly-born Pittstock may do to us, he will never crush our pride or our spirit.'

'You are right,' the girl replied. 'I forgot, for a moment, who I was, and I apologize for it.'

But Lady Wilton was no longer listening. Instead, she was gazing into the audience again, with a look of sudden inspiration on her face.

'There may yet be a way,' she said.

'A way, Mamma?'

'If I could reach Paris, and lay all the evidence in front of the Count de Balzac, then I am sure he would be able to devise a means of defeating this evil scheme which has been designed to destroy us.'

'But you *can't* get to Paris!' Elizabeth Wilton wailed, raising her hands to her face in despair. 'You know as well as I do that the vile Pittstock has his evil henchmen watching every railway station and every port in the land. They will be bound to stop you.'

'No, they will not,' the older woman said. 'Because I will use neither train nor ship for my journey.'

'Then how will you reach Paris?'

Lady Wilton threw back her head and laughed. 'I will travel by hot air balloon!' she said triumphantly.

The curtain descended. There was loud applause, but none of it came from Detective Inspector Sam Blackstone, who was seated in the gallery at the very back of the theatre. It was not that he refused to clap, merely that both his hands were busily engaged in loosening the maddeningly uncomfortable bow-tie which – along with the rest of his evening clothes – would need to be returned to the tailor he had rented it from some time the following morning.

Blackstone turned to speak to his companion for the evening, but she had already engaged herself in conversation with the woman who was sitting at the other side of her.

'Cor blimey, 'ooever would have fort that Mr Pittstock could be such a rum un?' Ellie Carr was asking.

The other woman, who – judging by her dress – was probably the wife of a moderately successful city clerk, looked distinctly unimpressed by Ellie's familiar and unwelcome approach.

'I'm afraid I simply couldn't comment on that,' she replied, in what was obviously an *acquired* drawl.

2

'Couldn't comment?' Ellie repeated, amazed. 'Could not comment? Well, *I* could comment, all right. It quite set me 'eart aflutter, the way 'e was carryin' on – an' if I wasn't spittin' fevvers, I don't know where I'd find the strenf to get meself to the bar.'

'Do please excuse me,' the other woman said, standing up and hurriedly edging her way towards the aisle.

'You really shouldn't do that kind of thing, you know,' Blackstone told his companion.

'What kind of thing?' Ellie Carr asked innocently.

'Come over all cockney, just because you know that it will embarrass a certain kind of person.'

'But I *am* a cockney, Sam, born and bred,' Ellie argued. 'And if women like her judge other people solely by the way they speak, then they *deserve* to be embarrassed.'

A faint smile appeared on Blackstone's lips. 'So that whole pantomime had no other purpose than to teach the woman a lesson in humility and tolerance?' he asked.

'Exactly. Clever of you to have spotted that.'

Blackstone's smiled broadened. 'And you got no personal pleasure out of it at all?'

Ellie grinned. 'Give me a break, guv, for Gawd's sake,' she said, reverting to her cockney persona. 'When a girl's been cuttin' up dead bodies all the livelong day, like wot I 'ave, she's entitled to 'ave her bit of fun of an evenin'. An' I was bein' honest about one fing to that corseted harridan.'

'And what was that?'

'I really *am* spittin' fevvers!'

'Well, if that's the case, I suppose I'd better buy you a drink, hadn't I, Dr Carr?' Blackstone asked.

'That's right, guv,' Ellie agreed. 'You better 'ad.'

The bar of the George Theatre was large enough to accommodate the great mass of people who habitually flooded into it during the interval, but not quite so vast that it was in any danger of being confused with a bar that might be found in one of the much less reputable music halls. Blackstone found it a pleasant enough place to be in, but couldn't help wishing that, like the music halls, it served its beer in man-sized glasses, instead of in thimbles which would scarcely get a leprechaun drunk.

3

'This is your first visit to the theatre, isn't it?' Ellie Carr asked, when they'd found a table and sat down.

'That's right,' Blackstone agreed.

But it was far from being *her* first visit, he reminded himself. Ellie, when she chose to do so, could move in circles as far above his own as his own was above those of a coster-monger.

'And what do you think of the play?' she asked.

He didn't know what to answer her, especially since the whole expedition had been her treat.

'I like it well enough,' he said, cautiously.

'You're being evasive, Sam!' Ellie said, with a warning note in her voice. 'Now tell me what you really think.'

'It's not very much like real life, is it?' Blackstone asked.

'Not like the real life you'll see on the streets of the East End, no,' Ellie admitted.

'Not like the real life you'll see in the homes of the aristocracy, either.'

'Oh, the homes of the aristocracy!' Ellie repeated. 'Pardon me for missing that point, Sam.'

'You're pardoned,' Blackstone told her.

'But, you see, I never realized you rubbed shoulders with the cream of society,' Ellie added mischievously.

'I don't,' Blackstone said. 'I'm not the sort of bloke they'd ever invite to go riding in St James's Park with them – but I *have* investigated a few of the buggers in my time.'

And once or twice, when they've been *really* important people I've investigated, it's almost cost me my job, he added mentally.

'Was there anything else about the play, apart from its unreality, that you don't like?' Ellie wondered.

'The sensationalist effects,' Blackstone said.

'Are you referring to the train crash?'

'For a start.'

The crash in question had occurred in the second act. The train had not been a full-sized steam engine, of course, but it had been large enough to fill the very large stage and had come off its rails convincingly enough to make the audience shrink back in its seats.

'What was wrong with the crash?' Ellie asked. 'Didn't you think it was well done?'

'I think it was *very* well done – but I don't see the need for it to have been done at all.'

Ellie gave him a searching glance, as if she were suddenly seeing a new side of him. 'Explain yourself,' she said.

'It was very dramatic, but it didn't do much to help the story along. I think the only reason they staged it was just because they could – because it was *technically* possible.'

Ellie laughed. 'You're quite right, of course.'

'I am?' Blackstone asked, surprised.

'You most certainly are. They *were* just showing off with that train crash. And it's a terrible play – all fur coat and no bloomers. Even those critics who normally have their noses so far up Sebastian George's backside that they haven't seen the light of day for years have been pushed to say anything good about it. And word's getting around. There's nearly a full house tonight, but I've heard that advanced bookings for next month are very slow.'

'So why did you bring me to see the play if it's so terrible?' Blackstone asked suspiciously. 'Was it some kind of test?'

'A test?' Ellie repeated, innocently.

'To see what I'm made of.'

'What you're made of?' Ellie said, and now there was no doubt that she was stalling.

'Were you trying to discover whether or not my fairly rough *exterior* was no more than a disguise to mask my very rough *interior*?' Blackstone asked.

Ellie laughed. 'That's rather good, you know,' she said. 'Almost epigrammatic.'

'Maybe,' Blackstone agreed. 'But is it true?'

'Not really.'

'No?'

'Well, perhaps a *little*.'

'And what conclusion have you reached?'

'That I'll never be able to turn you into a gentleman—'

'I don't want—'

'—which is something of a relief, because there are far too many so-called "gentlemen" in the world already. On the other hand, there are indications that if I work hard at it – and you don't resist me too much – I just might be able to broaden your horizons.'

He wasn't sure that he *wanted* his horizons broadened. More importantly, he wasn't sure that – even if they *had* both dragged themselves up by their own bootstraps from the slums of the East End – there was any future in this relationship between a Scotland Yard Inspector who owned little more than two second-hand suits, and a medical researcher at University College Hospital who had published her findings in learned journals.

'I'm nobody's case study . . .' he began.

'Of course you are,' Ellie interrupted him. 'We're all *somebody's* case study, whether we like it or not.'

She disconcerted him, he thought. She had a way of making him feel like a boxer who had just been knocked to the canvas – a way of jabbing at him with apparently outrageous ideas which, once they hit home, were near enough to the truth to make him groggy.

He was still mentally climbing to his feet – and searching for a knockout punch of his own – when a ringing sound announced that the next act was about to start.

Well, he consoled himself, he wouldn't be the first fighter who had been saved by the bell.

The curtain rose for the first scene of the final act. The previous backcloth – of Lady Wilton's drawing room in Park Lane – had been replaced by one which depicted Hampstead Heath on a dark and stormy morning.

A clump of bushes had been placed at one end of the stage, and a circus tent – miniaturized to make it seem as if it were much further in the background than it actually was – at the other. The centre stage was dominated by a large hot air balloon, and in its basket stood Lady Wilton.

'I wonder how she managed to get a license for that balloon without the evil and ubiquitous Pittstock finding out about it,' Blackstone thought fancifully. 'I wonder how she intends to launch the balloon on her own, and if she's checked the wind direction.'

And he wondered whether, if he repeated these comments to Ellie, she would find him incredibly witty – or merely incredibly dull.

Pittstock appeared from behind the fake bushes at the edge of the stage. Lady Wilton saw him, and threw the anchor out of the basket. And almost immediately – and certainly improbably – the hot air balloon began to rise.

The villain sprinted across the stage. By the time he reached the balloon, it had already risen several feet above the ground. Pittstock took a flying leap, and just managed to gain a hold on the top edge of the basket.

The audience gasped!

The balloon continued its ascent, and – to further gasps from the audience – carried the dangling Pittstock with it.

Blackstone, as bored by the faked action as only a man who has seen real action can be, switched his attention to the other parts of the stage. The tent and bushes both looked smaller now – not because they had actually shrunk in size, but because they were no longer quite as elevated as they had been.

Or to put it another way, Blackstone thought, they were being slowly lowered down below stage level, to create the illusion that the balloon had climbed even higher than it had.

Which was clever – but ultimately pointless.

The bottom of the basket was at least twelve feet from the stage floor now, but still the villainous Pittstock was hanging on.

'You thought you could escape me, Lady Wilton,' he roared, 'but you will *never* escape! In a moment, I will join you in that basket—'

No, you won't – not if you keep wasting the energy that you'll need to pull yourself up on making threats, Blackstone thought.

'—and then your fate will be sealed!'

'I am not the feeble woman you take me to be!' Lady Wilton told the dangling man. 'And though I am loath to take the life of another, yet I must do what I can to protect my own life, and the lives of my family, friends and servants.'

And Uncle Tom Cobbley and all, Blackstone added silently.

Lady Wilton reached into her handbag and took out a leather sheath. She allowed the audience a second to ponder on what it might contain, then produced a large and menacing dagger.

'With this knife, I will have my revenge for the evil you have visited on me!' she announced.

She swung the dagger in a wide, dramatic arc, and struck Pittstock in the neck. The villain slowly released his grip on the basket, and plummeted down to the stage.

The people in the audience gasped yet again. They all knew

7

it was faked, of course, but the fakery had been carried out with a flair and magnificence which had quite taken their breaths away.

It was only when Lady Wilton looked down at the body of her fallen foe, and began to scream uncontrollably, that they even started to suspect that perhaps it hadn't been faked at all.

Two

Even without the screams coming from the woman in the basket, the stage hands and actors who were watching the production would have known that something had gone seriously wrong the moment that William Kirkpatrick – 'the *great* William Kirkpatrick', as the theatre posters rashly proclaimed him – fell.

At every other performance of the play, he had milked the moments preceding the fall for all they were worth, never relinquishing his grip until he had first squirmed for some time like an electrified tadpole and wailed as a banshee might in the middle of a nervous collapse. This time, however, he hadn't put on much of a show at all. This time, he'd simply let go.

He'd landed badly, too, missing the cushioned matting completely, and hitting the hard wooden stage with a sickening thud.

It was at this point that Sebastian George – who always liked to watch the special effects which it had cost him so much money to create – signalled that the curtain should be lowered immediately.

Dominic Smedley, the stage manager, appeared from the wings, and bent over the fallen man. As if this were their cue, several other members of the company began to gather around, too.

'What are you all doing?' Sebastian George bellowed. 'We're in the middle of a play here. Get back to your positions, immediately, so that we can proceed with the next scene.'

Heads turned in his direction. Eyes looked at him, accusing him of callousness.

'This is the *theatre*,' George continued, still talking loudly, but now with a hint of defensiveness in his tone. 'We have traditions by which we all live, and one of the most hallowed of those traditions is that whatever else happens, the show must always go on.'

'But Mr Kirkpatrick's sick,' Dominic Smedley told him.

'I'm not a fool – I can see that for myself,' Sebastian George said exasperatedly. 'But I'm not asking him to act on through the pain, am I? Fortunately, he's already delivered his last line, so why not take the poor fellow back to his dressing room, where he can get some rest?'

'It wouldn't be a good idea to move him,' Smedley said. 'He's *very* sick indeed. Truth is, I think he's dying.'

Sebastian George shook his head in resigned frustration.

He'd have to give way, he told himself, because as loath as he was to abandon the performance, he could quite see that the body of dying man – lying in the centre of the stage – might well inhibit the feelings of *joie de vivre* which the closing scenes of the play were supposed to convey.

The curtain was pulled back slightly at the edge of the stage, and through the gap stepped a short man wearing a flamboyantly colourful frock coat.

'For those few of you who may not recognize me, I am Sebastian George, the owner and manager of this theatre,' he announced, 'and, in that capacity, it is my unpleasant duty to inform you that the remainder of this evening's performance has regrettably been cancelled.'

Several members of the audience booed, but Sebastian George chose to ignore them.

'I must therefore ask you to leave the auditorium in a quiet, orderly manner,' the impresario continued.

'We paid good money to see this show!' a man called out from the centre of the stalls.

'And you have received excellent value in recompense for it,' Sebastian George snapped back. 'There is not a single production that I can think of, anywhere else in the West End, which comes close to this one for . . .' He pulled himself up short. 'If you are prepared to leave your names and addresses at the theatre box office, I will personally ensure that you are given complimentary tickets for some future performance.'

'And what if we don't *want* to see another performance?' some troublemaker in the stalls asked.

'In that case . . .' the impresario visibly gulped, ' . . . in that case, I am prepared to refund the price of your tickets, which, given that you have already seen most of the play, is more than generous.'

'What happened to Pittstock?' a third member of the audience wanted to know.

'There is no Pittstock. There is only Mr *Kirkpatrick,* and he has been taken ill.'

'Taken ill?' the wag responded. 'I'll say he has! Looked to me like he was suffering from a serious case of *being dead.*'

'So what's the good of free tickets if the leading actor's dead?' a fourth voice demanded.

'Mr Kirkpatrick was no more than a *secondary* lead,' Sebastian George corrected the heckler. 'And, in any case, the production is much greater than the sum of its parts. But that is neither here nor there. The performance is over for the evening, and the sooner you leave your names at the box office, the sooner you will be able to go home.'

The quicker-witted members of the audience were one step ahead of him, having already worked out that the sooner they reached the box office, the shorter the queue to leave their names. They had already risen to their feet as he was speaking, and soon everyone else was following their example.

No longer the centre of attention, Sebastian George suddenly seemed to remember that there was something else that he had meant to say to the audience – possibly much earlier.

'Is there, by any chance, a doctor in the house?' he asked his now-fleeing customers.

The bouncer, who'd been posted to keep the riff-raff away, looked with suspicion on the two people who were now about to mount the stage.

The man was very tall and very lean, with a nose which was almost a hook, a square jaw, and sharp, penetrating eyes. There was almost something of the Old Testament Prophet about him. He did not give the outward appearance of being a particularly 'hard' case, but the bouncer's instinct immediately told him that was exactly what the man was.

The woman was much shorter than her companion – she was maybe five feet one or five feet two – and several years younger. She had dark brown hair, a delicate nose, and a mouth which was already developing laughter lines. Her body was lean and hard, like the man's, but there was a pleasant swelling of her chest which the bouncer found most appealing.

As they reached the stage, the bouncer stepped forward to block their passage. 'Authorized persons only allowed beyond this point,' he said.

'Your boss just asked for a doctor,' the woman said.

'And are you telling me *he's* a doctor?' the bouncer asked sceptically, noting that though the tall, thin man was wearing an evening suit, he certainly didn't look very at home in it.

'Of course he's not a doctor,' Ellie said. 'He'd be about as much use in an operating theatre as a eunuch would be in a knocking shop.'

'Come again?' the bouncer said.

'*I'm* the doctor,' Ellie explained.

'Then who's he?'

'He's somebody else you might need if, as seems likely, there's been a crime committed,' Ellie said.

'Meaning what?'

'Meaning *he's* the Filth.'

Behind the curtain, nothing much was moving.

Actors and stage hands stood in a frozen tableau, not looking at each other – and certainly not looking at the man who had fallen to the stage.

Sebastian George, having positioned himself somewhat apart from the rest of his company, was puffing away energetically on a huge cigar, but otherwise showed no sign of life.

The woman in the balloon had stopped screaming, and was now quietly sobbing to herself.

Ellie Carr strode quickly across the stage, and knelt down beside William Kirkpatrick.

'I need two bowls of water,' she said to the stage manager, after she had taken a quick look at Kirkpatrick's face. 'One of them should be very hot, and the other very cold.'

11

'Will that do any good?' Dominic Smedley asked hopefully.

Ellie looked down at Kirkpatrick again. 'Probably not,' she said. 'But we might as well try it, don't you think?'

Kirkpatrick was in a pitiful state, Blackstone saw. His eyes were so wide open – either through fear or pain – that they seemed far too large for his face. His skin was turning purple, and his tongue had begun to swell up.

'Can you speak?' Ellie asked.

A hideous gurgling sound came from Kirkpatrick's throat, and then he fell silent.

Ellie placed her finger gently against the pulse in his neck, then shook her head.

'If you're going to conduct a murder investigation, you might as well start it right now,' she told Blackstone, 'because there's absolutely nothing more that you can do here.'

'*Is* it murder?' Blackstone asked.

Ellie shrugged. 'A man's been stabbed – there's clear evidence of a knife-wound on his neck – and now he's dead. Whether or not you call that murder is, I suppose, up to you.'

Blackstone crossed the stage to where Sebastian George was standing. George seemed to be so wrapped up in his own reveries that he didn't even notice the inspector's approach.

'I hate to bother you, but I thought you might like to know that your leading actor has just died,' Blackstone said, holding up his warrant card for the theatre manager to inspect.

George snapped back into life. 'William wasn't my leading actor,' he said. 'He was only—'

'The secondary lead,' Blackstone interrupted. 'I know. Anyway, he'll be giving his next performance on the celestial stage.'

'He'll be a very great loss to the theatrical profession,' George said unconvincingly.

'Not to mention to the poor bloody wife and children he left behind,' Blackstone said dryly.

'He had no family,' George replied. 'Like so many of us, he was married to his art.'

'Even if he *was* only the secondary lead?'

'A secondary lead is still a man of consequence,' George said. 'There are people who would kill to be in his position.'

12

'Funny you should say that,' Blackstone replied.

He turned to look at Ellie. She was watching a couple of the stage hands bring a trestle table on to the stage. She showed them where to place it, then pointed to the dead man. As the stage hands lifted the corpse on to the table, the woman in the balloon began to scream again.

'Don't you think it would be a good idea to get her down?' Blackstone asked Sebastian George.

'What?'

'The woman in the balloon? Don't you think it would be a good idea to get her down?'

George nodded.

'Why are you just standing there, you idiots!' he screamed angrily at the stage hands who had been assisting Ellie. 'Yes, it's you that I'm talking to! Are you incapable of doing *anything* without an explicit order from me? Do you need my permission before you can even think of going to the crapper and opening your bowels?'

The two men looked confused. 'Sorry, sir? I don't quite understand,' one of them said.

'Look at Miss Devaraux, you fool! She's still hovering above the stage like a wounded bloody seagull. Lower her down, for God's sake!'

There were four of them in the leading lady's dressing room. The leading lady herself, Charlotte Devaraux, sat on a padded stool in front of her make-up mirror – sobbing softly – while her dresser, a tiny woman called Madge, fussed and fretted over her. The other two present – Blackstone and Sebastian George – were both standing, George by the door and Blackstone a couple of feet away from the woman who he was intending to interrogate.

Charlotte Devaraux was much younger than the airborne character she had been playing, the inspector thought, but not quite as youthful as her publicity photographs would tend to suggest. Still, he was probably being unfair to judge her on her appearance at that moment. No woman looked her best when she'd just witnessed a murder – when, in fact, she'd committed it herself.

Blackstone coughed discreetly. 'If you don't mind, Miss Devaraux, I'd like you to tell me what happened,' he said.

13

'I don't *know* what happened,' Charlotte Devaraux said, between sobs. 'I just don't know.'

'But you are aware that you did *stab* Mr Kirkpatrick, aren't you?' Blackstone asked, gently.

'Yes, but I . . . but I . . .'

'What was *supposed* to happen? Was it merely your intention to make it *look* as if you'd done it?'

'No, I . . . I . . .'

'It wasn't a real knife,' Sebastian George interrupted.

'It looked real enough to me,' said Blackstone, who had retrieved the dagger from where Charlotte Devaraux had dropped it in the balloon basket. 'Felt real enough, for that matter.'

'The one you picked up – the one Charlotte used tonight – *was* real,' George said. 'But it's not the knife she *usually* uses.'

'How's the one that she usually uses any different to the one I found?' Blackstone wondered.

'It's a *trick* knife. At the push of a button, the blade immediately retracts into the handle. When she stabs William in the neck, it's only the haft of the knife which actually touches him. Then, when she's pulled the knife free, she touches a button again, and the blade reappears.'

'Wouldn't it have been much easier – and much *safer* – to use a rubber knife?' Blackstone asked.

'We are talking of the dramatic arts here!' George said scornfully. 'We are talking of the magic of the theatre! A rubber knife would never even begin to scale the heights of perfection that I demand from my productions.'

Heights of perfection! Blackstone repeated silently. What heights of perfection?

He was beginning to suspect that he and Sebastian George had seen two entirely different plays performed on the stage – but he wisely kept the observation to himself.

'Even with a trick knife, it seems a pretty dangerous stunt to try and pull off,' he said.

'Perhaps that might be true if the "stunt", as you choose to call it, were carried out by a rank amateur,' Sebastian George countered, 'but in the hands of a true professional, it is safe enough. And that is what Charlotte is – above all else – a true professional.'

'A true professional!' echoed Madge the dresser.

And the True Professional herself merely nodded, as if all this went without saying.

'Still, there's no disputing the fact that the poor bloke *is* dead,' Blackstone pointed out, in fairness.

'That is because someone substituted a real knife for the fake one,' George countered.

'And nobody noticed?'

'That would seem to be self-evident.'

'Not the props master? Not any other member of the cast? Not Miss Devaraux herself?'

'As far as I can tell, the real knife is an exact copy of the fake one,' George said. 'I'll wager it even weighs exactly the same.'

So someone – a person with easy access to the props – had gone to a great deal of trouble and expense to stage an extremely elaborate murder, the inspector thought.

Well, that certainly did seem to rule out the possibility of a crime of sudden passion, didn't it?

The body still lay on the trestle table, and Ellie Carr was bent over it, giving it a thorough examination.

Blackstone told Ellie about the trick knife, then took a closer look at the body himself.

'I would have expected there to have been much more blood around,' he said.

'And you wouldn't have been disappointed, if this had been a deep stab wound,' Ellie replied. 'Even if it hadn't been deep, but had just managed to pierce the jugular, there would have been a veritable fountain of blood. But neither of those things happened – which is only logical, when you think about it.'

'Is it?'

'Of course. Based on what you've just told me, I'm assuming Charlotte Devaraux believed that she'd be touching Kirkpatrick's neck with the haft of the knife. Is that correct?'

'Yes.'

'But she'd still have exercised restraint, wouldn't she?'

'Because the haft, even on its own, could do serious damage if it struck hard enough?'

'Exactly. So while she'll have been aiming at making it appear as if she were using considerable force, her true intention will have been to achieve the merest whisper of a touch. But even a whisper of a touch can cause damage if the knife is as sharp as that one was.' Ellie Carr stepped away from the table. 'See for yourself, Sam.'

Blackstone bent over the corpse. The knife had indeed penetrated the skin on the neck, and while it would have been an exaggeration to have described the result as a mere pin-prick, it didn't really look like a serious wound either.

'So what actually killed him?' Blackstone asked. 'The fall?'

'The fall *could easily* have killed him. You can die rolling off a park bench, if you're unlucky.'

'But you don't really think that's what caused death in this case?'

Ellie sighed theatrically – which was quite appropriate, given their surroundings.

'Why are you asking me that now, Sam?' she asked. 'You know that I hate to give a definite opinion on a stiff until I've slit him open and rummaged around in all the goo.'

'Why don't you give me a *provisional* opinion, then?' Blackstone suggested.

'Take another look at him,' Ellie said. 'You see how his facial muscles are contorted?'

'Yes. But so would mine have been if I'd been stabbed in the neck and then fallen twelve or fifteen feet on to a hard-wood floor.'

'No, they wouldn't,' Ellie said dismissively. 'At least, not quite in the way Kirkpatrick's are.'

'So what's the answer?' Blackstone asked, restraining his natural impatience, because experience had taught him that sort of approach simply didn't work with Ellie Carr.

'Whoever wanted Kirkpatrick dead would have known that the knife wound – if properly administered – wouldn't kill him, and that the fall probably wouldn't either,' Ellie explained. 'So, in order to ensure his success, he will have decided to bring a third element into the equation.'

'And that third element was what?'

'My guess would be that it's some kind of quick-acting poison, which could have been smeared on the tip of the knife. The knife then serves as a perfect delivery system, much like a poison arrow would. Once the poison had worked its way into Kirkpatrick's blood stream, he was finished.'

'But why go to such elaborate lengths to kill Kirkpatrick?' Blackstone wondered.

'I wouldn't know about that, Sam,' Ellie said.

'You don't sound like you care much either,' Blackstone commented.

'Why should I?' Ellie asked. 'You're the detective, and so you're naturally interested in the "why" of things – but I'm a pathologist, and the "how" of a death is infinitely more intriguing to me. Fair enough?'

Fair enough, Blackstone agreed. His question had been addressed more at himself than at Ellie, anyway, and as he began to stride up and down the stage, the questions which followed it were also more for his own consideration than for the good doctor's.

'If he wanted him dead, then surely it would have been easier to follow him down some dark alley and stab him to death,' the inspector mused. 'Or, if that solution was too messy for the killer's taste, why not simply slip some poison into Kirkpatrick's tea?'

Either of those would have done the trick, but the killer had rejected both options. And instead of making the murder a purely private affair – as most murderers would – he had deliberately arranged things so that when Kirkpatrick died, he would do so in front of a couple of thousand witnesses.

Three

Blackstone stood at the front of the stage, and looked down at the dozen or so uniformed constables – and two uniformed sergeants – who were looking back up at him expectantly.

So this was what it was like to be a performer, he thought. It was quite intoxicating, in its own little way.

As he clasped the lapels of his rented evening jacket between his thumbs and forefingers, he felt a sudden temptation come over him to say something at least vaguely Shakespearean.

Then, recognizing it was not a good idea, he resisted it, and when he did speak it was in his Scotland Yard voice.

'Your sergeants will divide you into two groups,' he announced. 'One group will talk to everyone connected with either the play, or with the theatre. I want all their names and addresses taken down, and I want to know if any of them noticed any unusual occurrences in the two hours which led up to the murder.' He paused for a moment. 'The second group will search the theatre, both front-of-house and back-stage – and I mean search *every square inch* of it – for clues. Are there any questions so far?'

The two sergeants exchanged quick glances, and then one of the raised his hand.

'Yes?' Blackstone said.

'What clues will you want us to be looking for, exactly, sir?' the sergeant wondered.

'It would be rather pleasing if you could come up with a bloody big knife with a retractable blade,' Blackstone told him.

The sergeant nodded. 'Right, sir.'

'And it would be even more pleasing if the bloody big knife you found had a clear set of fingerprints on it,' Blackstone continued. 'Failing that, I'd like to see anything you discover that you think has no place in a theatre – or *does* have it's place in a theatre, but isn't in that place.'

Or to put it another way, he thought to himself, I'm buggered if I know *what* we're looking for!

As the uniformed officers set about their work with a slightly mystified enthusiasm, Blackstone found himself wondering where his invaluable assistant, Sergeant Patterson, was.

If there was one place Patterson *wouldn't* be, he reflected, it was in one of his favourite chop houses.

Not now.

Not since THE EDICT.

It was Patterson's fiancée, Rose, who had brought about the change in the sergeant's usual way of life, when she had informed him that though he might get away with describing himself as 'pleasantly plump' while they were still only walking out together, she did not want to be engaged to a man who others might perceive as bordering on being fat.

As a consequence of all this, a diet sheet had been drawn up, and handed down – by Rose, to Patterson – with much the same gravity and sense of purpose as God must have displayed when handing the Ten Commandments to Moses. And since he would rather face down half a dozen East End cut-throats than admit to Rose that he had fallen off the wagon – and under the wheels of the gravy train – Patterson had been following the diet with rigour, though not without pain.

'Is there anything I can do to hurry this whole awkward business along?' asked a voice to Blackstone's left.

Now that was a novel way to describe a murder, the inspector thought – a whole awkward business!

He turned to look at the man who addressed him. Sebastian George was standing not more than a couple of yards from the trestle table on which the body that had started the 'whole awkward business' still lay, and was puffing on the largest cigar Blackstone had ever seen.

'No, I'm afraid there isn't anything that you can do, Mr George,' Blackstone said.

'But surely, since, after all, this is my show . . .'

'It stopped being *your* show when Mr Kirkpatrick got himself killed,' Blackstone told the impresario. 'Now, in case you haven't noticed, it's very definitely *my* show.'

'I'm not sure I care for your attitude, Inspector,' Sebastian George told him, with some disdain.

'I'm bloody *certain* I don't care for yours,' Blackstone replied. 'But you were asking me if there was anything you could do to hurry matters along, and now I think about it, there is.'

'Yes?' George said eagerly.

'You can tell me who was in charge of the dagger before it came into Miss Devaraux's possession.'

'That would be the properties manager,' George said, his eagerness rapidly transforming itself into a sulk.

'Where might I find him?' Blackstone wondered.

'In the props room, of course.'

Blackstone sighed. 'And is there any danger of you telling me where that might be, do you think?' he asked.

Sebastian George took another puff of his huge cigar. 'It's in the basement, behind the stage,' he said. 'Where *else* would it be?'

* * *

19

There was a whole different world in the theatre basement – a world of narrow corridors with numerous doors leading off them.

It was, Blackstone thought, a little like being below stairs in one of the grand houses on the edge of Hyde Park. Here, as there, countless minions sweated and slaved to ensure that what appeared above ground was perfect and faultless. And the theatre audience, just like the grand families in their big houses, gave little thought to all the effort that had gone into creating that perfection for them – if they ever thought about it at all!

The properties room was located in one of these warrens. The far end of it was clearly used for storage, but in the area closest to the door was a very large table, presided over by a small, middle-aged man with receding brown-grey hair and very alert eyes.

'I'm Norman Foster,' he said, when Blackstone had shown him his warrant card. 'I'm the props master.'

He made the announcement with some considerable pride. But that was hardly surprising, for just as some men are born warriors or born painters, he had the look of a born custodian about him. He was the kind of man, Blackstone thought, who probably came out of the womb fretting about whether or not the doctor would put his instruments away properly, and then proceeded to spend the rest of his life worrying over objects most other people considered of little importance.

'Am I right in thinking that it's your job—' Blackstone began.

'Do you know what's wrong with my job?' Foster interrupted.

'No, I—'

'Actors! That's what wrong with it! It'd be a perfect position for anyone to hold if it wasn't for the bloody actors. You have no idea what they're like. I tell them all to look after the props, but do they listen?'

'I imagine not.'

'Do they hell-as-like! Some of them don't even know *which* prop I've assigned to them.'

'What do you mean?'

'Well, take a "for instance". We did *Julius Caesar* a couple of years ago, and I made sure each one of the conspirators had his own personal dagger right from the start – this one for Brutus, that one for Casca, the other one for Cassius. I even had their character's names painted on the hafts in tiny letters. It made no bloody difference at all to the actors. They'd come into the property room and just grab the first dagger that came to hand.'

'And did that matter?'

'Of course it mattered! You have to have order in this life. You never get anywhere without order.'

'What about the dagger that killed William Kirkpatrick?'

'Wasn't one of mine,' the props master said, with a finality which suggested that since it didn't come within his realm of responsibility, it could be of no possible interest to anybody. 'He wouldn't be lying there stone dead now, if it had been one of mine.'

'But Miss Charlotte Devaraux thought it *was* one of yours,' Blackstone pointed out.

'I'm not surprised. One of your men showed the one she actually used. I couldn't tell it from one of my own, and I'm an expert.'

'So it was probably made by the same craftsman who provided the fake dagger,' Blackstone mused.

'Highly unlikely,' Norman Foster said dismissively. 'Virtually impossible, in fact.'

'What makes you think that?'

'The men who strive for perfection in the gentle art of prop creation – those unsung heroes, those da Vincis of theatrical illusion – would never soil their hands with anything so sordid as producing a murder weapon.'

'Unless they didn't know *what* the knife they were producing was intended to be employed as,' Blackstone said. 'Where was the fake dagger kept, when it wasn't being used?'

'Under lock and key. Every night, when the curtain goes down for the final time, I check through the props, and then I lock them up. I have to do that, you know, or some of them would go missing.'

'They'd be *stolen*?'

'Oh yes. You'd be surprised at the number of things that I've lost in my time. Swords, helmets, even complete suits of armour!'

'Really?' Blackstone said.

'A grandmother clock!' Foster pressed on. 'A *grandfather* clock! One night, during a production of *Hamlet*, I lost Yorick's skull. It turned up eventually, of course – in some pub or other, where, no doubt, one of the so-called actors had been using it to get a cheap laugh from his lowlife friends – but by then it was too late.'

'Too late?' Blackstone asked, curious despite himself.

'"Alas, poor Yorick, I knew him, Horatio." That's what Hamlet's supposed to say as he looks down at the skull – but it's hard for him to make it sound convincing when all he's talking to is his own bloody hand, isn't it? So I had to get another skull before the next performance, didn't I? And don't ask me where I got it from—'

'I wouldn't.'

'—because I won't tell you, you being a policeman, and all that. But let me assure you, it was bloody expensive!'

Blackstone sighed, and found himself wishing he'd left the questioning of the props master to his sergeant.

'When do you *unlock* the props, Mr Foster?' he asked.

'Just before the start of the performance. Then I lay them out on this table, all in the right order – the first one to be used in the top left-hand corner, the last in the bottom right. I ask the actors to put them back exactly where they found them, but of course, they never do.'

'So at the start of every performance of this particular play, you place the dagger on the table?'

'Yes.'

'And does Miss Devaraux come and collect it?'

'You must be joking!'

'Must I?'

'She's an *artiste* – and you'd better not forget it, because she never does. It would be beneath her dignity to actually pick up a prop herself, however vital the part it's about to play in her performance.'

'So you deliver it to her, do you?'

'Certainly not! I have my professional standards to maintain, too, you know! If I'd wanted to be a delivery boy, I'd have bought myself a bicycle and gone to work for a butcher.'

'So how *does* she get her hands on the dagger?'

'One of the errand boys comes for it. She usually sends

Horace, who is halfway to becoming her own personal little monkey.'

'And was it Horace who picked it up tonight?'

'Yes.'

'So am I correct in assuming that you had the dagger under close observation from the time you took it out of the cupboard until the moment you handed it over to Horace?'

Foster suddenly began to look a little uncomfortable. 'Well, not exactly,' he confessed.

'Why not?'

'In the middle of the first act, I got called away to the tele-phone. They said it was an emergency.'

'*Who* said it was an emergency?'

'The errand boy who delivered the message.'

'And who told him?'

'Whoever was calling.'

Blackstone sighed again, and *really* began to wish that he'd waited for Patterson to arrive.

'What was the name of this caller of yours?' he asked.

'I don't know,' Foster admitted.

'Didn't he tell you?'

'I never got to speak to him. The phone's in the porter's office, and by the time I reached it, there was nobody on the other end of the line.'

Now wasn't that convenient, Blackstone thought.

'How long were you away, answering this non-existent telephone call?' he asked.

'It couldn't have been more than five or ten minutes.'

'And when you got back, the dagger was still here?'

'I *assumed* it was still here. Why wouldn't I? But it was in its sheath, wasn't it? And even if it hadn't been, I'd never have noticed, because, like I said, the real one and the fake one are as alike as two peas in a pod.'

Four

There were occasions on which Detective Sergeant Archibald Clarence Patterson told himself that whilst his decision to join the police may have been a great gain for the forces of law and order, it was a correspondingly great loss to the fields of science and technology. But these moments were rare. Most of the time, he happily conceded that though he had boundless enthusiasm for both these areas of study, he was also cursed with a lack of the brain power he would have needed in order to make any significant contribution to them.

And so, denied the chance to become a technical innovator himself, he settled for being a *follower* of innovation, and pursued his chosen course with a dedication which would have made avid stamp collectors question their own commitment, and keen bird watchers wonder if they were not, perhaps, being a little too lukewarm towards their feathered friends.

Thus, it would scarcely have surprised anyone who knew Patterson at all that, on arriving at the George Theatre, he did not immediately set out in search of his boss – as he should have done – but instead found himself irresistibly drawn to the theatrical machinery below stage.

What he found down there amazed him. The days of ropes, pulleys and hand-operated levers were now gone, and in their place was a complicated network of machines which could do anything and everything, from rotating the stage one hundred and eighty degrees to drenching it with artificial snow. But it was the electric 'bridge' which truly took his breath away – for it was one thing to read about a machine which could be used – and *had* been used – to raise fully-grown elephants up on to the stage, but it was quite another thing to have the opportunity to actually stand next to it.

As his hunger for the new and innovative began to abate

a little, he was becoming aware of a different kind of hunger – a purely physical one – which had been gnawing away at his insides ever since Rose had decided that he needed to slim down a little.

'Very nice of you to finally turn up, Sergeant, even if it is only in the pursuit of your hobby,' said a voice from somewhere behind him.

Patterson turned. 'I'm not here for my own pleasure, sir,' he said, with mock-indignation. 'I'm working.'

'Working?' Blackstone repeated.

'Working!' Patterson reaffirmed.

He did not sound entirely convincing – even to himself – but considering he was arguing his case in the face of the overwhelming evidence against it, he thought it was not a bad effort.

Blackstone gave him a sardonic grin. 'And precisely what *kind* of work are you currently involved in, Sergeant?' he asked.

What kind indeed, Patterson wondered.

'You've always taught me that the three vital strands of a murder investigation are means, motive and opportunity, sir,' Patterson said, improvising wildly. 'And that the "opportunity" strand of the equation is as much a factor of physical geography as it is of timing. So that's why I'm down here – I'm thinking about the physical geography of the theatre.'

'Very useful, considering the murder took place at least fifty feet above where you're standing now – and is separated from it by a floor several feet thick,' Blackstone said dryly. 'Anyway, you weren't thinking about the murder at all – you were thinking about *food*.'

'I most certainly was not.'

'You most certainly *were*. I could hear your stomach rumbling, nineteen-to-the-dozen, even from upstairs.'

'Not true,' Patterson said, trying to avoid blushing. 'A scientifically calculated diet, such as the one I have been following, is well known to be both nutritious and filling.'

But not as nutritious as a beefsteak! he added silently. Not as filling as a suet pudding!

'What I don't understand,' he continued, in an attempt to quickly move away from the twin subjects of food and his presence in the machine-room, 'is why the killer should have chosen the method he did. You have to admit, sir, it was pretty hit-and-miss.'

'Hit and miss? It worked, didn't it? Kirkpatrick *is* dead! And you don't get much more "hit" than that.'

'But it might *not* have worked,' Patterson argued. 'Charlotte Devaraux could have realized the knives had been swapped. Or she could have missed her target completely, and—'

'She's a professional,' Blackstone interrupted. 'Everybody – from Sebastian George himself, right down to Madge, her dresser – has been at great pains to point that out to me. The murderer could have been pretty sure that she'd strike where she was intended to.'

'But even so, there are much more reliable murder weapons down here,' Patterson argued.

'That electric bridge must weigh several tons,' Blackstone said. 'Even a big lad like you would be hard pressed to pick it up and bang somebody over the head with it.'

'You're missing the point, sir,' Patterson told him.

'I rather thought that I might be,' Blackstone agreed. 'So what *is* the point, Sergeant?'

'The murderer could have opened a trapdoor when he knew the victim was standing over it.'

'The fall might not have been fatal.'

'It would have been if he'd left something nasty – like a nice big spike – for William Kirkpatrick to fall *onto*. Impalement very rarely fails to achieve the desired result.'

'That's certainly true enough – as any vampire will probably testify,' Blackstone said.

'Alternatively, the murderer could have knocked Kirkpatrick out with a blow to the head, then placed him under the electric bridge and let the machinery crush him. In either case, it would have looked like a pure accident, and we wouldn't even be here now.'

'You may be right,' Blackstone agreed. 'But maybe he's not as fond of all this new technology as you are, Sergeant. Maybe, at heart, he's a bit of a purist – a good, old-fashioned murderer.'

'Yes, there are people who refuse to move with the times,' Patterson agreed, giving his boss a significant look.

'Anyway, if he'd done what you've suggested, he would

have been directly involved in the death,' Blackstone continued. 'Whereas, by choosing the method he has chosen, he didn't even need to be in the bloody *theatre* when Kirkpatrick met his end.'

'I hadn't thought of that,' Patterson said glumly. 'He's a clever bloke, isn't he?'

'*Fiendishly* clever,' Blackstone replied.

'Fiendishly clever,' Patterson repeated. 'I'm not sure I'd go quite that far, sir,' he cautioned.

'I'm not sure I'd go that far myself,' Blackstone agreed. 'But you can bet your last brass farthing that all the popular newspapers will.'

By the time Blackstone returned to the stage, the body of William Kirkpatrick had been removed, but Sebastian George was still there, pacing up and down, and puffing on his huge cigar.

'There are uniformed policemen all over the place,' the impresario complained to the inspector.

'Are there?' Blackstone replied, looking around him in mock-amazement. 'Now why should that be? Maybe somebody's told them there's been a murder in the theatre. Do you think that could be it?'

George was not amused. 'How much longer will they be cluttering the theatre up?' he demanded.

'I imagine the "cluttering up" will continue until I'm happy they've completed all the necessary inquiries.'

'Can't you give me a definite time, my good man? Will it be an hour? Might it be as long as two?'

'Do I look like a chimney sweep or a knife-grinder to you?' Blackstone wondered.

George gave his evening dress a quick inspection. 'Not at the moment, no,' he admitted. 'Why do you ask?'

'Because you're addressing me as if I was,' Blackstone replied. 'I am not "your good man", I'm a police officer investigating a serious crime, and I have to tell you now that the work my men are involved in will take much more than an hour or two.'

'I simply can't permit that to happen,' Sebastian George said. 'My cast can't stay up half the night being questioned by policemen. They are artists. They need their rest. Besides,

I have workmen arriving at first light, and they will need space to be able to go about their tasks.'

'Your cast will have plenty of time to rest once we've finished with them,' Blackstone said. 'A couple of days, at least.'

'What complete and utter nonsense!' George replied. He made a great show of checking his pocket watch. 'As I calculate it, none of my players will be in their beds until two or three in the morning, yet they have to be back here, refreshed and re-invigorated, by noon at the very latest.'

'Hang on!' Blackstone said. 'You're talking as if you think you'll be putting on a performance tomorrow night.'

'The evening performance has not even entered my consciousness yet,' George told him. 'For the moment, I am far more concerned about the staging of the extra matinée.'

'The extra matinée!' Blackstone repeated, incredulously. 'There'll *be* no matinée of any kind. And no evening performance, either. Until I'm satisfied that my men have completed all their work, your people won't even be allowed back in the theatre.'

'I'm afraid you're wrong about that,' the impresario told him, though there was not even the slightest trace of regret in his voice.

'And I'm afraid you don't quite seem to understand the powers of the police,' Blackstone told him.

'But I do understand,' Sebastian George responded. 'I particularly understand the power of *some* policemen – policemen like Sir Roderick Todd, your Assistant Commissioner. Do you happen to know him?'

Oh yes, I know the bastard all right, Blackstone thought. I know him from Russia, when he almost buggered up the case of the missing golden egg. And I know him from the investigation into the fire bug, when he seemed to spend most of his time trying to get me kicked off the force.

But aloud, all he said was, 'You may well be an acquaintance of Sir Roderick's, sir—'

'I am much than a simple acquaintance, I can assure you of that. In fact, I would go so far as to count him as being among my closest friends.'

'He could be your long-lost brother as far as I'm concerned,' Blackstone said, barely managing to keep his temper reined

28

in. 'He could be your identical twin, for all the difference it makes. When a police investigation is underway, nobody, not even the Assistant Commissioner—'

'I spoke to Rodders not more than an hour ago,' Sebastian George interrupted. 'He can see no harm at all in the show being put on as normal. In fact, he agreed to honour us by personally attending tomorrow night's performance, and I have already reserved the Royal Box for him.'

So that was the way it was, was it?

'But how can you put on a show when your leading actor's *dead*?' Blackstone said.

'As I think I've explained to you at least five or six times already, *Miss Charlotte Devaraux* is the leading light of this company,' George told him. 'Mr Kirkpatrick, for all his undoubted talent, was no more than the secondary lead, and his understudy is more than ready to step into his shoes.'

What was the other thing Sebastian had said earlier? Blackstone wondered. Something about the workmen needing space to do their work?

'What exactly will these workmen of yours be doing when they get here?' he asked.

George looked suddenly guarded. 'The workmen?' he repeated, clearly to give himself time to think. 'Ah, yes! The stage will need to be tidied up a little after Mr Kirkpatrick's unfortunate collision with it.'

'You don't need *workmen* in the plural for that. *One* workman would be enough.'

'True, but you see, there are some of other . . . er . . . minor structural changes to be made.'

'Such as?'

'You need not concern yourself with that,' Sebastian George said airily.

'But I *am* concerned,' Blackstone insisted.

George sighed. 'Very well, since you seem intent in sticking your nose into matters which are absolutely no concern of yours, I suppose I might as well tell you that the seating arrangements are in need of readjustment.'

'You're going to put more seats into the theatre, aren't you?' Blackstone demanded.

'We may possibly decide to add two or three more rows,' George replied vaguely.

'You're expecting to get a packed house, as a direct result of the murder, and you want to cram as many paying customers into the theatre as is humanly possible?'

'I would not put it quite like that.'

'Then how *would* you put it?'

Sebastian George took another puff on his big cigar, something Blackstone had already noted he had a tendency to do when he was about to be either bombastic or pompous.

'I feel a keen responsibility to my public,' the impresario said. 'I would not wish to disappoint those who thirst after culture, by having to turn too many of them away.'

'Thirst after culture!' Blackstone said, sceptically. 'Disappoint them by turning them away!'

'You, as a common-or-garden policeman with little or no imagination, plainly underestimate the enthusiasm of devoted theatre-goers,' Sebastian told him. 'There have been instances – though fortunately never at this theatre – where the refusal of admission has led to an out-and-out riot.'

'Well, if you think there's any danger of a riot here, you'd definitely better cancel tomorrow night's performance after all,' Blackstone suggested. 'The matinée, as well.'

'That won't be necessary,' George replied. '*Some* policemen – and my good friend Sir Roderick Todd happily among them – have the ability to see *beyond* the end of their noses. *Some* policemen, rather than just reacting to a situation, can see the value of advance planning.'

'And what's that supposed to mean?'

'It means, *my good man*, that Sir Roderick has kindly agreed to draft in a number of uniformed officers – twenty, I think, was the number he mentioned – to patrol the area around the theatre before tomorrow's performances. Thus, if we do have the demand for tickets we are anticipating – and if those people turned away do become disgruntled – the situation can be very easily contained.'

'The Metropolitan Police can't spare twenty men, just so you can cash in on the murder like some kind of bloodsucking ghoul!' Blackstone said, outraged.

Sebastian George smiled. 'That might be your opinion,' he said, 'but the Assistant Commissioner – whose opinion carries *much* more weight – would appear to disagree with you.'

Five

The King's Head Tavern and Oyster Bar was not more than a few doors down the street from the George Theatre, with the consequence that most its customers were either connected with the theatre in some way or fervently *wished* that they were connected with it.

On the basis of this clientele alone, Blackstone would normally have been persuaded to find somewhere else to drink, since he disliked men who spent most of their time prancing and posturing – actors, con men, Assistant Commissioners in the Metropolitan Police, and people of that ilk – and whenever possible, steered well clear of them.

That night, however, he decided he had two quite compelling reasons for giving the King's Head his patronage. The first was that he would very likely find people on the periphery of his new case drinking in there. The second – slightly less professional – was that it was eleven fifty by the time he left the theatre, so with only forty minutes drinking time left before the pubs closed up for the night, it was a question of any port in a storm.

'What do you want, Archie?' the inspector asked his sergeant as they entered the saloon bar. 'A pint of the usual?'

'Yes, I could use a . . .' Patterson began. Then his mouth froze, and his right hand unconsciously reached for his stomach. 'No, I think I'll have a glass of soda water tonight, if you don't mind, sir,' he continued, somewhat mournfully, as his hand patted the bulge.

Blackstone bought the drinks, and then walked over to a table in the corner which gave him a good view of the rest of the room.

Patterson sat down heavily, and took an unenthusiastic sip of his glass of soda water.

'Well?' Blackstone asked.

31

'Well what, sir?'

'What's it taste like?' Blackstone wondered.

'Very refreshing,' Patterson replied, though without much conviction. Then he noticed the amused look on his boss's face, and added defiantly, 'I'm doing this through my own choice, you know. Rose isn't forcing me into it.'

'Of course she isn't,' Blackstone agreed, trying his best to look as if he really believed his sergeant's protestation.

'Anyway, sooner or later we all give in to what our women want,' Patterson said, seemingly unaware that he was undermining his own argument. 'Nobody's immune to it – not even you.'

'Not even me? What do you mean by that, Sergeant?'

Patterson smiled knowingly. 'You were at the theatre tonight, weren't you, sir?'

'Yes? What of it?'

'And when was the *last* time you went?'

'Quite recently, as a matter of fact.'

'I'm talking about the legitimate theatre now, not the music hall,' Patterson pointed out.

'In that case, it was some time ago,' Blackstone admitted.

'Some time ago!' Patterson repeated derisively. 'What does that mean, exactly? A month? A couple of months? Six months and a day? I'd be willing to bet that it must have been years!'

'You'd probably win that bet,' Blackstone conceded.

'And the reason you went this time was not because you felt a sudden urge for culture – it was because *your* woman told you to.'

'Ellie Carr's not my woman,' Blackstone said.

And there was some truth in his assertion. They were not sleeping together. They hadn't even kissed. Yet they were very comfortable in each other's company – *uncomfortably* comfortable, as far as Blackstone was concerned.

The inspector looked around the saloon bar. 'Who do you know in here?' he asked.

'Changing the subject, are we, sir?' Patterson asked.

'Yes,' Blackstone said firmly. 'So who *do* you know?'

'A few people,' Patterson replied.

By which he probably meant at least half the customers, Blackstone thought. That was the thing about Patterson. Aside for his undeniable loyalty – a rare virtue in the back-stabbing atmosphere which Assistant Commissioner Todd had imported with him into the Met – his greatest value was in his large circle of acquaintances. Patterson knew people *everywhere* – journalists and barristers, costermongers and watermen, prostitutes and pickpockets. It was impossible to walk down any London street without Patterson stopping to greet at least ten or twelve people.

'Anyone from the play here?' Blackstone asked.

Patterson made a quick survey of the room.

'Yes. All the people at that table,' he said, making a discreet gesture with his podgy index finger.

The table which he was pointing to had two men and two women sitting at it, and from the flamboyance of both their dress and attitude, Blackstone had already guessed they were connected with the theatre.

'The two woman are just bit players,' Patterson continued. 'Walk-ons. Faces in the crowd. I don't know their names. Probably the only reason they're in the play at all is that they're on very friendly terms indeed with a couple of the backers of the production.'

'Very delicately put,' Blackstone said.

'The man on the left is Binsley Hough,' Patterson said.

Hough was a very round man, Blackstone noted, a living – *waddling* – warning to Sergeant Patterson that he should stick to the diet his young lady had put him on.

'Can't see a barrel of lard like him being very convincing as the dramatic lead,' Blackstone said.

'That's probably why he doesn't *play* the dramatic lead,' Patterson replied, with a slight air of superiority. 'He's usually the kindly uncle, the clown or the evil mastermind.'

'What if there isn't a kindly uncle, a clown or an evil mastermind in the play they're putting on at that moment?' Blackstone wondered.

Patterson shook his head. 'There's always *one* of them in every play,' he said, almost pityingly.

'What about the other man?' Blackstone asked.

'He's Richmond Clay.'

Richmond Clay! Didn't any of these people have proper Christian names, Blackstone asked himself.

Still, he was forced to admit that the name did appear to suit Clay. He was tall and good-looking, with that slightly arrogant curl of the lip that some women found appealing.

'Our Mr Clay certainly looks very pleased with himself tonight,' the inspector said.

'He should do,' Patterson replied. 'He was William Kirkpatrick's understudy. Now that Kirkpatrick's dead, he'll be given the lead role.'

'You mean the *secondary* lead role, don't you?' Blackstone asked, getting a little of his own back.

'Perhaps I do,' Patterson admitted. 'It is a little bit ironic, though, isn't it, sir?'

'Isn't *what*?'

'That Richmond Clay should keep on following in Kirkpatrick's footsteps like that.'

'*Keep* on following?'

'After Martin Swinburne.'

'I don't think this soda water's doing your brain any good,' Blackstone said. 'You're not making any sense at all.'

'Aren't I?' Patterson asked. 'You surely know what happened to Martin Swinburne, don't you?'

'As a matter of fact, I don't.'

'But it was in all the papers.'

It probably had been, Blackstone agreed, but he came across enough sensationalist horror in his job, without looking for any more of it in the pages of the popular press.

'I must have missed that particular story,' he said.

'Martin Swinburne was the leading actor in the George Company,' Patterson said, speaking slowly now, as if explaining it to a rather dim-witted child. 'Then, a few months ago, he was the victim of a tragic accident.'

'What kind of tragic accident?' Blackstone asked, discovering a sudden new interest in theatrical gossip.

'It was in another of the sensationalist plays at the George Theatre. This one was about a flying machine.'

'A play about a flying machine!' Blackstone scoffed. 'Even by the standards of what they normally try to get you to swallow at the theatre, *that's* got to be rather far-fetched.'

'No, it isn't!' Patterson protested. 'It's only a matter of time before a heavier-than-air machine—'

'Stick to the point,' Blackstone told him. 'What happened to Martin Swinburne?'

'In this particular drama – I think it was called *Taking Wing*

– Swinburne played the inventor of the flying machine, and his big moment comes when he's standing on the stage, and it flies above his head . . .'

Martin Swinburne, a true leading man by any standards, is alone on the vast stage. Behind him is a painted back-cloth of Hackney Marshes. From off-stage comes the sound of a distant engine.

'How I have yearned, for so long, to command my flying machine with my own two strong hands,' he says to himself in a poignant whisper, loud enough for those at back of the theatre to hear. 'And so I would have done, had I not lost my good right arm.'

He turns, in order to remind the duller members of the audience that where there was once an arm, there is now only an empty sleeve.

'Yet what choice did I have?' he asks. 'The building was burning, the child needed to be saved. If I had not responded to her cries, I would have been the lesser man for it, and even the great triumph I am about to observe would have brought me no pleasure. For surely, the life of a sweet child is of greater value than any man's own dream.'

The flying machine appears at the edge of the stage, so high in the air that it is just within the line of visibility of most of the audience. It is the shape of a cigar, and halfway down its body there are wings – made of many small pieces of wood, and modelled on the wings of an eagle – which are flapping furiously.

'At last, the miracle I have worked for, so hard and so long!' Martin Swinburne says.

He waves his free arm – the one which is not strapped to his side – high in the air.

'You fly it like a master, my son!' he calls out to the pilot who is supposedly inside the contraption.

Halfway through its slow journey across the stage, the flying machine begins to shake in a most alarming – and unscripted – manner.

'Hold your nerve, my son,' Swinburne calls out, improvising wildly. 'For great glory was never won without first enduring a rough passage.'

He is so convincing that most of the audience still believe the flying machine is performing just as it was intended to, but even they begin to have their doubts when it hurtles down towards the stage.

Martin Swinburne has no time to run, and though he tries to lift both his arms above his head – as if that would protect him – one of them remains stubbornly strapped to his side. So it is his unrestrained left arm alone which feels the initial impact. A split second later, of course, the rest of his body is allowed to share the experience.

'They say it was the weight of the electrical engine that actually killed him,' Patterson said.

'The engine?' Blackstone repeated. 'You don't mean to say it really was a flying machine, do you?'

'How could it be when, according to you, such things are impossible?' Patterson asked, with a grin.

'Stop being such a smart alec, and tell me what happened,' Blackstone growled.

'The engine was only there to make the wings flap,' Patterson explained. 'The flying machine itself was suspended from a series of cables which ran along a track. Some of the cables must have come unhooked, and the rest, unable to bear the strain on their own, simply snapped. So the flying machine fell, and Swinburne was flattened.' The sergeant paused. 'Do you see now what I mean about Richmond Clay following in William Kirkpatrick's footsteps, sir?'

'I think so,' Blackstone said. 'William Kirkpatrick was Martin Swinburne's understudy, just as Richmond Clay was William Kirkpatrick's understudy. Have I got that right?'

'Exactly right!' Patterson said. 'Overnight, Kirkpatrick went from being a nobody to being the star of the show. And that's just what's about to happen to Richmond Clay. So one of them got his big chance through a tragic accident, and the other through a murder.'

'Or?' Blackstone said.

'Or they both got their big chances through a murder!' Patterson exclaimed.

'That's just what I was thinking,' Blackstone said.

Jed Trent looked around the empty morgue with the trained

eye of a man who had served in the Metropolitan Police for over twenty years.

Not that there was much to see with his trained eye, he thought. Not at that time of the morning.

He had been employed by the morgue at University College Hospital since he retired from the police in his early forties. He was supposedly a general factotum, but had heard more than one doctor complain that there was very little 'general' about the way he did his job, and that in reality he had become no more than a personal assistant to Dr Ellie Carr.

He was forced to admit that there was some justice to the complaint. He did spend much of his time working for Dr Carr, partly because he found the kind of research that she was involved in interesting, and partly because ... well ... because there was just something about the bloody woman which made it very hard to say no to her.

Trent looked around the morgue again. Nothing had changed in the previous couple of minutes. The building – like its customers – was perfectly still.

'Doesn't it ever strike you as odd that it's so often the case that we're the only people here?' he asked.

'What?' Ellie Carr responded absently, her eyes – and her thoughts – still very much concentrated on the body of William Kirkpatrick.

'I mean to say, there are plenty of dedicated doctors who work in this building – dozens of them – but *their* dedication doesn't seem to stand in the way of their going home from time to time,' Trent amplified.

'*We* go home from time to time,' Ellie said impatiently. 'You were at home when I called you.'

'Yes, I was,' Trent agreed. 'In bed! Asleep!'

'And I was out at the theatre, enjoying myself. So, since we have both been away from this place for several hours at least, I don't think that anyone can say that we're chained to the job, now can they?'

'Well, there are people who might say that the fact we're here at one o'clock in the morning proves we *are* chained to the job,' Trent said. 'But they'd be wrong, would they?'

'Of course they would.'

'So why *are* we here?'

'Luck,' Ellie Carr said. 'Pure, blind luck.'

'Luck?'

'If I hadn't been at the theatre tonight, someone else might have got his hands on this body.'

'And that would have been a bad thing, would it?'

'It would have been a *very* bad thing.'

'Why? Is it because William Kirkpatrick's famous that you're getting so much pleasure out of slicing him up? Are you hoping to get an earl or a cabinet minister on the slab next?'

'You do talk nonsense sometimes,' Ellie said.

'Or are you hoping a little of his fame will rub off on you? Do you want to be pointed out in the street as the doctor who dissected Kirkpatrick?'

Ellie clicked her tongue disapprovingly. 'I have no desire to be recognized in public,' she said. 'Nor am I impressed by the cadaver's pedigree. William Kirkpatrick was a mediocre actor – at best. He wasn't half as interesting to me alive as he is now he's dead.'

'And what is it that makes him so interesting now?'

'The *way* he died. He was poisoned.'

'Huh, that's nothing unusual,' Trent said, clearly unimpressed. 'Poison's the weapon of choice for half the murderers in this country. There must be dozens of rich widows who've bought arsenic claiming they needed it to keep down the rats – when what they really wanted it for was to feed to their husbands.'

'Some husbands *are* rats, and undoubtedly get what they deserve,' Ellie Carr said mildly. 'But that's neither here nor there. The interesting thing, as you've just pointed out, is that most English poisoners use arsenic – and this one didn't.'

'How can you be so sure of that?'

'Arsenic's a powder or a solution. This poison was some kind of paste, which had been smeared on to the tip of the dagger.'

'Maybe there's some new kind of arsenic that comes in a paste form,' Trent suggested.

'There isn't,' Ellie Carr said dismissively. 'And even if there were, you'd need much more of it than could be smeared on the point of a dagger to get your result.'

'Maybe this new kind of arsenic—' Trent began.

'Then there's the speed of the reaction,' Ellie Carr ploughed on. 'Kirkpatrick was dead within a very few minutes of being poisoned. Arsenic never works as quickly as that. And neither do any of the other metallic poisons. So we can dismiss the whole lot of them out of hand, can't we?'

'I suppose we can, if you say so.'

'I *do* say so. I think that what we may be dealing with here is some kind of vegetable alkaloid. It could be digitalin, which is a great favourite over the water in France.'

'I never did trust the French,' Trent grumbled. 'They've always been a sneaky lot.'

'Yes, it might well be digitalin – I'll know for certain when I've done the tests – but I've got this feeling that it isn't that at all.'

'And *if* it isn't, you're stumped?'

'Exactly, Jed! Completely and utterly stumped! I've no idea at all – for the moment – what else it could *possibly* be.'

'You don't sound overly depressed about your incredible ignorance on the subject,' Trent said.

'I'm not,' Ellie told him. 'In fact, I'm very excited. Don't you realize that this may be a completely new kind of poison – or, at least, one that's never been seen in London before?'

'Yes, I may not be a sharp-as-a-razor scientist like you, but the thought had occurred even to me.'

'And what are the implications of that, Jed?' Ellie Carr asked. 'What does that mean for us?'

'Does it mean that we're at a total loss to know what to do next?' Jed Trent suggested.

'Not at all! It means that you and I, Jed, will have to set ourselves the task of tracing this hitherto unknown poison back to its source. Isn't that thrilling? Doesn't that set your heart racing?'

'Absolutely,' Trent said, in a dead-flat voice. 'If you want to know the truth, Dr Carr, I can barely contain my enthusiasm.'

Six

Most Englishmen considered themselves to be experts on the rain, but in Blackstone's case, there was some justification for this belief. He had travelled widely, and known rain in all its forms – the torrential downpours in India, which seemed to be unleashing all the wrath of the angry gods; the harsh rains of Afghanistan, stabbing like the daggers of a thousand tiny tribesmen; the gentle, caressing showers of an English country spring.

The rain that early morning was none of these. It was a typical London rain – a fine drizzle which was persistent rather than fierce, and *through* its persistence managed to penetrate even the most waterproof of clothing, and soak to the bone those who dared face it. The people out on the streets knew this all too well. Those on their way from one place to another hurried along, while those whose business dictated that they stay in a single spot – like the newspaper vendors – sought out whatever cover they could find in doorways and under awnings.

Despite the depressing atmosphere, the newspaper vendors seemed to be on fine form that morning. And why wouldn't they be, Blackstone thought, as he hurried along. After all, there was nothing like a good headline for selling papers – and the one they had been handed that morning was a beauty.

'Thespian's Mysterious Demise!' one of them shouted from his doorway shelter. 'Read all about it!'

'Final Curtain for William Kirkpatrick,' called out another.

But it was a third, positioned quite close to the George Theatre itself, to whom Blackstone would have awarded the prize for inventiveness.

'The Balloon of Death!' the man screamed. 'Read all about the Balloon of Death!'

Despite the rain – and despite the fact that the box office

would not be opening for another three hours – a long queue
had already built up outside the theatre. The people who made
up the queue had their shoulders hunched up against the
elements. They looked a little like the vultures that he had
seen in the East, Blackstone thought – and *just* like those
vultures, these people were prepared to tolerate a certain
amount of personal discomfort if there was some promise of
blood and gore at the end of it.

The inspector made his way to the stage door, knocked,
and was admitted by a porter whose face was covered with
so many unsightly red blotches that it was practically impossible to detect the areas of normal skin which almost certainly
lay between them.

'Well, well, well, if it isn't Sam Blackstone,' the man said.
'Fancy us meeting up again like this, after all these years.
What a turn-up for the books that is, eh?'

'Yes, it's certainly been a long time,' Blackstone replied,
searching the recesses of his mind for a name to fit to the
face. 'How long is it, exactly, do you think?'

'Must be twenty-five years, if it's a day,' the porter told
him.

Blackstone did a quick mental calculation. Twenty-five
years! Then they must have met in Dr Barnardo's!

'Whoever would have thought that any of us poor orphans
would ever amount to anything?' the porter continued.

'Who indeed,' Blackstone said, still buying himself time to
gather up his recollections.

'Yet here I am, in charge of the porter's lodge of one of
the biggest and most important theatres in London,' the porter
continued. 'And as for you,' he added, almost as an after-
thought, 'well, you haven't done so badly for yourself, either,
have you?'

'Spotty Wilberforce!' Blackstone exclaimed.

'*Tommy* Wilberforce,' the porter said, with offended dignity.
'Or *Thomas*, as I'm better known these days.'

There'd been all kinds of kids in Barnardo's, Blackstone
recalled. Kids who could be happy anywhere, however tough
the conditions – and they could be *very* tough in the orphanage;
kids who were so miserable that they viewed catching a disease
– and dying of it – as almost a welcome release; kids who
knew how to play the system, and kids who didn't.

41

Spotty Wilberforce, even without his horrendous spots, would not have been an attractive child. He'd lacked the wit to be amusing, the courage to attract admiration, and the empathy to engender love. And yet, despite all the evidence to the contrary, he had been one of the kids who consider themselves superior types, and so made themselves the natural targets for bullies.

Blackstone, who – even then – had despised those who used their own power solely for their own purposes, had kept the bullies away from Wilberforce for years, though the other boy had never thanked him, or even acknowledged that he was doing it. In the time that had passed since, he had occasionally asked himself *why* he had protected Wilberforce – getting bruises aplenty himself, in the process – and had come to the conclusion that while it is easy to protect a worthy object, protecting an *unworthy* one is a real test of character.

'You must think it's a real stroke of luck, finding me here,' Wilberforce told him.

'Must I?' Blackstone replied.

'Of course you must. Half the theatre porters in the West End don't have the brains to tie their own bootlaces, so I can imagine how you will have been dreading questioning the one who works here. Then you suddenly discover it's me – a man who really knows his onions – a man who can give you a real insight into what goes on in this place. You must feel like all your birthdays have come at once.'

'Something like that,' Blackstone agreed. 'Were you on duty here last night, Sp . . . Thomas?'

'I'm on duty *every* night. Mr George wouldn't trust anybody else to be in charge.'

'So you'll have been here when the phone call came through for Mr Foster, the props manager?'

'The *properties* manager,' Wilberforce corrected him. 'Yes, I was here. And I ordered the boy to bring Mr Foster to the phone straight away.'

'Who made the call?' Blackstone asked.

'Caller didn't say. Just said it was urgent.'

'But was it a man? Or a woman?'

'It was . . . er . . . a man,' Wilberforce said.

'You don't sound so sure about that.'

'It was a man,' Wilberforce said, more definitely. 'I'd guess

42

he was middle-aged. He had a South London accent. I'd say he probably came from somewhere in Southwark.'

Spotty Wilberforce had always been a liar when it suited him, Blackstone thought, and it suited him now – because, having bragged so much already, he wanted to seem more competent than he actually was.

'It's understandable, given all the other things you have to do during a show, that you don't really remember something as insignificant as one phone call,' Blackstone said, giving the other man a way out.

'But I *do* remember,' Wilberforce insisted. 'As I said, he was thirty-five or thirty-six, and he came from Southwark – possibly from the area quite close to St Saviour's workhouse.'

Give him another minute, and he'd be pinning it down to the street – or even the house, Blackstone thought.

Wilberforce had backed himself into a corner, and could now never admit to the truth without considering that he had lost face. And there was no way he would be prepared to do that in front of a man who he thought had got on in life *almost as well* as he had.

So if they were ever to get any leads on the man who made the phone call, they would have to come from the *other* end of the line, where Sergeant Patterson was currently making enquiries.

Patterson had never overcome his initial awe of the telephone. It seemed to him that it was, quite simply, the greatest invention which had ever been devised in the history of the world.

It was an instrument which allowed him to indulge in two of his three great passions, his fascination for technology and the love of conversation. He made use of the telephone constantly, and – in his more optimistic moments – even dared to dream that he might some day possess one of his own.

Thus, while the spring in his step that morning may well have been a reflection – in some small measure – of his recent weight loss, it had much more to do with the fact that he was heading for the building which, in his mind, was the palace of modernity and progress – and in the minds of others was merely the Post Office Central Telephone Exchange in St Paul's Churchyard.

The Exchange did not exactly live up to his expectations.

The room itself was so prosaic – a large, oblong-shaped space with a supervisor's desk in the centre, and perhaps sixty switchboards against the wall. And the operators fell even further below the standards he had been anticipating. True, they looked quite smart in the dark gowns which covered their street clothes. And true, they answered the flashing lights on their switchboards with a brisk efficiency. But where was the flair, Patterson thought forlornly. Where was the magic?

Didn't these young women realize what an exciting thing it was that they were doing? Didn't they understand what a privilege it was to be there, at the beating heart of civilization?

'Is there something I can do to help you, young man?' asked a distinctly chilling voice to his left.

Patterson turned, and saw a small woman, with her hair in a tight bun, glaring at him.

He produced his warrant card. 'Sergeant Patterson,' he said. 'And you are Mrs . . .'

'I am *Miss* Dobbs,' the woman told him. 'The Postal Telephone Service does not employ married ladies.'

'And quite right, too,' Patterson said, before he could stop himself.

'I beg your pardon?'

'For important work like this, you need a clear head, free of all the distractions that married life brings with it,' Patterson continued, convinced, even as he spoke the words, that he was merely digging himself into a deeper hole than the one he already found himself in.

But instead of being angered by his tactless comments, the tiny harridan beside him actually began to smile.

'Yes, it is important work, though not enough people realize it,' Miss Dobbs said. 'We provide a valuable service here. The business of the City would be much less efficient without us.'

'You provide a *vital* service,' Patterson corrected her. 'And without you, the business of the City would grind to a halt.'

Miss Dobbs's smile was now so broad it seemed in danger of cracking her face. 'What can I do for you, Sergeant?' she asked.

'I'm trying to track down a telephone call which was made last night to the George Theatre,' Patterson explained. 'Do you keep any records of who called whom?'

Miss Dobbs shook her head regretfully. 'Each of our subscribers has his own personal meter in our central office, and every time he calls, it clicks up another penny that he owes us,' she replied. 'But while we know how many calls our subscribers have made, we have no idea who they called or when they called them.'

'Then perhaps the operator herself might remember placing the call,' Patterson suggested.

'It's possible,' Miss Dobbs agreed. 'At what time was this particular call made?'

'As near as we can estimate, it was placed at around half past eight.'

'Then my operators will certainly not have dealt with it.'

'No?'

'No. The company has ruled that none of the young ladies should work after eight o'clock. And I think that they are quite correct in that belief.'

'Any particular reason for that ruling?' Patterson asked idly.

'Indeed there is.' Miss Dobbs glanced around at her operators, then said, in a much lower voice, 'In the evening, there are some men who drink to excess, you know.'

'So I've been told,' Patterson replied.

'And once the drink has taken hold of these reprehensible men, they lose all restraint, and abandon any kind of civilized behaviour.'

'True,' agreed Patterson, who had collected more bruises from handling drunks than he had ever done from arresting murderers.

'And some of these men, in their wild state, then decide to make telephone calls.'

'They do?'

'And that is why there are no female operators on duty. Many of my young ladies are the daughters of clergymen, lawyers or doctors. I would not want them to be subjected to the foul-mouthed calls that the male operators who replace them sometimes have to deal with.'

'So I really need to come back tonight, and talk to the male operators,' Patterson said.

'That is the case.'

'Well, thank you for your time,' Patterson said.

'It has been a pleasure to talk to a young man who is intelligent enough to appreciate our calling,' Miss Dobbs told him.

Patterson turned towards the door, then stopped, and swung round to face Miss Dobbs again.

'I do have one more question,' he said. 'It's nothing to do with my official inquiries. It's more a case of satisfying my own curiosity.'

'Please feel free to ask it,' Miss Dobbs told him.

'I was wondering why all the young ladies in this office wear dark over-gowns.'

'Ah, that is for their own protection – a kindly and thoughtful gesture on the part of the management.'

'Is it? How?'

'Most young ladies, as you have no doubt observed yourself, cannot help noticing what their friends and colleagues are wearing. It is not their fault, it is simply the way that God made them. By providing them with gowns, we are shielding the sensitive and modestly-garbed operator from being distracted by the extra-smart frocks on either side of her.' Miss Dobbs paused. 'You see nothing wrong with that, do you, Sergeant?'

'Not at all,' Patterson assured her, admiringly. 'As a matter of fact, I think it's a brilliant idea.'

Spotty Wilberforce had insisted that Blackstone accompany him back to his own little office, and since there seemed to be nothing else to occupy his time at that particular moment, the inspector had agreed.

It was more of a cupboard than an office, but Wilberforce was plainly immensely proud of his own little kingdom, which contained not one battered old armchair but *two*.

'I could tell you some stories about what goes on this company,' Wilberforce boasted once they were seated. 'I could tell you tales that would make your hair stand on end.'

'Then please feel free to do so,' Blackstone suggested.

Wilberforce shook his head. 'Can't.'

'Why not?'

'I'm like a doctor, or a lawyer, in that respect. Anything I see, I have to keep to myself.'

The appalling, self-important little boy had grown up into an appalling, self-important little man, Blackstone thought. But that still didn't mean that nothing he had to say was worth listening to.

'Of course, I can quite see that if you don't think I'd believe your stories—' he said.

'Why wouldn't you believe them?' Wilberforce interrupted.

'—or if you think that they would bore me, because, in my job, I'll have been bound to see things which were much more interesting—'

'There's nothing more interesting than the things that go on here,' Wilberforce said firmly. He paused for a second, as if weighing the advantages and disadvantages of being indiscreet. 'You probably think this is a highly successful theatre company, don't you?' he continued.

'Well, yes, I suppose I do.'

'Then that only shows your ignorance. Mr George has been teetering on the brink of financial disaster for years. Why, only last year, he had to lease the theatre out to another company. And while the other company was using the theatre, do you know what he did with his own?'

'No, I don't.'

'He took them on a tour of South America.'

'I see,' Blackstone said, and as his response was obviously not enough to satisfy Wilberforce, he added, 'South America, eh?'

'Not *North* America, where the population can at least act a little bit civilized on occasion,' the porter said, 'but *South* America, which is well known to be full of nothing but Indians and Dagoes! I ask you, Sam! How desperate do you have to be to go there?'

'But presumably, however dreadful the tour might have been, it did at least serve the function of putting the company back on a sound financial footing again, didn't it?' Blackstone asked innocently.

'So that's what you think, is it?' Wilberforce said.

'Am I wrong?'

'Couldn't be wronger. The whole trouble with these sensationalist plays, Sammy-boy, is that while you've got no choice but to stage them – because that's what every other theatre management in London is doing – they cost an absolute fortune to put on. Which means – as you could no doubt work out for yourself, given time – that even before the first ticket is sold to the first customer, the company's already up to its ears in debt.'

'I can understand that. But surely, once they *have* sold the tickets—' Blackstone began.

'And even the best sensationalist effects in the world won't guarantee you an audience,' Wilberforce interrupted him. 'To be assured of a success, you've got to have a male lead who's capable of pulling in the crowds – and Sebastian George doesn't have one!'

'Why is that?' Blackstone asked. 'Because William Kirkpatrick's been murdered?'

'William Kirkpatrick!' the porter said contemptuously. 'Why even mention him? That clown was never a crowd-pleaser. It's *Martin Swinburne* I'm talking about. Now he was a star, if ever there was one. All men admired him, and all women swooned at his feet.'

'All men admired him,' Blackstone mused. 'Are you sure about that? There must surely have been *somebody* who disliked him.'

'The public loved him!'

'I imagine they did. But I was thinking more about the people who he worked with.'

'Oh, if it's the *company* you're talking about, that's a different matter altogether. Actors always put on a great show of affection in public, but really they can't stand one another in private. It's the jealousy, you see – they're always worried that one of the others is getting more lines, or a better part, than they are.'

'Yes, I can see that.'

'And when you *do* get the biggest parts and the best lines – which Swinburne always did – you're not going to have a lot of friends in the company, *especially* among the men.'

The stage door opened, and Sebastian George entered the building. He did no more than glance at the tiny cupboard-office as he swept majestically past it, but even that was enough to unsettle the porter.

Wilberforce rose quickly to his feet. 'I'd better go and have a word with Mr George,' he said.

'He didn't seem to eager to have a word with you.'

'That's just his way. But he'll be wanting a full report. He relies on me, you see.'

'I'm sure he does,' Blackstone replied. 'After all, if he's

even half as useless as you say he is, you must be the one person who's keeping this company from falling apart.'

A look of panic crossed Wilberforce's blotched face. 'You won't tell him what I've been saying to you, will you?' he asked.

'Of course not,' Blackstone said.

'Only he might get the wrong idea, if you do.'

Or the *right* idea, Blackstone thought.

'I'll treat your confidences to me with the respect that they so obviously merit,' he said.

'And I'll treat yours in exactly the same way,' Wilberforce said, sounding somewhat reassured. He held the office door open. 'Since I'm going out myself, I'm afraid I shall have to ask you to leave, too.'

'Couldn't I stay?' Blackstone asked, as meekly as if he took Wilberforce at his own evaluation.

Wilberforce frowned, causing the blotches on his forehead to merge into one red mass, then separate again into smaller, angry islands.

'Well, I'm sure I don't know about that,' the porter said. 'You're not supposed to be here, and—'

'I just need a few minutes to collect my thoughts together,' Blackstone cajoled.

'I suppose that'll be all right then,' Wilberforce conceded. 'Though I have to say that, as far as I'm concerned, a job that's got a lot of sitting and thinking about it is not much of a job at all.'

'You're probably right,' Blackstone agreed, 'but we can't all be porters at the George Theatre, can we? I'm stuck with the job I've got, and I'll just have to make the best of it, won't I?'

Wilberforce nodded sagely. 'It's a wise man who accepts the lot that fate has imposed upon him,' he said, before opening the door and stepping out into the corridor.

Blackstone gave Wilberforce a minute to get clear of the cupboard-office before he began his search of it.

He wasn't expecting to find much of any significance in the place, so he wasn't too disappointed when all his search uncovered was a hidden bottle of gin and a few illegal betting slips.

The porter knew nothing, and saw even less, he decided.

He was far too wrapped in the limiting world of his own self-importance to be either an accurate observer or a reliable witness.

Blackstone lit up a cigarette, and allowed the acrid smoke to snake around his lungs.

It had been a salutary experience meeting Wilberforce again, he thought. It had reminded him that however difficult his own life could be from time to time, he still had a great deal to be thankful for.

True, his line of work led him to see sights of human depravity that would turn the stomach of even the strongest man.

True, he had to endure taking orders from a jumped-up baronet who thought that he knew all there was to know about policing, but in fact knew virtually nothing at all.

And true, his own particular approach to policing would probably mean that would eventually lose his job and – if he didn't have the guts to slit his own throat when that happened – that he was destined to spend his declining years in the workhouse.

But at least he hadn't been born Spotty Wilberforce!

Seven

It was the sound of the two men's voices – in earnest, though not yet quite heated, conversation – which drew Blackstone towards the theatre stage. And it was a sudden thought – that he might learn more by listening than he ever could by interrupting them – that brought him to an abrupt halt when he reached the wings.

The men were standing at the very centre of the stage itself, almost like thespians giving a performance, but there was no audience seated in the auditorium to appreciate it, and the show each man was putting on was purely for the benefit of the other.

One of the 'actors' in this little drama was Sebastian George himself – small, plump, flashily dressed, and puffing on the inevitable cigar.

The other was much taller, and probably somewhere in his early sixties. He wore a sober – though expensive – frock coat, and a silk top hat. His face was long and thin – the sort of face that Blackstone was used to seeing in pictures at the National Portrait Gallery – and was framed by a set of distinguished silver side-whiskers. But it was the way he carried himself which was the most fascinating. He had about him an air of confidence and authority which could possibly have been acquired, though it was much more likely, the inspector strongly suspected, to have been inherited along with the family estate.

'The play was written with Miss Devaraux specifically in mind. It is her vehicle,' Sebastian George was saying, in a wheedling tone that was a million miles away from his normal arrogant delivery. 'Please understand – I beg you – that that without her presence, the drama is nothing,'

'I do understand that,' the other man replied. 'And what *you* must understand, George, is that my primary concern is not the success or failure of your little commercial venture, but the state of Charlotte's health.'

Who was the bugger? Blackstone wondered. Archie Patterson would have come up with his name in an instant, but then he could have done the same with the names of half the chimney sweeps and watermen in London, too.

'I wish you would reconsider, my lord,' Sebastian George said, in the verbal equivalent of throwing himself at the other man's feet.

My lord! Blackstone repeated silently.

So the man with the silver whiskers was an aristocrat. That surely should be enough of a clue to enable a smart-as-paint detective inspector from New Scotland Yard to identify him. He ran quickly through his mental list of the dinosaurs who not only assumed that they still had the right to run the country, but very often – far *too* often – chose to exercise it.

Lord Bixendale! He groaned inwardly.

Why did it have to be someone like him who was involved in all this?

Why couldn't it have been some backwoods peer instead?

Because, he supposed, backwoods peers, by their very nature, *stayed* in the backwoods, while peers like Lord Bixendale had their fingers in more pies than a baker.

Bixendale was a true grandee of the Tory Party. He had served in several governments, and even when his own party was out of office, he still had considerable political influence. He was the steward of one of the more prestigious race courses, and the Bixendale Cup was to jockeys what the Victoria Cross was to soldiers. But, as far as Blackstone could remember, there had never been any talk of him being involved in the theatre.

The two men on the stage, still unaware of the inspector's presence, were continuing their conversation.

'I can understand your – quite proper – concerns for the lady, my lord, but I can assure you that Miss Devaraux is in perfect health,' Sebastian George was gently protesting.

'Perfect health!' Bixendale repeated. 'Physically, what you say may well be true. But, need I remind you, she has just witnessed a murder. Indeed, she has inadvertently played a part in that murder herself. For someone of her delicacy and sensibilities, that will have been a great strain.'

'Delicacy and sensibilities!' George said, his diplomatic skills seeming to suddenly quite desert him. 'Charlotte Devaraux! She's a bloody actress, for God's sake!'

'I am quite well aware of her profession,' Lord Bixendale said coldly.

'And she's as tough as old boots!' Sebastian George continued, ignoring the warning implied in Bixendale's tone. '*All* actresses are – especially the successful ones like her. If she'd been the wilting flower that you seem to imagine her to be, she'd never have got where she is today!'

'Old boots?' Bixendale repeated, his voice now pure ice.

'I didn't mean . . .' George began, finally beginning to understand how slippery the ground beneath his feet was turning.

'I will thank you not to use such gutter phrases when referring to the lady we are currently discussing,' Bixendale said.

Sebastian George seemed to physically shrink under the other man's freezing gaze.

'I apologize, my lord,' he said, in a shaky voice. 'I meant no harm, I can assure you of that—'

'That is not how it appeared to me.'

'—though I fully realize, of course, that I may, *by impli-cation*, have given the wrong impression. In truth, I fully appreciate, as you do yourself, that whilst Miss Devaraux may be an actress, she is, as you have yourself stated – first and foremost – a lady.'

Sebastian George was wise to stick to the business of *managing* theatres, Blackstone thought, because, as his current performance was quite clearly demonstrating, *acting* in them was certainly not his forte.

'Your apology is accepted,' Bixendale said graciously.

'But I still feel that you are underestimating Miss Devaraux's tremendous fortitude and true strength of character if you believe that last night's upset will in any way—'

'I have reached my decision and am not to be moved from it, especially by such a man as you,' Bixendale interrupted. 'However, I will ensure that you do not suffer financially as a result of it—'

'That's more than generous of you, my lord,' George gushed.

'—and since you probably appreciate that having a theatre without Charlotte is better than having no theatre *at all*, you would be wise to give that decision your full support.'

It was at that moment that Blackstone noticed that Charlotte Devaraux had appeared in the wing opposite the one in which he was standing.

It was almost as if she had been waiting for her cue, he thought. And perhaps she had!

She could have seen him as clearly as he was seeing her, but never so much as glanced his direction. Instead, she appeared to be looking into herself – preparing for the role which she was just about to play.

Her preparation completed, Charlotte Devaraux glided across the stage like a tragic heroine who was crossing a dark and desperate place.

'Charlotte, my dear!' Lord Bixendale exclaimed. 'We were just talking about you.'

'Were you, Robert?' the woman asked.

Robert! Blackstone noted. She did not call him 'my lord' – as Sebastian George had wheedlingly done – but *Robert*.

'I have just been addressing George here on the subject of the distress you were made to endure on stage last evening, Charlotte,' Bixendale said. 'I have, furthermore, been pointing out to him the obvious fact that you are in need of a complete rest.'

'I'm not sure—' Charlotte Devaraux began.

'And he agrees with me completely, don't you, George?' Lord Bixendale interrupted.

'Yes, my lord, I certainly do,' Sebastian George said, swallowing hard as he spoke.

'And so I have taken it upon myself to reserve a suite for you in a private sanatorium in the Scottish Highlands,' Lord Bixendale continued. 'There, you will get the tranquillity you sorely require, and perhaps, after a little while, you will feel strong enough to return to London.'

'But I couldn't go away now!' Charlotte Devaraux said. 'My public *demands* that I appear before them nightly.'

'Your public will have to learn to do without you,' Bixendale told her. 'I know what is best for you, and I want no arguments about it.'

The tragic stance which Charlotte Devaraux had been assuming began to melt away, and was replaced by one that was altogether less dramatic and much more human.

'But you'd miss me if I was away, Robbie,' she said, in what was almost a little girl's voice. 'You know you would.'

'I will bear it all with fortitude, because I understand that it is for your benefit,' Bixendale said. 'Besides, I have every expectation of being in Scotland myself, later this month.'

Blackstone was beginning to think that perhaps he'd been rather too hasty in judging Sebastian George to be a poor actor, for though the manager was still standing where he had been all along, he had somehow contrived to make himself appear almost invisible.

Charlotte Devaraux reached up, and gently stroked one of Bixendale's silver whiskers with her index finger.

'It would be wonderful to have you there in Scotland with me, Robbie,' she cooed. 'Indeed, if you could stay there all the time, I don't think I would ever want to leave the place myself. But your visit will be no more than a short one, won't it? How could it be otherwise?'

'Well, I . . .'

'A man of your importance has a great many responsibilities and duties that he must attend to in the capital. And you have never been one to shirk your duty, Robbie, however much you might wish to.'

'It's true that I don't think I could stay in Scotland for much more than a week,' Bixendale admitted.

'And what would I do up there in those Highlands – entirely on my own – once you'd gone away again?' Charlotte Devaraux asked, as her index finger moved under his chin and began to caress it gently.

'You'd soon get used to it, Charlotte,' Bixendale said, though it was quite obvious to Blackstone that the more the woman's finger explored his jaw line, the harder the noble lord was finding it to concentrate on the subject under discussion.

'I should go quite mad, if I were left alone,' Charlotte Devaraux said. 'I know that I should. And what would happen then? Would you want to take a *mad* woman out to dinner with you? Would you invite a *mad* woman to visit you in your private apartments.'

'Well, I . . .'

Charlotte removed her finger from under Bixendale's chin, and placed one of her hands on each of his shoulders.

'Don't be cruel to your little Lamb-Chop, Bobbity,' she implored. 'Let me stay where you know I'll be at my happiest.'

Bixendale hesitated, but it was more than clear that he had already lost the battle.

'We'll let you continue performing for another week, and see how it goes,' he conceded.

'Thank you! Thank you so much!'

'But if I feel that you're under any strain at all, I shall insist that you abandon this foolishness and go straight to the sanatorium in Scotland.'

Charlotte stood on tiptoe to kiss him on the nose. 'That's my wonderful Bobbity,' she said tenderly.

He'd seen enough, Blackstone decided, stepping quietly backwards out of view.

More than enough.

It was possible that Charlotte Devaraux did have some genuine affection for the older man, but still he could not wipe completely from his mind the idea that what he'd just witnessed was a little drama which could have been entitled *The Whore, her Pimp and her Lover*.

55

Eight

Patterson was sitting in the bar of the Crown and Anchor Tavern, a pub often used by officers from Scotland Yard, and facing him across the table was Detective Sergeant Hector Chichester.

Archie Patterson had always had mixed feelings about Chichester. On the one hand, he was forced to admit that Chichester was a good bobby, who worked hard at his job, would never have thought for a moment of taking a bribe, and sometimes found solutions to crimes that a duller policeman might have overlooked entirely. In addition – and still trying to be completely fair to the man – he was a loyal comrade, who watched your back as well as his own, and wouldn't think twice about doing you a favour.

On the other hand, there were things about him that made Patterson occasionally wish he could bundle the bloody man into a sack and drop him over the side of the nearest paddle steamer. He could be smug – no one admired him more greatly than he admired himself – and he could be superior. When he had been clever, he went out of his way to let you know it. And – though Patterson accepted this should not have tipped the balance of judgement about him one way or the other – most women took one look at him and fell swooning at his feet.

'Are you *sure* you want to drink that stuff, Archie?' Chichester asked, looking down with disdain on the glass of soda water which Patterson held in his hand, but was otherwise ignoring.

'It's all right once you get used to the taste of it,' Patterson said unconvincingly. 'Anyway, I haven't come here to be sociable. I want some information.'

'On what?'

'On the tragic and dramatic death of one Martin Swinburne, as it occurred in the latter part of the play *Taking Wing*.'

56

'Almost sounds like the title of a play in itself,' Chichester said.

'Clever of you to notice that,' Patterson countered, feeling as if he'd scored a point. 'You were part of the team that investigated that particular case, weren't you, Hector?'

'I most certainly was,' Chichester confirmed. 'What would you like to know?'

'Well, we could start with you telling me whether or not you think it really was an accident,' Patterson suggested.

'It could have been,' Chichester said enigmatically.

'Does that mean that you think it was an accident – or that you don't?'

'It means that I can't be sure – one way or the other.'

'But you must have an opinion.'

'Not necessarily,' Chichester said, looking as if he thought *he'd* scored a point. 'By their very nature, opinions must be at least *based* on facts – and the facts in this case are very murky indeed.'

'Even so . . .'

'Look at it this way, young Archie – by their very nature, sensationalist effects are dangerous things to perform. Would you like me to explain to you why that should be so?'

'You can do – or perhaps I could explain it to you,' said Patterson, not wanting to give his old comrade any more opportunities to show off than he absolutely had to.

'Go right ahead,' Chichester invited.

'The audience knows it's not a real steam train – or a real flying machine – that they're watching on stage,' Patterson said, 'but they don't want that fact rubbed in their faces by seeing too many ropes and wires. So the people who create the sensationalist effects have to do without a lot of the things they could use – and that would make the effects safer – in the interests of making them look more realistic.'

Chichester smiled encouragingly, as if Patterson were a pupil of his who had made surprisingly good progress. 'Most of the time, the designers get away with cutting corners,' he said. 'But sometimes, they don't.'

'You're not really telling me anything more than I could have worked out for myself in the comfort of my own office,' Patterson said, 'and frankly, I'm a little disappointed.'

'I can't help that, my old mate,' Chichester said cheerfully.

'All I can give you is the facts of the case, and they are that Martin Swinburne was killed because a couple of hooks broke, and a bloody big weight – an electrical motor – fell right on top of him. Now, did the hooks break because they weren't strong enough to hold up the machine? Or did they break because somebody had weakened them before the performance? I don't know, but there certainly wasn't any direct evidence that it was a murder.'

'What about *indirect* evidence?' Patterson said hopefully.

'Are you asking me who had the opportunity to murder him, and might also have had a motive?'

'Exactly.'

'The flying machine was only on stage for the one scene in the whole play, so if somebody had wanted to doctor it, they could have done it at any time in the previous twenty-four hours. And that means that anybody connected with the theatre would have had the *opportunity* to do it.'

'What about motive?'

'The ground's still shaky, but there is a little bit more to go on there. A couple of nights before Swinburne met with his accident—'

'Or before he was murdered!'

'—or before he was murdered, he got into a fight with another member of the company. It was quite a bloody fight, by all accounts, and if they hadn't been quickly separated by some of the other actors, they could have done each other some serious damage.'

'What was the fight about?' Patterson asked.

The superior smile was back on Chichester's face. 'There are only two things that most men will ever fight over,' he said. 'Do you know what they are, Archie? Or have you forgotten at least one of them now that you're engaged?'

'No, I haven't forgotten,' Patterson said. 'The two things most men fight over are women and money.'

'And in this case, it was a woman.'

Patterson took a sip of his soda water, and wished it was beer. 'Tell me more,' he said.

'Her professional name's Tamara Simmons, though it wouldn't surprise me if she'd been christened something far more ordinary, like Nellie Clegg. She's twenty-one years old, if I recall correctly. At the time, she wasn't one of the leading actresses, by any manner of means – the only opportunity she'd ever had to be at centre stage, she told me, was when she'd stood in for the principal actors during rehearsals – but she was a lovely-looking girl, with a figure that makes me go all a-quiver, just thinking about it.'

Patterson grinned. 'You're showing all the signs of eventually turning into a dirty old man,' he said.

Chichester seemed to be trying to choose between being amused and annoyed at the remark. 'I have many years left to me yet as a dirty *young* man,' he said, opting for the former, 'but when the time does come for me to make the change, I trust I shall play that role with honour and dignity.'

Patterson laughed. 'You're full of shit,' he said.

'We all are,' Chichester countered. 'It's a biologically established fact. But to get back to Tamara Simmons—'

'Yes, I wish you would.'

'These theatre girls are not like the girls that you and I know. Our girls are virgins – or at least have the decency to pretend to *us* that they are. These theatre girls, on the other hand, have lovers left, right and centre, and make absolutely no bones about it at all.'

'And this Tamara Simmons had a lover?'

'She did. It was Martin Swinburne. But it seems that one of the other actors was sniffing around her – not that I can blame him for that – and she told Swinburne all about it. Swinburne didn't like that at all, as you can imagine, and that's how the fight started.'

'Is Tamara Simmons still a member of the company, or did she leave it when her lover died?' Patterson asked.

'She's still a member of the company. In fact, she's done rather well for herself since his death. She's still not one of the stars, but she is getting much bigger roles these days.'

'Now how would you know that?' Patterson wondered.

Chichester grinned, self-consciously. 'I happened to run into her in a tea shop on the Strand.'

'Did you now? That is strange.'

'Why?'

'Because, knowing you as I do, I can't see you even going into a tea room through choice.'

'All right, I followed her from the theatre, and made it *seem* as if I'd bumped into her by accident,' Chichester admitted.

'And whatever made you do that?'

'What do you *think* made me do it? We got on well when I was interviewing her – *very* well, as a matter of fact – and I thought that if I gave her a little time to get over Swinburne's death, she might be open to new offers.'

'And was she?'

Chichester shook his head sadly. 'No.'

'Now that is surprising,' Patterson said, sarcastically.

'The only reason is that I'd left it *too* long, isn't it?' Chichester said, on the defensive for once.

'Is it?' Patterson asked. 'How would that work?'

'Like I said, she'd gone up in the world since we last met, and a detective sergeant – even a detective sergeant as incredibly handsome as I am – obviously wasn't good enough for her any more. Oh, she was polite enough to me, but I could see that she couldn't get away from me quickly enough.'

'I think I'll have a word with her myself,' Patterson said.

'You!' Chichester scoffed.

'Yes, me!' Patterson retorted.

'Look, I don't want to seem rude, my old mate, but you've absolutely no chance of succeeding where I've failed,' Chichester warned him. 'Besides, Rose would kill you if she ever found out. Or even worse than that – she might take it into her head to do some permanent damage to your wedding tackle.'

'It's not *that* kind of word I want,' Patterson said severely. 'I wish to speak to her in a purely professional capacity.'

Chichester grinned. 'We've all used *that* line in our time,' he said, 'but good luck to you, anyway. You'll certainly need it.'

'You never told me the name of the man who was sniffing round her – the man Martin Swinburne got into a fight with,' Patterson reminded him.

'Didn't I?' Chichester asked, as if he were about to deliver a punch-line to a very good joke.

'No, you didn't.'

'It was William Kirkpatrick – the bloke who got himself murdered last night.'

Nine

London was not really a city at all, Ellie Carr thought, as she stood at the corner of two roads and looked down a street of dilapidated terraced houses.

Ancient Athens was a city, and so was classical Rome, but this was a collection of different towns – of different *worlds*, almost – which touched, but did not merge. The boundaries which existed between these independent entities did not, it was true, appear on any of the official maps – but they were there, right enough. And woe betide anybody who was foolish enough to cross one of these boundaries without realizing that the rules had changed – that the laws of *this* land were not the same as the one they had just left behind them on the previous street.

She turned to the man who was standing rigidly next to here. 'This is as far as you go, Jed,' she said.

'I was against you doing this right from the start, even with me along to protect you,' Jed Trent said, 'but if you think that I'll allow you to go on with it on your own, then you must be out of your mind.'

'I'm much better on my own,' Ellie Carr said calmly. 'On my own, I've only got myself to worry about. If we go down that street together, I have you to worry about as well.'

'I'm deeply touched by your worry and concern for me, Dr Carr,' Trent said sarcastically.

'And so you should be,' Ellie Carr replied. 'I'm almost like a mother to you, Jed.'

'But though it may have escaped your attention, I'm perfectly capable of taking care of myself. I used to be a policeman, don't forget – and a bloody hard one at that.'

'And *when* you were a policeman, did you ever go down that street?' Ellie asked.

'I may have done,' Trent replied evasively. 'Or if not that particular one, then dozens like it.'

'Did you go down it alone?'

'I don't remember,' Trent said. 'It was a long time ago.'

'No it wasn't! It's no more than a couple of years since you left the Force. And even if it *had* been a long time ago, you'd still remember – because I know you, Jed Trent, and you've got a memory like an elephant's. So now, if you don't mind, I'd like a straight answer to a straight question.'

'No, I probably wouldn't have gone down it alone,' Trent admitted reluctantly.

'Of course you wouldn't. You'd have taken five or six of your comrades with you to back you up. But you haven't got that back-up available now, and if some of the villains who live round here so much as catch sight of you, they'll turn you into mince before you can say "meat grinder".'

'And what about you?' Trent asked worriedly. 'What do you think they'll do to you?'

'They won't do nuffink to me, me ole cock-sparrer,' Ellie said, slipping into her cockney accent. 'Why would they? I'm in disguise, ain't I?'

And so she was, in a way. The dress and hat she was wearing were third-hand – at best – and the dirt she had smeared on her face and hands looked as if it had been there for days.

Yet, to some extent, this was no disguise at all, she thought. She might well *be* Dr Eleanor Carr, who attended important medical conferences and lectured to vast halls full of eager students, but somewhere – not too far below the surface – lurked *little* Ellie Carr, who had been born in the slums, and, for much of her childhood, could not even have conceived of life being lived anywhere else.

'I still don't like it,' Jed Trent said.

'Let's reach a compromise, then,' Ellie suggested.

'What kind of compromise?'

'Let's say that if I'm not back here within the hour, you'll have my permission to call up your old mates in the Met and drench the whole area with bobbies.'

'If you're not back within the hour, I'll call the police out whether I've got your permission or not,' Jed promised her.

The two uniformed constables had been far from thrilled when they'd reported for duty that morning and been handed a long list of names and addresses by their sergeant.

'Who *are* all these people, Sarge?' Constable Baker, the more senior of the two, had asked.

'They're all the sword-makers, knife-grinders and general cutlery makers who conduct their businesses within the London area,' the sergeant replied, with all the chirpiness of a man planning to spend *his* day sitting in front of the police station's stove.

'And why should they be of any interest to us?' Constable Davenport wondered.

'They're of interest to you because they're of interest to Inspector Blackstone, who just happens to be your superior,' the sergeant explained. 'The inspector would like you to visit all these establishments, and show the people in charge of them this photograph of a knife.'

'But if they're running that kind of establishment, they'll already *know* what a knife looks like,' Davenport said, then seeing the change of expression on his sergeant's face, added a hasty, 'Sorry, Sarge.'

'And so you should be,' the sergeant told him. 'This particular knife was used in a sensational murder only last night, and you two have been given the honour of playing a vital part in the investigation.'

'Couldn't we play a vital part that won't involve so much walking?' Baker asked hopefully.

'No, you could not,' the sergeant said. 'This is the job that has been assigned to you, and this is the job that you'll do. I want all the shops on this list to have been canvassed by the time you go off duty, and I don't want to hear any excuses for you missing even a single one of them out.'

'Can we take cabs?' Davenport asked hopefully.

'No,' the sergeant said sternly. 'You most certainly can not.'

The boy was twelve or thirteen, and said his name was Horace. He was scrawny but tough, and his deep brown eyes were ever-alert and ever-watchful. At first, Blackstone couldn't work out why he should look so familiar. And then it came to him – the boy reminded him of his own, much younger, self.

'What exactly is your job here?' he asked.

'A bit of everyfink, to be honest wiv yer,' the boy told him.

'For instance?'

'A bit of paintin', a bit of cleanin' up, a bit of keepin' the vermin down . . .'

Blackstone smiled. 'Vermin?' he said. 'You're not talking about the actors, are you?'

'No,' the boy said, missing the point completely. 'We get all kinds of wild fings comes to pay us a visit. Mice as big as rats. Rats as big as cats. Cats as big as young lions. We've had foxes an' hedgehogs, once or twice. The uvver night, there was even a frog in 'ere.'

'And what did you do with that? Flush it into the sewer?'

'Would 'ave done, if I could 'ave found it. But I didn't. I could hear the bugger croakin', all right, but I couldn't find neither hide nor hair of it, so I suppose it might still be here.'

'Tell me about some of the other things you do,' Blackstone suggested. 'You sometimes run errands for the actors, don't you?'

'That's right,' the boy agreed, puffing out his thin chest. 'That's where the trainin' comes in, you see.'

'The training?'

'I want to be an actor myself, one day. They have a grand life, you know. They sleep in proper feather beds. An' they can eat three meals a day, if they feel like it. So when I'm runnin' their errands for them, I'm watchin' them as well. Learnin' all the tricks of the trade, as you might say.'

'You were the one who picked up the knife for Miss Devaraux last night, weren't you?'

'That's right. Same as I've done every night while this partic'lar play's been runnin'. I like doin' fings for 'er. She's a nice lady, an' sometimes she'll give me a bit of spendin' money out of 'er own purse.'

'Did you notice anything unusual about the knife last night?' Blackstone wondered.

'Unusual? 'Ow do you mean?'

'Well, did it feel like a different knife to the one you usually took her?'

'Nah, it felt the same as always. If it 'ad been different, I would 'ave told Miss Devaraux.'

'Then let me ask you another question. Did you see anybody in the props room who shouldn't, by rights, have been there at all?'

The boy grinned. 'You mean a mysterious stranger wiv a foreign accent an' blood drippin' from his teeth?' he asked.

Blackstone returned the grin. 'I was thinking more of any member of the cast – or any of the stage hands, for that matter – who wouldn't normally be in that area, but put in an appearance last night.'

'No,' the boy said. 'Everyfink was perfectly normal – right up until Mr Kirkpatrick got killed, of course.'

'Of course,' Blackstone agreed. 'Did Mr Kirkpatrick have any particular enemies that you know of?'

'Well, he didn't 'ave a lot of friends, if that's what you're askin',' the boy said. 'Leadin' actors never do. But I can't fink of anybody who'd dislike him so much as to actually go an' kill the bleeder.'

Especially, Blackstone thought, to go and kill the bleeder in such an elaborate manner.

The house she was heading for was midway down the terraced street. It looked no worse than the ones which flanked it, Ellie Carr thought – but in this street of decay and desperation, that really wasn't saying very much.

Ellie knocked on the door, and her knock was answered by a grotesquely fat woman with a skin which would not have looked out of place if it had been worn by a rhinoceros.

'What d'yer want?' the woman demanded, looking at Ellie as if she were something the cat had dragged in.

'Do yer know Mrs Minnie Knox?' Ellie asked.

The fat woman scratched her armpit. 'Yes, I know 'er. She's me muvver. What's that to you?'

'I'd like ter see 'er.'

'What for?'

'Cos she's famous, ain't she?'

The fat woman thought about it. 'It'll cost yer a shillin' to see 'er,' she said finally.

'A shillin'!' Ellie repeated. 'If she was in one of them shows on the Mile End Road, it'd only cost me a penny.'

'But she ain't in one of them shows, is she? She's upstairs in 'er bed. An' if you want to see 'er, it'll cost yer a shillin'.'

'Fair enough,' Ellie Carr agreed.

Ten

Police Constables Baker and Davenport had already checked out half a dozen shops on the list they'd been given by their sergeant. So far, they had met with no success at all, and their feet were beginning to complain about the punishment they were unfairly being asked to endure.

The seventh shop on the list – Delaney and Company (established 1786) – looked to be no more promising than the previous ones had been. It was located on a narrow side-street, and though it boasted the family crests of several of its patrons over the door, it seemed highly unlikely that any member of the aristocracy had set foot in it for at least twenty years.

The man behind the counter was in his forties. He wore a khaki smock, and the spectacles, which rested precariously on his nose, had lenses as thick as the bottoms of beer bottles.

'Are you Mr Delaney?' Constable Baker asked.

'That's me,' the man agreed.

'So, how's business?' Constable Davenport inquired.

Baker scowled. He wished his partner wouldn't always ask that question. Davenport claimed that he did it to put the person they were questioning at his ease. Maybe it did. But it also exposed them both to the danger of hearing much more on the subject than they ever needed to know.

And so it proved to this time.

'Business isn't what it used to be at all,' Delaney complained. 'Seven generations of my family have been involved in this firm, but it looks like I shall be the last one to uphold the tradition.'

'I'm sure that's very interesting in its way, Mr Delaney, but—' Constable Baker began.

'In the old days, people took a real pride in their weapons,' Delaney interrupted him. 'Gentlemen of quality always wanted the best dress swords that money could buy them, and even a lowly cut-throat wanted to own a knife that he wouldn't be ashamed to show to the other members of his gang. It's not like that at all, these days. If a knife just does the job, then that's all they care about. Why, I can remember when—'

'Have you seen this knife before?' Baker asked, slapping the photograph of the murder weapon on the counter.

'Have I seen it before!' Delaney scoffed.

'Well, have you?'

'I should say that I have. I made it to order. And a lovely job I did of it, too, if I say so myself as shouldn't. And it wasn't easy, you know.'

'Why wasn't it easy?' Davenport wondered.

'It's never easy to make a *really* good knife, a knife that says immediately that craftsmanship isn't for—'

'But it was no easier, and no more difficult, than most of the knives you've been asked to make?' Baker said.

'It was *much* harder,' Delaney said rebukingly. 'In this case, my task was complicated by the fact that the customer demanded that the knife was a certain weight. I told him, a knife weighs what a knife weighs, and if you start messing about with that – going against the laws of nature, as you might say – you'll probably ruin the balance. And do you know what he said to me?'

'No,' Baker asked impatiently. 'What *did* he say?'

'He told me he didn't *care* about the balance! Can you imagine that? I mean, *can you*?'

'Never really thought much about it,' Davenport admitted.

'I make him a beautiful knife – and charge him through the nose for it – and he doesn't give a damn about the balance!' Delaney said, as if he still couldn't quite believe it.

'Do you happen to remember what this customer looked like?' Constable Baker asked.

'Well, of course I remember. It's not every day somebody hands you that kind of commission. Like I told you before, all they usually care about is whether it will cut or not.'

Baker sighed. 'What *did* he look like?' he asked.

'He was a little old man.'

'How old?'

'I couldn't say for sure.'

'Sixty? Seventy?'

'Maybe. But it wouldn't surprise me if he turned out to be even older than that.'

The fat woman led Ellie Carr into a corridor which was crammed with rusting prams and broken chairs, and pointed to the stairs.

'Muvver's up there,' she said. 'Don't take too much time about it, or I shall 'ave to charge you extra.'

As if I'd stay in this place any longer than I had to, Ellie thought, placing her foot gingerly on the first of the rotting steps.

The bedroom at the top of the stairs was as mean and dirty as the rest of the house. The bed itself looked – and smelled – as if it had last been changed when Queen Victoria came to the throne, and lying in it was a very old woman. She was almost skeletally thin and had a skin which was nearly translucent, but there was a fire in her eyes which said that though her body might be close to death, her mind was still very much alive.

'There used to be 'undreds of people 'oo wanted to see me, just for the privilege of shakin' me 'and,' the old woman said. 'Course, that was just after the trial. I don't get many admirers comin' to see me these days.'

'Well, yer've got one now,' Ellie said. 'Did yer do it?'

'Do what?'

'Did you poison yer 'usband an' 'is fancy-woman both?'

The old woman gave a rasping laugh. 'The jury found me not guilty, didn't they?' she asked.

'Well, they were bound to, weren't they? I mean to say, when one of 'em dropped dead in the street on the way to the court, it was only natural for the rest of 'em to wonder 'oo was goin' to be next.'

'That was an 'eart attack wot that juror 'oo yer talkin' about died of,' the old woman said.

'It was poison, an' everybody at the time knew it,' Ellie contradicted her. 'The bobbies couldn't prove 'e'd been poisoned – an' even if they could 'ave, they'd never have bin able to pin it on you, what wiv you bein' locked up inside the prison an' everyfink – but every member of that jury knew that if 'e voted to convict you, 'e might be the next one to feel a sudden sharp pain in 'is chest.'

The old woman cackled. 'The judge was bloody furious wiv that jury,' she said. 'Told 'em there was enough evidence to 'ang me three times over, an' it was a disgrace that they'd found me not guilty. But for all 'is shoutin' an' screamin', there was nuffink he could do about it, was there? They'd reached their verdict, an' 'e 'ad to let me go.'

'An' you were more careful after that, wasn't you? There was never enough evidence to arrest you a second time.'

The old woman's eyes narrowed. 'Maybe that's 'cos I didn't do no more poisonin's,' she said.

Ellie put her hand on her hips. 'Pull the uvver one,' she said. 'It's got bells on.'

'But if I *'ad 'ave* done any more poisonin's, it would only 'ave been 'cos I 'ad no choice,' Minnie Knox said. 'After all, I was a poor widder woman after me 'usband got taken. I 'ad to do somefink to earn a crust, didn't I?'

Ellie reached into her purse and produced a gold guinea. She held it up for the old woman to see.

'Speakin' of earnin' a crust,' she said, 'I need some advice – an' I'm willin' to pay for it.'

Minnie Knox's eyes clouded over with dark suspicion. 'I've retired,' she said.

'Well, now, that is a real pity,' Ellie replied, putting the money back in her purse.

''Ow do I know yer not workin' for the police?' the old woman asked, her eyes following the progress of the coin with longing. ''Ow do I know yer not just tryin' to trap me?'

'It's thirty years since you was arrested,' Ellie said. 'All the policemen involved in the case will be dead by now, an' them that 'as replaced them ain't interested in you no more.'

'Yer prob'ly right. It's a terrible fing to be forgotten,' the old woman said wistfully.

'But since you are, an' since – as far as the bobbies are concerned – yer've got away wiv it, will yer 'elp me now?' Ellie said.

'If I tell yer 'ow to kill somebody, I'll be just as guilty as what you are yourself.'

'I don't want yer to tell me 'ow to kill somebody,' Ellie explained. 'I want yer to tell me 'ow somebody was killed.'

'Now why would yer want to know that?'

They'd reached a point at which it was time to stop playing

games, Ellie decided. 'I'm a criminal pathologist,' she said in her normal voice.

'A what?'

'It's a special kind of doctor. I cut people open to find out exactly how they died.'

'You *are* a woman, ain't you?' Minnie Knox asked suspiciously. 'You ain't a man, wearin' a disguise?'

'No, I am a woman, I promise you.'

'An' yer weren't lyin' when you said you was a doctor?'

'No.'

'Well, good for you!' the old woman said. 'Yer've made somefink of yerself.' She sighed. 'Wiv what I know, I might well 'ave 'ad the same sort of job as you meself – if I'd been born thirty years later.'

Ellie laughed. 'You might well have had,' she agreed. 'Shall I tell you about the case now?'

'Why not. It'll be a pleasure to talk to somebody 'oo's more or less in the same business as I was in meself.'

Ellie described the death of William Kirkpatrick.

'Sounds like 'ooever killed 'im really knew 'ow to do 'is job,' Minnie Knox said.

'That's just what I was thinking,' Ellie agreed.

'Don't sound like arsenic, though.'

'It wasn't. I knew that right from the start. But I tested his organs for traces of it, anyway.'

'What did yer use?' the old woman asked. 'The Marsh test?'

'Yes, but how did you know about that?' Ellie asked, astonished.

Minnie Knox cackled again. 'It's always best to find out what yer enemy can prove an' what 'e can't,' she said. She thought for a second. 'The murderer might 'ave used digitalin, I s'pose, like the bloke wot murdered Madame de Pauw did, over in France.'

'It wasn't that either. I tested for all the plant alkaloids, and came up with a blank.'

'Then yer lookin' for a new kind of poison – one that 'as never bin used in England before.'

Ellie smiled. 'I knew I'd come to the right person,' she said. 'We think alike, you and I, but you're the one with the greater experience.'

'If I was you, I'd start by takin' a much closer look at places around the world where there ain't much in the way of what you might call law an' order,' Minnie Knox said.

'Why?'

''Cos it's a *secret* poison.'

'A what?'

'A poison yer know nuffink about. But yer will, won't yer? By the time yer've finished examin' it, yer'll know all about it.'

'That's certainly what I'm hoping,' Ellie admitted.

'But poisons – even secret poisons – don't just drop from the sky, do they? It must 'ave been used somewhere else before it was used 'ere. So why ain't there no record of it?'

'You tell me.'

''Cos it's like I said before – in the places where it's bin used, there ain't no real law an' order. So there also ain't no bright gals like you to identify the poison proper.'

'I see what you're getting at,' Ellie said, admiringly.

'It's 'eathen countries what yer should be lookin' at,' the old woman advised her. 'Places like India an' China.'

'I think you're right,' Ellie said. 'You've been very helpful,' she continued, reaching into her purse again.

'I don't want yer money,' Minnie Knox told her.

'You don't?'

'I do not. An' shall I tell you why?'

'Yes, I'd be pleased if you did,'

'It's because you're an expert, an' I'm an expert. An' any advice I might 'ave bin able to give you 'as been . . . wot-d'yer-call-it.'

'A professional courtesy?' Ellie suggested.

'That's right,' the old poisoner agreed. 'A professional courtesy.'

Eleven

When Blackstone had arrived at the theatre at eight o'clock that morning, there had only been Spotty Wilberforce there to greet him – if 'greeting' was what you chose to call it. By nine, Sebastian George, Charlotte Devaraux and Lord Bixendale were also present, playing out their little three-cornered drama of 'should-she-go-to-Scotland-or-should-she-stay-in-the-theatre' on the stage. But it was not until around ten thirty that the building began to fill up with those people whose job it was to provide the entertainment that the ghoulish public – which had been queuing in the rain for over three hours – demanded.

The actors and stage hands arrived at the theatre in dribs and drabs. None of them looked more than half awake. They were all sluggishly uncommunicative, and seemed to be holding a grudge against the world in general – and anyone who accidentally happened to cross their paths in particular.

It was scarcely an inspiring sight, Blackstone thought. A military commander, observing his troops in this kind of state just before the start of a major offensive, would have all but given up hope of winning the battle. A City stockbroker, noticing his jobbers wrapped up in such a heavy blanket of lethargy, would already be anticipating huge losses on the day's trading. And a police duty sergeant, sending his constables out on their morning beats, would have foreseen an easy time for the criminals operating on his patch.

It was an hour before the curtain was due to go up for the afternoon matinée that the atmosphere changed. Suddenly, the actors began to radiate a presence which would thrill even those members of the audience at the very back of the balcony. In a flash, the technicians and stage hands transformed themselves from grumbling time-servers into men with the confidence and competence to handle any disaster that might possibly occur.

The sleeping beast that had been the theatre had come to life, and was ready to take on its public.

Sergeant Hector Chichester had told Patterson that Tamara Simmons was a peach of a girl. And – from a distance – Patterson could see that Hector Chichester had not been wrong. It was only when you got nearer to her that the magic disappeared.

It wasn't that a closer inspection revealed flaws in her skin – which was near perfect – Patterson thought. It wasn't that

72

her stunning figure was any less impressive once you could almost touch it. The problem lay with her eyes. True, they were as deep blue as the Pacific Ocean – but they were also quite as empty of thought and feeling as that vast stretch of water.

There was no absolutely spark about the woman at all, Patterson decided – no sign of intelligence, or sensitivity, not a hint of a zest for life.

'I'm appearing in the second act of the play, so I can't stay here long,' Tamara told him as he ushered her towards a table in the tea room next to the theatre. 'Anyway, there wouldn't be any point in staying. I've already told that other bobby everything I know.'

'That other bobby?' Patterson repeated. 'Do you mean Sergeant Hector Chichester?'

'Was that his name? I don't remember.'

Oh, you poor deluded bugger, Hector, Patterson thought, as he experienced only the mildest touch of malicious pleasure. Chichester had imagined he was getting on so very well with Tamara Simmons, hadn't he? Yet the truth was that he'd made so little impression on her that she didn't even recognize his name when it was brought up.

'So, can I go now?' Tamara Simmons asked.

'No, you most certainly cannot,' Patterson said, in his deepest – most official – voice. 'You may well have told Sergeant Chichester all you know, but that's neither here nor there. I need to hear your statement for myself.'

'Oh, all right, if that's what you want,' Tamara Simmons replied, with an acceptance which was almost bovine in its quality.

'You were having an affair with Martin Swinburne just before he died, weren't you?' Patterson asked.

Tamara Simmons shrugged.

'Weren't you?' Patterson persisted.

'I wouldn't say we were having an *affair*, exactly.'

'Then what would you say?'

'That he was my *gentleman friend*.'

'But you were having sexual relations with him, weren't you?'

'Well, yes, I suppose I was.'

'So how long had this *affair* of yours been going on?'

'A few weeks.'

'And how did it start?'

'Start? What do you mean?'

'How did you first become friendly?'

'Oh, he asked me out to dinner one night.'

'And how long after that first dinner was it that you actually went to bed with him?'

'A few days.'

'How did you feel about the relationship? In your own mind, did you see it as the Grand Romance?'

'Pardon?'

'Were there fireworks when you were together?'

The girl seemed to be making a real attempt to search through the overgrown jungle of her memory. 'We did see fireworks *once*,' she said finally. 'It was in Hyde Park. I think it must have been the Queen's birthday or something.'

Patterson sighed. 'Were you in love with him?'

'In love?'

'In love.'

'Well, yes, I suppose I must have been.'

Having this conversation was harder than trying to pull teeth, Patterson thought.

'Tell me about what happened between you and William Kirkpatrick,' he suggested.

'Nothing happened.'

'But he wanted something to happen, didn't he?'

'That's what he said.'

'Exactly what *did* he say?'

'I don't know. I suppose it must have been something like, "I want to sleep with you".'

'Very romantic,' Patterson said. 'And what did you do, once he'd made this almost irresistible proposal to you?'

'I told Mr Swin ... I told Martin ... all about it. He was very angry, and went to see Mr Kirkpatrick right away. Then they had a big fight. And that's really all I know.'

Patterson tried to imagine himself fighting over this woman, and found that he just couldn't even begin to picture it.

'Did you ever have the suspicion that Martin's accident might not have been an accident at all?' he asked.

'Why should I have?'

'Well, both he and William Kirkpatrick were mad with desire for you, weren't they?'

'I wouldn't say they were exactly *mad* with it.'

'And when Martin Swinburne was killed, Kirkpatrick no longer had any other rivals for your affection. Isn't that true?'

'Yes.'

'So maybe Kirkpatrick *arranged* the accident.'

'He could have done, I suppose. I never thought about it that way before,' the woman admitted.

Tamara Simmons never actually thought about *anything* very much, Patterson decided.

'Had William Kirkpatrick tried to woo you again *since* Martin Swinburne was killed?' he asked.

'No. Not really.'

'That's strange, isn't it? What made him suddenly lose his passion for you?'

'I don't know.'

Hopeless, Patterson thought. Completely bloody hopeless. He'd get more information from interrogating a sack of potatoes.

'Hector Chichester tells me you've started to get bigger parts in the plays since Martin Swinburne died,' he said.

'That's right.'

'And why do think that is?'

'Because Mr George *gave* me bigger parts.'

Patterson resisted the strong urge to lean across the table and shake the bloody woman until her teeth rattled.

'But *why* did Mr George give you bigger parts?' he asked exasperatedly. 'Was it because he felt sorry for you after your lover was killed? Was it because he thought you'd now gained the necessary experience to take them on?'

The girl was still looking at him blankly.

'Was it because a green owl appeared to him in the dead of night and told him to?' Patterson asked desperately.

'I don't think it was that last thing you mentioned,' Tamara Simmons said. 'We've had rats and frogs in the theatre, but I don't ever remember seeing an owl, especially a green one.'

'But you *can't* get to Paris!' the actress playing Elizabeth Wilton said, speaking to Charlotte Devaraux, but looking out into the packed auditorium. 'You know as well as I do that the vile Pittstock has his evil henchmen watching every railway station and every port in the land. They will be bound to stop you.'

'No, they will not. Because I will use neither train nor ship for my journey.'

'Then how will you reach Paris?'

Charlotte Devaraux threw back her head and laughed. 'I will travel by hot air balloon!'

The curtain began to descend. Charlotte Devaraux maintained her stance as it was coming down – even when only her feet were visible to the audience – but the moment it had finally touched the floor, a change came over her. She was no longer the grand lady, who even the villainous Pittstock could not intimidate. Now, free from her public's gaze, she was suddenly a perfectly ordinary woman who had clearly been exhausted by the traumatic events of the previous eighteen hours.

And that ability to mask her true feelings – to project an entirely different self – was why they called what she did *acting*, Blackstone supposed, as he watched from the wings.

From the audience's side of the curtain came the sound of thunderous applause, but Charlotte Devaraux, instead of staying to revel in it, immediately left the stage.

And Blackstone, for his part, abandoned his position in the wings in favour of one in the props room.

The props were laid out on the table in just the manner that Norman Foster had described them the previous evening. The dagger, with its wicked-looking blade sheathed in its leather case, was amongst them.

'How did you manage to get a replacement dagger so quickly?' Blackstone asked.

'I didn't,' Foster told him. 'With a complicated prop, like this one is, I always make certain we have a spare to hand. But I'm not at all happy about using it – if this one disappears like the last one, we'll really be stuck.'

'You'd have thought that the murderer would have borne that in mind, wouldn't you?' Blackstone said, with his tongue firmly in his cheek. 'I mean to say, how much effort would it have taken, once he'd done the swap, for him to leave the fake dagger somewhere you could find it?'

'No effort at all,' Foster said. 'But I'm not surprised that he didn't. Actors, managers, murderers – nobody in this place ever shows any consideration for *my* problems.'

Unable to keep his face straight any longer, Blackstone turned his head and looked out on to the corridor. There was a constant stream of people rushing past the door of the props room, he noted.

He turned around to face the props master again, and as he did so, he forced himself to look serious again.

'Tell me, Mr Foster, is it always as busy as this?' he asked.

'Always,' the props manager replied. 'Sometimes, depending on the nature of the play, it can be even worse.'

Which meant that it was unlikely the murderer *could* have entered the props room – which he would have to have done in order to make the substitution – without anyone seeing him do it, Blackstone thought.

Which meant, by extension, that either the people who'd seen him had forgotten all about it, or that he had had a perfectly legitimate reason for entering the room, so they'd not even given it a second thought.

'Can you remember which of the props were collected during the time you were out of the room taking the phone call?' he asked Foster.

'I didn't take a call,' Foster said. 'There was nobody on the other end of the line.'

Blackstone sighed. 'But you were out of the room?'

'Yes.'

'And some props *were* removed while you were away?'

'They had to be. The production doesn't stop just because I've been called away.'

'And do you know who normally picks up the props that were taken while you *were* away?'

'Of course I do. I'm the props master.'

'Then I'd like you to make me a list of them – the props *and* the people – if you wouldn't mind,' Blackstone said.

The boy, Horace, appeared in the doorway. 'I've come for the dagger, Mr Foster,' he said.

'Well, you know where it is,' Foster told him.

'An' you're sure it's the fake one this time, are you?' the boy asked cheekily. 'I don't want to go carryin' no more murder weapons this week, thank you very much.'

'It's the fake,' Foster replied, giving no indication that he even realized the boy had been joking. 'And it's the only one we've got left now, so you'd better take care of it.'

'No worries, Mr Foster,' Horace assured him. 'It's as safe as houses in my hands.'

'He's a smart lad,' Foster said, approvingly, when the boy had disappeared down the corridor. 'He could make a halfway decent props master one day, if he really applied himself to it.'

Pittstock appeared from behind the fake bushes, and Lady Wilton, seeing him, threw the anchor out of the basket.

How would Charlotte Devaraux handle this scene, Blackstone wondered, observing her from his position in the wings.

How would she cope with reenacting an incident which, only the night before, had caused a man's death?

The audience was obviously having similar thoughts. At the performance Blackstone had attended as a paying customer – or rather, as a *paid for* customer, since Ellie had footed the bill – they'd gasped when the balloon began to rise. Now there was no more than an expectant hush.

Pittstock – or rather Richmond Clay, the understudy who'd so unexpectedly found himself promoted to secondary lead – sprinted across the stage, grabbed hold of the edge of the basket, and was lifted off the stage. And still the audience was perfectly silent.

'You thought you could escape me, Lady Wilton!' he roared. 'But you will never escape! In a moment, I will join you in your basket, and then your fate will be sealed.'

'I am not the feeble woman you take me to be . . .' Charlotte Devaraux told him.

And she didn't sound feeble, Blackstone thought.

Not at all.

But the real test of her character was yet to come – when she had to produce the dagger.

' . . . yet I must do what I can to protect my own life and the lives of my family, friends and servants.'

She reached into her handbag, and suddenly the sheathed dagger was in her hand.

The audience, though still completely silent, was finding it increasingly hard to sit still.

Charlotte Devaraux pulled the dagger from its sheath, and held it above her head for everyone to see.

'With this knife, I will have my revenge for all the evil you have visited on me,' she said.

This was what they'd all been waiting for, Blackstone thought. This was why they'd queued in the rain for over three hours without complaint.

Charlotte Devaraux swung the knife through an arc with such speed that it was almost a blur. And at the end of that arc – as everyone in the theatre knew – was Richmond Clay's neck.

The knife struck its target. Richmond Clay screamed, released his grip on the basket, and plummeted to the stage.

Charlotte Devaraux held the knife aloft again, where the audience could see it gleaming it all its evilness, and from the stalls there were several screams equal to Clay's.

The blade had failed to retract, Blackstone thought in horror.

And for the second performance in a row, Charlotte Devaraux had killed a man!

But Charlotte Devaraux did not scream as she had done the previous evening. Instead, she put her free hand to her brow, and looked out into the audience.

'God forgive me for killing him, but I did not have a choice!' she said dramatically.

Then the curtain fell, and – with all agility of a trained athlete – Richmond Clay jumped to his feet.

There were two more scenes to be played out before the end of the melodrama, but even a normal audience would have regarded them as no more than a necessary tying-up of loose strands of the plot, and thus tolerated – rather than actively enjoyed – them. For this particular audience of ghouls, the scenes were an almost unbearable anticlimax, and when Richmond Clay appeared on stage to take his final bow, the applause he received was somewhat tinged with disappointment.

Blackstone was standing in the wings when Charlotte Devaraux came off-stage after taking her bows.

'I thought you did that magnificently, especially considering all you've been through,' he told her.

'Why, thank you,' the actress replied. 'I won't say that it was easy for me, but my dear father always taught me that when you've been thrown from a horse, the only thing to do is to mount it again immediately, and that is a lesson I have carried with me throughout my life.'

'I really thought that you'd stabbed Richmond Clay,' Blackstone said, realizing he must be sounding like a fumbling, bumbling stage door Johnny, but not being able to help himself. 'I've been involved in knife fights myself—'

'You have? How interesting for you,' Charlotte Devaraux said, with a slight smile playing on her lips.

'—so I know what it's like. I know all the moves – the left-hand feint, the right-hand feint – and even with that knowledge, I still truly believed that you'd actually stabbed him!'

'It is the essence of my art to make the highly artificial seem excessively real,' Charlotte Devaraux replied. 'And as I think I indicated to you last night, I pride myself on being a true professional.'

And there was no disputing that was just what she was, Blackstone thought.

Twelve

The King's Head Tavern and Oyster Bar was full to overflowing with those members of the audience who had seen the matinée from the cheaper seats, and, to a man, they were talking excitedly about the performance.

'Do you know, Oswald, I've never actually been to what you might call the proper theatre before,' said one young man at the bar, who – judging from his style of dress – was probably a junior clerk in a brokerage house, or else worked as a wharfinger's assistant at one of the warehouses down by the river. 'To tell you the truth, the music hall's normally more my style of thing.'

80

'Is that so, Reginald?' asked his companion, who looked to be in a similar line of business. 'Well, that is a surprise. I've always pictured you as being a well-known face Up West.'

'But I have to say, it's been an eye-opener,' Reginald continued, missing the irony. 'And well worth playing the "sick" card for and taking the afternoon off work. Do you know, when I saw that Pittstock fall from the balloon, I was convinced – really, truly convinced – that he'd been stabbed.'

'Richmond Clay,' Oswald corrected him superciliously.

'What?'

'Pittstock's only the name of the character. The actor's called Richmond Clay. If you'd been to the theatre as often as I have, you'd soon be able to tell the difference.'

'Who are you trying to fool?' Reginald asked, turning like a worm which has only just seen the gardener's sharp spade.

'Why should I be trying to fool *anybody*?' Oswald asked, apparently mystified.

'"Been to the theatre as often as I have",' Reginald repeated, in a fair imitation of his friend's voice. 'It's all as new to you as it is to me. You only went this time because you thought you might see somebody getting killed.'

'That's not true at all,' Oswald protested. 'I've always been very interested in the theatre, and if I haven't been to it as often as I'd have liked to, that's only because I couldn't find the time.'

'So coming to see this play today had nothing to do with what happened last night?'

'I won't deny that last night's events might have added a little edge of excitement to the whole proceedings,' Oswald said weakly.

'Little edge of excitement!' Reginald repeated, with a show of derision. 'You thought you'd see Pittstock – or Richmond Clay, if you'd prefer it – get himself topped!'

'And it's a bloomin' wonder that he didn't,' Oswald agreed, abandoning all attempt to appear to be above the baser curiosity of his companion. 'Did you see that knife?'

'I most certainly did.'

'If Charlotte Devaraux had misjudged it by just an inch – or even *half* an inch . . .'

'And who's to know if she'll get it right next time? They

81

say that when you play with fire, you're almost bound to get burned eventually.'

'So will you be going to see the show again?'

'I should say so. And you?'

'Definitely!'

The tall thin man standing next to them had placed an order for a pint of bitter and a glass of soda water, but so far said nothing. Now, he decided to speak.

'The way I heard it,' he told the two clerks in a confidential whisper, 'you're not even allowed to play the role of Pittstock unless you're suffering from an incurable disease.'

'Is that right?' Reginald asked incredulously.

'Absolutely,' Blackstone confirmed. 'Well, it makes sense, doesn't it?'

'Does it?'

'Of course. They're not going to risk having a healthy man involved in a dangerous stunt like that, now are they?'

The two young men nodded wisely. 'No, of course they're not,' they agreed in unison.

Blackstone took the drinks over to the table in the corner, where Patterson was waiting for him.

'The vultures are circling,' he said.

'Sorry, sir?'

'Sebastian George had better pray the government doesn't suddenly decide to bring back public execution, or he'll lose half his new-found audience to it overnight.'

'Yes, death must seem quite exciting – when you don't come across it quite as often as we do,' Patterson said, philosophically.

Blackstone took a sip of his pint of bitter and – in deference to poor Archibald Patterson's suffering – tried to look as if he really wasn't enjoying the experience too much.

'How did your interview with Tamara Simmons go?' he asked.

'I might as well just have stayed at home and plucked my nose hairs,' Patterson said.

'Which, I take it, means that you didn't actually find the interview very helpful at all.'

'You've heard the saying that beauty is in the eye of the beholder, haven't you, sir?'

'Yes?'

'Well, all I can say is that if Martin Swinburne and William Kirkpatrick both fell in love with Tamara Simmons, then they were both sorely in need of a pair of very thick spectacles.'

'She's not attractive?'

'She's *attractive* enough, I suppose. If you were running a matrimonial agency, and showed one of your clients three photographs, one of Tamara Simmons, one of my Rose and one of your Ellie—'

'She's not *my* Ellie,' Blackstone interrupted.

'—if you showed him a picture of all three of them, he'd probably choose Tamara. But there's nothing to her, sir. She's an empty shell. And talk about stupid – she makes a bucket of jellied ells look like a mastermind.'

'Perhaps she was only *pretending* to be stupid,' Blackstone suggested. 'When all's said and done, she *is* an actress.'

'And not a very good one, as far as I could tell,' Patterson countered. 'But if she *was* acting – which I don't believe for a minute she was – then it was a truly brilliant performance.'

'How do you think the case is going otherwise?' Blackstone asked. 'Do we have any suspects?'

'I should say so. We stand amidst a veritable forest of suspects,' Patterson replied.

Blackstone almost choked on his beer.

'Less than a day of brushing shoulders with the bloody theatre folk, and you're already starting to sound like one of them,' he said, when he'd cleared the obstruction in his throat. 'You'll be wearing tights by the time this investigation is over.'

'Maybe I will at that – if I can ever slim down enough to find a pair that will fit me.'

'Be of good cheer – the fat's positively melting off you, even as you speak,' Blackstone said encouragingly. 'Now, why don't you tell me about this "veritable forest of suspects" of yours?'

'Everyone in the company is a suspect, as far as I'm concerned – with the possible exception of Tamara Too-Stupid-To-Live Simmons – but I think a couple of them stand out above the rest.'

'And they are?'

'Well, for a start, there's Sebastian George himself.'

'You think he'd kill off his own leading actor?'

'If needs be. But according to what your mate Wilberforce told you, Kirkpatrick wasn't much of a leading actor at all,' Patterson pointed out. 'Martin Swinburne was the real attraction of the George Theatre, and he was already dead. And as you've just seen for yourself, Kirkpatrick's murder has been a real spur to ticket sales. I rang up earlier, just to see how they were going, and I was told the play's booked up for weeks.'

'Even so . . .' Blackstone began.

'People kill to protect the things they love, sir,' Patterson said earnestly. 'And there's no doubt that George loves his theatre – after all, he named it after himself.'

'I don't think you're right on that particular point,' Blackstone contradicted him.

'So what are you saying? That he named it after somebody *else* called George?' Patterson asked sceptically.

'As I recall, it was his father who first opened the theatre, about forty years ago. Sebastian wasn't even born then, so the chances are that it was named after Mr George Senior, don't you think?'

'Good point,' Patterson conceded. 'And what happened to Mr George Senior?'

'I should imagine what happened to him is the same as will happen to all of us, in the course of time.'

'Do you mean that he's dead?'

'As far as I know, he is. And if he's not, he must be a bloody old man by now. But let's get back to *Sebastian* George, shall we? Can you really see him committing murder?'

'Why not? We know he's got the motive, and he's got the means and the opportunity, as well,' Patterson said. 'You wondered who was where they shouldn't have been at the time of the murder. Well, George had the right to be anywhere he damn-well pleased. He's the boss. It's his theatre. Nobody would question his right to be in the props room at any time of day or night.'

'There's some truth in what you say,' Blackstone agreed. 'But you mentioned two suspects. Who's your second one?'

'Richmond Clay.'

'The understudy?'

'Not any more, he isn't, sir. As from today, his name is as

prominently displayed on the marquee as Martin Swinburne's once was.'

'So, if I understand you correctly, you're saying that he killed both Swinburne *and* Kirkpatrick?'

'Maybe – but not necessarily. Swinburne's death *could* have been an accident, but, even so, it could also have put the idea of killing Kirkpatrick into Clay's head.'

'He sees how Kirkpatrick benefits from Swinburne's death, and realizes he'd benefit in the same way if Kirkpatrick died?'

'Exactly. On the other hand, Clay could have seen that there were *two* men standing in the way of his fame, and decided to kill them both. There's a saying in the theatre which goes something like, "I'd kill for that part," and perhaps some people take it much more literally than you or I might.'

'So why the delay? Why were there several months between Swinburne's death and Kirkpatrick's?'

'Well, Clay wouldn't have wanted to make it too obvious, now would he?' Patterson said.

Blackstone nodded thoughtfully. 'I've got one more name to toss into the ring myself,' Blackstone said.

'And who might that be?'

'Lord Bixendale.'

'Bixendale!' Patterson exploded. 'Why would you ever consider him a suspect?'

'Well, for a start, it would be just about par for the bloody course, wouldn't it?' Blackstone asked.

'Would it?'

'Definitely. Haven't you ever noticed how we seem destined to investigate crimes in which the guilty parties happen to have titles?'

'And not just titles, but power,' Patterson said gloomily.

'Indeed,' Blackstone agreed.

'Power they've been prepared to use in an attempt to destroy us the second they felt we were getting close to feeling their collars.'

'Well, exactly. It's become almost a habit with us.'

'A habit we could well do with breaking ourselves of, in my opinion,' Patterson said. 'Is it *only* the fact that it'd be just our luck to have to deal with another bloody aristocrat that makes you suspect Bixendale could be the murderer?'

'Of course not.'

'Thank heavens for that! So are you going to tell me what your main reason actually is?'

'He's in love with Charlotte Devaraux. I've been convinced of that ever since I saw the way he behaved in her presence this morning.'

'So?'

'I don't think he likes her being involved in the theatre one little bit. But since he can't offer to marry her—'

'Can't he? Why not?'

'Because he's married already, and anyway, lords don't marry actresses if they put any value at all on their place in society. So, since marriage is out of the question, he didn't think there was anything he could offer her which would persuade her to leave the life she's currently leading. But then, possibly, he might have come up with a scheme which he thought might make her do just that.'

'What kind of scheme, sir? Killing William Kirkpatrick? How could that help?'

'You're looking at it from the wrong angle, Archie,' Blackstone said. 'If I'm right, it's not who was actually killed that's important.'

'Then what is?'

'Who did the killing!'

'So your theory is that he just wanted Charlotte to kill *someone*?'

'No! What he wanted her to do was to kill someone *on stage*.'

'But why?'

'To turn her against the theatre for ever, of course! Imagine it. She goes on stage, and accidentally kills a man. That's got to be a terrible shock to anyone's system, hasn't it?'

'I suppose so.'

'He thinks to himself that after such a terrible thing has happened, she'll never be able to bring herself to perform again. But the flaw in his plan – and it's a bloody big flaw – is that he's underestimated Charlotte. She's shaken – there's no doubt about that – but she's also determined to climb right back on the horse immediately.'

'It's a bit far-fetched, isn't it?' Patterson asked dubiously. 'I mean, surely he would have to have considered the emotional and mental damage that it might well do to her?'

'We always hurt the ones we love,' Blackstone said. 'Besides, you know yourself how capable people are of self-delusion when they really want something. He may well have persuaded himself that she'd get over the shock eventually and return to being her normal self – except that that normal self would no longer want to be an actress.'

'I'm still not convinced,' Patterson said.

'My theory is the only one that comes anywhere near to fitting the facts,' Blackstone told him. 'If Richmond Clay had wanted to kill William Kirkpatrick, why would he have chosen that method? Why not poison his food? Or hire some thugs to waylay him in a dark alley, and make it look like a robbery gone wrong? But as far as Bixendale is concerned, the death had to be connected with the stage, because the whole point of it would be its effect on Charlotte Devaraux.'

'If I'd been Richmond Clay, and decided to kill Kirkpatrick, I'd have done it in exactly the way it was done,' Patterson said.

'Why?'

'Because now that he's the leading actor of the company, he's just as interested in playing to packed houses as Sebastian George is in selling tickets for them.'

'So?'

'And as you said yourself, it's because Kirkpatrick was killed on stage that the demand for tickets has suddenly shot through the roof.'

'You're right,' Blackstone agreed morosely. 'What I keep forgetting is that we're not dealing with normal people here. Instead, we're dealing with theatricals – and almost every-thing they *do* is theatrical.'

Patterson looked at his watch. 'The night-time telephone operators will be reporting for duty soon, so it's time I set off for the telephone exchange again,' he said. 'What will you do, sir? Go and see the play again?'

'No, I think I'll give it a miss tonight.'

'And why's that? Have you had enough of the magic of the theatre for one day?'

'It's not the theatre I can't face,' Blackstone said, 'it's the audience. Or, more particularly, one member of the audience.'

'Of course! Sir Roderick Todd!'

Blackstone nodded. 'Our beloved Assistant Commissioner

will be there in the Royal Box – reaping his reward for being a good little boy and allowing the theatre to stay open despite the fact that a murder inquiry's going on.'

'Are you're afraid that if you see him, he'll ask you how the investigation's going?'

'Not exactly. I'm afraid that if I do see him, I won't be able to resist the temptation to smash him in his big, fat, stupid face. And that could be very bad for my career, you know.'

'Yes, it might be something of a set-back to promotion,' Patterson agreed. He stood up and adjusted his waistcoat over his still-ample girth. 'There is just one more thing we haven't discussed yet, sir,' he said.

'And what might that be?'

'The little old man. I still don't quite see how *he* fits into the picture that we're building up.'

Blackstone looked at him blankly. 'What little old man are you talking about?' he asked.

'The one who the knife-maker described.'

'You're still talking in riddles,' Blackstone said.

'The constables who were sent out to question the knife- and sword-makers have found the man who made the murder weapon. It's in all their report. Haven't you seen it?'

'Obviously not,' Blackstone said. 'It's probably sitting on my desk back at the Yard. So what did this knife-maker have to say for himself?'

'That he made the knife on a commission. And that the person who commissioned it was a little old man.'

'A little old man?' Blackstone repeated.

'Apparently.'

Blackstone put his head in his hands. 'This was never going to be an easy case to solve,' he said, to nobody in particular, 'but at least we knew where all the suspects were. Now this little old man pops up from out of nowhere. Isn't that just what we bloody-well needed?'

Thirteen

Many of the books Ellie Carr had withdrawn from UCH's library earlier that day had lain undisturbed on the shelves for years. Now, still coated with the dust of neglect, they stood in dangerously unstable towers on every available inch of her desk.

Ellie looked at the books with something akin to mild despair.

'Bloody toxicology,' she said loudly to herself. 'Bloody, bloody – *buggering* – toxicology.'

The word itself was simple enough to explain, she thought: toxicology, from the Greek, *toxicon*, meaning poison for arrows.

'But the subject itself is *far* from simple,' Ellie informed her empty room. 'In fact, there's so much written on toxicology that a bright young doctor could go completely off her head trying to read it all!'

Her tired eyes needed a rest – or, at least, a change – and she forced herself to tear them away from the heavy book in front of her and focus on the far wall of her office.

It had taken her a long time to accept the room for what it was. As her *office*! As *her* office!

She remembered being shown it for the first time, by the hospital administrator – remembered the lump that had formed in her throat as she looked around.

It was the sheer size of the place which had overcome her. The office, which had been designated *for her use alone*, took up almost as much floor space as the rented rooms in which she'd been brought up – rooms in which she, her mother, and her seven brothers had not only eaten and slept, but also *worked*.

In those rooms they had made hat-boxes and paper flowers when there had been a call for them, and produced scrubbing brushes when there hadn't. They had boiled up beetroot, and sold it down at the market on a Friday night. They had – to put it simply – done just about anything and everything that they could to keep their heads above water.

The whole family had known, even then, that Ellie was brighter than the rest of them put together. But not one of them had ever even dreamed that she would some day have an office like this one. And they still couldn't *quite* comprehend it.

Her mother was dead, and two of her brother had succumbed to the endemic illnesses of the slums in their early teens. But five brothers were still alive – three of them soldiers, the other two stokers on transatlantic steamships – and whenever they were in London and came to visit her, they looked around this office with expressions on their faces which said – more clearly than words – that not only did *they* have no right to be in this posh place, but they strongly suspected that *she* didn't, either! And the worst thing of all was that, from time to time at least, she almost half-agreed with them.

'Don't you think it's time that you called it a day?' a voice asked from the doorway.

Ellie peered at Jed Trent through the space between two towers of musty books.

'I can't just abandon my grand tour of the poisons of the world when I've only got as far as Africa,' she said.

'Why not? You haven't actually learned anything very useful, now have you?' Trent asked.

'What makes you think that?'

'Because if you had, I wouldn't have heard you saying "Bloody, bloody, buggering toxicology" when I was walking past.'

'Was I that loud?' Ellie asked, slightly embarrassed.

'Everybody with an office on this corridor would have heard you, if they'd been there *to* hear,' Trent said. 'But, of course, they're *not* there. They've all gone home – and it might be a good idea if you followed their example.'

'Did you know there's a poison called ricin which has been round for thousands of years?' Ellie asked.

'No, I can't say that I did. Nor can I honestly say I feel any better for knowing it now.'

'There are references to it in something called the Susruta

Ayurveda, which was written in Sanskrit in the sixth century *BC*!'

Jed Trent held up his hand. 'Please, Dr Carr, don't feel under any obligation at all to enlighten me further on the matter,' he said, even though he knew it was a waste of breath.

'It's made from the castor oil plant, and there are records of its use in East Africa to poison unwanted children. But – and this is much more significant, Jed – there have been cases in India of people stabbing their enemies' cattle with rusty nails which have been smeared with extract of the castor bean.'

'And this ricin is what you think was used to poison William Kirkpatrick, is it?'

'Regrettably not,' Ellie Carr admitted. 'Its toxic effects have a latent period. They take at least two hours – and possibly as much as twenty-four – to develop. Kirkpatrick, on the other hand, died almost immediately. But at least I seem to be on the right lines, don't I?'

'Do you?' Trent asked. 'Being as I'm just a simple ex-bobby, I wouldn't know. And another thing I don't know – don't think I'll *ever* know – is why you push yourself so hard.'

Ah, but you *would* know if you'd seen the house I was brought up in, Ellie Carr thought.

The morning visit to the telephone exchange had been a depressing and disillusioning experience for Sergeant Patterson. The women operators – who had always been, in his mind, the high priestesses of the religion of new technology – had refused to see themselves in the role he'd assigned to them, and instead treated their sacred task as if it were nothing more than just an ordinary job.

The evening visit was even worse. The women had at least had *a little* respect for the expensive equipment they had been entrusted with – if only because it *was* expensive – but the swaggering and posturing male operators of the night shift showed no respect of any kind at all.

'What do they matter – these panels with their flashing lights and bits of wire hanging from them?' their very attitude proclaimed loudly. 'The mere machinery is nothing at all without the heroes who are here to operate it.'

The night supervisor was a man called Blaine, and like the men who worked under him, seemed to Patterson to have a highly inflated opinion of his own importance.

Miss Dobbs, the sergeant was sure, would have addressed her team of operators as a strict schoolmarm might have lectured her pupils – firmly but kindly, with her eyes moving from one face to the next as she spoke, and her index finger occasionally wagging to emphasize a point. Blaine, on the other hand, spoke to *his* operators with his hands on his hips and his eyes fixed on the distance – as if he were the captain of a whaling ship which was braving stormy seas.

'The police need our help,' he said, his tone almost suggesting that the police were actually quite useless, and what they really needed was for the operators to do their job *for them*. 'They want to know about a call which was placed at about half past eight last night to the George Theatre. Which of you men was it who handled that call?'

The operators looked first at each other, and then at Mr Blaine. None of them spoke.

'Since the call was made, one of you must have handled it,' Blaine said impatiently.

And if he doesn't admit to it now, it's ten strokes of the cat-o'-nine-tails for him, followed by an invigorating keel-hauling, Patterson added silently.

'The George Theatre!' Blaine said, as if simple repetition would make things clearer. 'Last night!'

The operators continued to look blankly at him, except for one man – a thin-faced, shifty-eyed character – who didn't look at him at all.

'What's your name, sir?' Patterson asked, pointing at him.

The man jumped, as if he'd suddenly become aware of the fact that he was sitting on a needle.

'Me?' he asked.

'You,' Patterson confirmed.

'H . . . Henry Woodbine.'

'Is there somewhere I could speak to Mr Woodbine in private?' Patterson asked Blaine.

'Will it take long?' the supervisor replied.

'I rather imagine that's up to Mr Woodbine,' Patterson told him enigmatically.

'I don't like being one man short on a busy shift like this one,' Blaine grumbled.

'I imagine you don't,' Patterson agreed. 'I not sure that I would care for it myself.'

'So I don't see how I can—'

'But I'm sure that if any man can manage being short-handed in a time of crisis, that man is you,' Patterson added.

The exchange supervisor bit back the rest of the comment he'd been about to make. 'You're a very shrewd judge of human nature – for a policeman,' he said grudgingly. 'All right, you can take him. But make sure I get him back as soon as you've finished with him.'

The play was done, the cast was already on its way home – and Sebastian George sat in his office, smoking a big cigar and mentally adding up the day's takings.

The knock on the door shattered his mood of self-congratulation, and his annoyance was only increased when he saw who it was that had come calling on him.

'What can I do for you, Miss Simmons?' he asked brusquely.

Tamara Simmons advanced into the room and simpered. 'Aren't you going to ask me to sit down, Mr George?' she said.

Before Martin Swinburne's death, she wouldn't have dared to come to his office *at all* without an invitation, Sebastian George thought crossly. Now she not only expected him to give up his free time to listen to her inane witterings, but wanted to sit down as well.

He was in half a mind to tell her she wouldn't be there long enough to need a seat, but then the more cautious – and rarely seen – side of his nature took over, and he heard himself say, 'By all means, make yourself comfortable.'

Tamara Simmons sat, and placed her hands on her lap like a demure Sunday school teacher.

'One of the policemen – the chubby one – bought me after-noon tea today,' she said.

'That was very nice of him,' George replied, thinking to himself that if Patterson imagined he could get Tamara into his bed for the price of a cup of tea and a piece of cake, he was heading for disappointment.

Tamara Simmons looked surprised at his comment. 'Oh,

he didn't do it because he wanted to be nice to me,' she said. 'He did it because he wanted to *question* me.'

Alarm bells were starting to ring in George's head. 'Question you?' he repeated. 'What about?

'What do you think it was about? He asked me about Martin Swinburne and William Kirkpatrick.'

'And what did you tell him?'

'That Mr Swinburne was my lover, and William Kirkpatrick wanted to take his place in my affections.'

'Do you think he believed you?'

'Of course he believed me! I'm an actress, after all, aren't I? And a very good one.'

George kept silent.

Tamara Simmons tapped the toe of her shoe impatiently on the floor. 'In case you didn't hear me, Mr George, I said I'm a very good actress, aren't I?'

'Yes,' Sebastian George agreed reluctantly. 'You are indeed a very good actress.'

'So, if that's the case, then why am I still only playing minor parts?' Tamara Simmons wondered.

'I wouldn't say you were only playing *minor* parts at all, Tamara, my dear.' George said, with sudden fake joviality. 'Why, in this current play alone, you have two major roles.'

'Major roles? Is that what you call them? The maid, and Lady Wilton's cousin?'

'Neither character may have that many lines, but – as I'm sure you fully appreciate yourself – both roles are absolutely pivotal to the development of the drama.'

'Maybe they are, but I'm not likely to set the West End alight with them, am I?'

George sighed. She wasn't likely to set the West End alight with *any* roles he gave her, he thought.

'So you're saying that you're not happy with the parts I've given you, are you?' he asked.

'That's right.'

'And what other role did you have in mind?'

'Have you noticed how tired Miss Devaraux's been looking since the murder?' Tamara Simmons asked.

'Good God, you surely don't want to take over the *lead*, do you?' George exploded.

Tamara Simmons laughed, quite prettily. 'No, of course not.'

'Good!'

'That would be very selfish of me, wouldn't it?'

'That's certainly one way of putting it.'

'But I did think I could take over the role in the some of the matinée performances – just to give Miss Devaraux a rest.'

'I'm afraid that wouldn't be—'

'And later on, of course, *she* might do the matinées, and *I* might do the evening performances.'

'Do be sensible,' George coaxed. 'The only reason this play is suddenly such a great success is because the public want to see Charlotte. And why do they want to see her – and her alone? Because she's the one who actually stabbed William Kirkpatrick. They'd feel cheated if they saw anybody else – and I can't say that I'd entirely blame them.'

'All right, she can keep the lead for the run of this play,' Tamara Simmons conceded graciously. 'But what about the lead in the next one you put on? Who'll be given that?'

'I haven't even thought about it yet.'

'Well, I think you should. And I'd like you to know that if I'm not given the leading role myself, I shall be very disappointed indeed.'

'I said you were a good actress, and so you are,' George said, keeping his temper under control – but only just. 'However, you must see yourself that Charlotte Devaraux is more than that – she is a *great* actress.'

'And so will I be . . . given time.'

The jumped-up little snot! George thought. The talentless little tart. Had she no concept of gratitude?

'Hell will freeze over before you'll be ready to fill Charlotte Devaraux's shoes,' he said.

'You think so?'

'I do! She is as different to you as chalk is to cheese.'

'Oh, I wouldn't say that,' Tamara Simmons replied airily. 'In fact, I think we have many things in common.'

'You have *nothing* in co—'

'And one of those things is that we both have the power to bring this company to its knees, should we choose to.'

'What?'

'Now, I don't think Charlotte would ever do that. Why

should she want to destroy the company, when – as the leading lady – she has so much to lose? But for the moment, you see, I do have not have quite as strong an incentive to keep my own mouth shut.'

Sebastian George felt the blood in his veins turning to ice. 'You're not as stupid as you sometimes seem, are you?' he asked.

Tamara smiled. 'No, I'm not,' she agreed.

'And it's because I'm now coming to appreciate you for your intelligence that I've just decided to take the time to explain something to you,' Sebastian George continued.

There was a new, hardened edge to his tone, and Tamara Simmons suddenly began to look a little less confident.

'Go on,' she said, hesitantly.

'You've been here long enough to remember when my father was in charge of this theatre, haven't you?'

'Yes, I—'

'And what did you think of him?'

'He . . . he was a nice old man.'

'Yes, he was,' Sebastian George agreed. 'He was a very nice old man indeed. And I loved him deeply – as only a son can love a father. But he did have one fatal failing, didn't he?'

'I . . . I don't know.'

'I think you do. His failing was that he wanted to remain in charge here long after it was time for him to retire and let someone else take over. And since he owned the theatre, you see, he thought there was nothing I could do about it. But he was wrong – very wrong. *Wasn't he*, Miss Simmons?'

Tamara Simmons was beginning to turn quite pale. 'I . . . I . . .' she said, gasping for air.

'You remember what happened to him, don't you?' George asked. 'Or do I need to remind you of it?'

'No, I—'

'Perhaps I'll remind you of it anyway. One morning, two men with black bags appeared at the theatre door, didn't they?'

'Yes.'

'And where did they go?'

'I don't—'

'*Where did they go?*'

'They . . . they went to your father's office.'

'And when they left again, did they do so alone?'

'No. Your father left with them.'

'He didn't *leave* with them at all. *Leaving* with them would suggest he had some choice in the matter. And he had no choice at all.' Sebastian George paused for a moment to let the words sink into Tamara's woolly brain. 'What actually happened was that they *took* him away, didn't they?' he continued. 'And why would they have done that?'

'Because they thought he was—'

'Because they thought what I *paid* them to think!' Sebastian George said, slamming his hand down violently on the desk. 'And they will think the same again – about another person – if I instruct them to. If it were my wish, they would think it about *you*.'

'Please . . .' Tamara said, clearly distressed.

An unexpected smile replaced the angry look on Sebastian George's face. 'Don't get upset, my sweet Tamara,' he said. 'I did not wish to sound as if I were threatening you, as I'm sure you did not wish to sound as if you were threatening me earlier. You *weren't* threatening me, were you?'

'No.'

'You have a great future in this company, if you are only prepared to be a little patient. Do you understand that?'

Tamara nodded. 'Yes.'

'Good,' Sebastian George said. 'Then I'll see you tomorrow, and we'll both pretend this conversation never happened. But keep in mind, Tamara, that there are many worse stations in life than the one you currently occupy – as my father has undoubtedly already found out.'

Fourteen

The telephone company did not provide meals for its staff, but it did employ a cook who prepared the food that the operators themselves had either ordered from the butcher's or else brought with them from home. These meals were eaten in a civilized-but-plain dining room, which was bustling at meal-times, but was completely empty when Patterson shepherded a reluctant Henry Woodbine through the door.

Woodbine looked desperately around the room, as if searching for some kind of escape hatch, and when he heard Patterson close the door loudly behind him, he almost jumped out of his skin.

'I . . . I think you must have made some kind of mistake, Sergeant,' the operator said. 'I don't know why—'

'Sit down!' Patterson ordered, pointing to a bench which ran along one of the long tables.

'If I'd been the one who put the call through to the George Theatre, I'm sure that I'd have remembered it,' Woodbine protested – but he reluctantly sat down anyway.

Patterson took a seat on the opposite side of the table. It was much easier lifting his leg over the bench now that he had started to lose weight, he thought.

'Tell me, Henry, have you ever been in trouble with the police before?' the sergeant asked casually.

'No, I . . .' the operator began. Then he implications of Patterson's words sunk in, and he said, 'What do you mean – in trouble *before*? I'm not in any trouble *now*.'

'Oh, how I wish that that were true, Henry,' Patterson said mournfully. 'I really do. Still,' he continued, brightening some-what, 'let's not be too pessimistic about the situation you find yourself in. If you're totally open and straightforward with me now, I suppose it is just possible I might be able to find a way to get you off the hook.'

'I'm innocent!' Woodbine said.

'Of what?' Patterson wondered. 'Of putting a call through to the George Theatre?'

'Yes.'

'I didn't know that was a crime,' Patterson mused. 'I had rather thought, in my own simple policeman's way, that it was the job you were paid to do. Yet you say you're *innocent* of it.'

'That's not fair! You're twisting my words around,' Woodbine complained.

'What I still don't see is why you'd *want* to deny putting through the call,' Patterson continued, as if the other man had never spoken. 'It doesn't make any kind of sense at all to me.'

'I did *not* put that call through,' Woodbine said firmly.

Sergeant Patterson's stomach rumbled loudly. 'What's the food like here?' he asked.

'The food?' Woodbine repeated, as if suspecting this was yet another clever interrogator's trick. 'You want to know about the *food*?'

'Don't you understand plain English?' Patterson demanded. 'Yes, I want to know about the food! What's it like?'

'It's all right.'

That wasn't nearly good enough to satisfy even *mental* hunger, Patterson told himself.

'What do they normally serve you with?' he pressed. 'A joint of meat and three veg? Side of beef? Leg of lamb? That kind of thing?'

'Well, yes.'

'With onion gravy?'

'I suppose so.'

'You suppose so!' Patterson repeated, contemptuously. 'I wouldn't *need* to suppose if I was in your situation! And is there a sweet to follow the meat dish? Jam roll with custard, for example?'

'Usually.'

Patterson shook his head, despairing of all non-dieting humanity, and Henry Woodbine in particular.

'The trouble with most people is that they never appreciate what they have until they've lost it,' he told the other man. He paused for a second, as if reliving tastes past and flavours long gone, then said, 'Tell me, Henry, do you know anything about Random Shellac Flat Disc Sound Retrieval System?'

'Never heard of it.'

Which is hardly surprising, since I just made the whole thing up, Patterson thought.

'It's a system of recording telephone calls on to a flat disc. They invented it in America,' he said. 'Don't you, as a telephone operator, find that absolutely fascinating?'

'No.'

'Well, you certainly should. It has all kinds of interesting possibilities, you know. In America, for example, they've been using it as a way of finding out whether their employees are doing their jobs properly. And your own company has been so impressed with the results they've had over there, that, on a purely experimental basis, it's introduced the same system itself.'

'They're recording *all* the calls?' Henry Woodbine asked, starting to look alarmed.

'No,' Patterson said. 'Remember, Henry, it's the "Random System". If they recorded all the calls, they'd have to refer to it as the "Universal System", wouldn't they?'

'I suppose so.'

'But let's concentrate on the calls they *have* recorded – like the one you made to the George Theatre last night.'

'Have you . . . have you heard it yourself?'

'Indeed I have. And a very fine recording it turned out to be, from a technical standpoint. Having listened to it just once, I would have recognized your voice again anywhere. '

This new information seemed to worry Woodbine, but it also seemed to perplex him.

'If you've heard it yourself, why are you asking me who placed the call?' he asked.

'I don't understand,' Patterson admitted.

'Well, if you've heard the recording, then you'll know that *nobody* placed it, won't you?'

'I . . . er . . . yes, I know that, of course I do,' Patterson said, extemporizing wildly.

'Then why did you—?'

'It was a trick question, Henry.'

'A trick question?'

'I was testing you, to see if you'd lie to me again. It's one of the first things they teach us to do when we're at the police training school.'

'So you're saying that you *do* know that there was nobody on the other end of the line?'

What! Patterson thought. Nobody on the other end of the line?

'Yes, that's what I'm saying,' he agreed.

'Well, then, why—?'

'I'd still like you to tell me, Henry – in your own words – exactly what happened.'

'But if you already know—'

'There are strict procedures which must be adhered to, whether

I know or not,' Patterson said solemnly. 'That's the *second* thing they teach us at police training school. So let's have it!'

'I was told to ring the George Theatre at exactly half past eight last night,' Woodbine said. 'I was to ask for the props manager, and say that there was a caller on the other end of the line with an urgent message to deliver to him. But there *was* no caller.'

'No caller?'

'I wasn't connecting anybody at all. The only line that was operating was between the switchboard and the theatre.'

'Go on,' Patterson said.

'I was told to keep the line open until the props manager picked up the phone, then I was to break the connection. And that's exactly what I did.'

'And you were *paid* to do this?' Patterson asked accusingly.

'I didn't know I was doing anything wrong. I swear I didn't,' Woodbine babbled.

'Which means you *were* paid!'

'He came up to me on the street. He said that he knew I was a telephone operator, and he also knew how little we got paid by the exchange. He said I could probably use a bit of extra cash, and he was willing to provide it. He told me that all he wanted to do was to play a practical joke on this friend of his.'

'And you believed him?'

'Yes. After all, he looked harmless enough. You'd never have thought somebody like him was up to no good.'

'Somebody like him?' Patterson repeated.

'I mean to say, if you can't trust a little old man, who *can* you trust?' Woodbine whined.

The book was called *The Power Struggle Within the Ottoman Empire from a Purely Toxicological Perspective,* and its author, Ellie Carr had already decided, must have been one of the most boring men who had ever lived.

She had so far skimmed over two hundred pages of the writer's dreadful, laboured prose, and she had learned – in gruesome detail – that it was not always good for the health to be a member of the Turkish ruling family. As far as her own personal quest went, however, she was no closer to an answer to her questions than she had been at the start.

'I thought you might like *yet another* cup of black coffee,' said a voice behind her.

Ellie turned in the direction of the speaker. 'Are you still here?' she asked Jed Trent.

Trent patted his powerful chest, as if to check. 'So it would appear,' he said. 'I take it, from the look of pure annoyance on your pretty face, that you've haven't had any luck in finding what you were looking for yet.'

'None at all,' Ellie admitted. 'It's the speed of the reaction that's creating the problem. All the metallic poisons and vegetable alkaloids I've come across so far are lethal in the long run – some of them can even kill within the hour – but none of them is capable of producing the effect that the poison administered to William Kirkpatrick did.'

'Then maybe it's a different kind of poison altogether that you're looking for,' Trent suggested.

'Brilliant!' Ellie said sarcastically.

And then – almost immediately – she felt guilty.

'I'm sorry, Jed,' she continued. 'I'd never have said that if I hadn't been so exhausted.'

'Which is why I've been telling you, for the last three hours, that you should go home,' Trent pointed out.

'But how *can* I leave, when I feel in my bones that the answer's here in one of these books, if I could only put my finger on it?' Ellie asked. 'Do *you* have any ideas, Jed?'

'You must be really desperate, if you're asking my opinion,' Jed Trent told her.

I am, Ellie thought.

'*Do* you?' she persisted.

'Well, I did have one idea,' Trent said cautiously. 'But as I've no training in any formal kind of—'

'I'd like to hear it.'

'You're not just saying that, are you?'

'Why would I?'

'To make up for being so sarcastic with me earlier.'

Ellie smiled. 'You have quite a sensitive soul lurking some-where beneath that bluff exterior, don't you?' she asked.

'I wouldn't go as far as that,' Trent said, beginning to look distinctly uncomfortable.

'I truly do want to hear your idea,' Ellie said. 'I'd want to hear it even if I hadn't been so ungracious to you earlier.'

'Well,' Trent began reluctantly, 'you've already examined mineral poisons and vegetable poisons, haven't you?'

'Yes?'

'So why not *animal* poisons? I got bitten by a viper once. It didn't kill me – I wouldn't be here now, if it had – but it was distinctly unpleasant. And from what I've heard, there are snakes much more poisonous than vipers. Of course, like I said earlier, I'm no expert on—'

'A snake!' Ellie interrupted, discarding her book on the Ottoman Empire, and reaching for another volume from the top of one of the tottering towers. 'Why *couldn't* it be a snake? Or a *spider*?' She flicked the book open, and impatiently scanned the index. 'You're a genius, Jed,' she said. 'Did you know that?'

'No, I didn't,' Jed Trent confessed. 'As a matter of fact, that particular piece of information comes as something of a surprise to me.'

Blackstone had lodged with Mrs Huggett for years. He paid her a little more than anyone else would have been willing to offer for the tiny back bedroom he occupied in her terraced house, but he knew she needed the money, and he was happy enough with the arrangement.

The other lodger, Mr Dimmock, was a commercial traveller in patent tooth powder. He spent most of working life outside London, but on the nights he was back at his base, he announced his presence with snores which would have penetrated the walls even if they hadn't been quite so paper-thin.

Dimmock was there that night, but it was not the sound of his snoring which was keeping Blackstone awake. It was not the investigation, either, though thoughts of that would normally have been quite perplexing enough to keep sleep at bay for a while.

Instead, he was thinking about Dr Ellie Carr – or rather his own relationship with the woman.

If, indeed, they *had* a relationship.

If, indeed, he *wanted* them to have a relationship.

The problem was that Ellie Carr was so very passionate about her work, and that was almost bound to lead to difficulties.

Twice before, he had made the mistake of falling in love with women who cared more about what they saw as their mission in life than they did about him, and he was not sure he wished to run the same risk a third time.

And yet . . .

And yet love was not a tap, that a man could turn on and off at will. It came uninvited – an unwelcome guest – and stayed, however uncomfortable its host tried to make it feel.

The quality of Mr Dimmock's snores had changed. Previously, he had been snorting like a bull that had just been presented with a red rag. Now the snores were less confident – almost apologetic – like those of a weak old man.

Where did the old man in *this* investigation fit in? Blackstone found himself asking.

He had commissioned the knife, but that single action did not, by any means, put him at the very centre of the murder plot. It was more than possible that he was a harmless dupe, a pauper whom the killer had picked up on the street, and had used to muddy the trail.

Yet Blackstone's gut instinct told him that this was not the case at all – that the old man had somehow played a much more vital part in the death of William Kirkpatrick.

In the other room, Mr Dimmock had changed position again, and had now embarked on a symphony of snoring which could have filled a space the size of the Royal Albert Hall.

Blackstone felt the urge for sleep coming over him – and this time he gave way to it.

As Tamara Simmons watched the two unsmiling men with black leather bags enter the theatre, she knew that none of it was real. As she saw them walk towards old Mr George's office, she understood that this was all no more than a dream. Yet she still dreaded the drama which was about to unfold.

It is five o'clock in the evening. The cast will not arrive for another hour, and the only reason Tamara herself is in the almost empty building is that she forgot to take her script home after rehearsals, and has come to retrieve it. Now, standing in the corridor which leads to the dressing rooms – and invisible to anyone who is not actually looking in her direction – she watches the men walk purposefully up to old Mr George's office door, and knock on it loudly.

Old Mr George comes to the door. 'Why are you making such a noise?' he demands. 'What is it that you want?'

'They've come to examine you, Father,' replies Sebastian George, who has joined the men in the doorway.

'Examine me?'

'They're doctors.'

'But I'm not ill.'

'Perhaps not physically.'

'Not in any way!'

'We'll see about that. Both these doctors are very familiar with mental illness. One of them has even trained as an alienist.'

'I don't want to see them,' the old man says.

'You have no choice in the matter. They have the authority of the Lunacy Commission to conduct this examination, which means that the law is entirely on their side.'

The dream-Tamara knew that she should remove herself to some other part of the theatre as quickly as she possibly could, but just like the real Tamara back then, she found herself unable to move.

'You can't come in,' the old man says, with an edge of fear evident in his voice now.

'They will come in,' Sebastian George tells him.

And then he takes a step forward, and pushes the old man – pushes his own father *– back into the office.*

He enters the office himself, the doctors follow him, and Sebastian George closes the door behind them.

Tamara Simmons moves a few steps closer, in order to be able to hear what is going on.

For some minutes, all she can discern is the soft mumble of voices from the other side of the door. Then voices begin to be raised.

'I won't submit to this!' the old man screams.

'Restrain him before he does himself any damage,' the doctor who is an alienist shouts.

There is the sound of a struggle – of tables being over-turned and glass being shattered.

And then there follows an heavy, unnatural silence which chills Tamara to the bone.

The door swings opens again – almost in slow motion – and still Tamara cannot bring herself to move away. Then she sees something that makes her wish she had.

Sebastian George is in the doorway, and just behind him is his father, standing between the two doctors like a thin piece of meat sandwiched between two thick slices of bread.

And then she realizes that he is not standing at all – that the two doctors have his arms clasped firmly, and are holding him up.

Old Mr George is not protesting. Not struggling. He is doing – and saying – nothing at all. But that is hardly surprising, because, judging from the blank look on his face, he has been doped.

Sebastian George sees Tamara for the first time. 'What are you doing here?' he demands.

'My script,' she burbles, holding it up to him as proof that she is not lying. 'I forgot my script.'

'You should be more careful,' Sebastian George tells her, with a menace in his words that has nothing to do with her forgetfulness.

'I will be,' she says.

'And now, I would like you to get out of the way, so that these two doctors can take my father to the hospital.'

'Of course,' Tamara says, and she knows full well that it is not an ordinary hospital they will be taking the old man to, but a lunatic asylum.

The doctors push past her. They are handling Mr George as if he were a sack of potatoes or a side of beef, rather than a weak and doped old man.

Later, Sebastian George will tell the cast that his father has been taken suddenly ill, and it may be some time before he returns to the theatre.

But Tamara knows that he will never return.

She was sitting bolt upright in bed. Her body was soaked in sweat, and her eyes full of tears.

It had been a mistake to even try and put pressure on Sebastian George, she told herself in a panic. He had locked away his own father without a second's thought, and he would have absolutely no hesitation in doing the same to her.

She would go to see Sebastian George again, the first thing in the morning, she resolved. She would tell him that she was perfectly happy with the roles she had been given in the plays so far, and would be equally happy with whatever roles he might choose to give her in the future.

And she would do more than that. She would promise to continue telling the same lies for him that she had been telling all along.

She might go even further, if this did not seem to reassure him, she thought, looking down at her trembling hands.

She might promise that she would say or do anything – however reprehensible or degrading it might be – if that meant she could avoid the same fate as had befallen his father.

Fifteen

Other people, who knew no better, might sometimes refer to Marcus Leighton as the 'police artist', but it was certainly not a term that he would ever have used about himself.

In his opinion, the two words – one of them potentially sublime, the other invariably crude – could not coexist happily in a single phrase. Even used in the same sentence, they required *at the very least* to be separated by a preposition and a definite article. Thus, when asked about his occupation, he would invariably reply by describing himself as 'artist to the police'.

But for all his quibbling over the terminology, he quite liked the work. For a start, it paid well. Furthermore – with the exception of those rare occasions when the Met failed to keep the lid on the barrel and crime spilled out all over London – it left him ample time to pursue his own experiments in painting. Most importantly of all, the police did not want the pictures he produced to flatter the subject – as so many of his patrons had done in the past – they instead prized accuracy above all else, and he was more than happy to provide them with it.

That morning, he had produced two sketches. They had been drawn from descriptions provided by two separate witnesses, though he was pretty sure that both those witnesses had been describing the same man, and when he laid out the sketches on Blackstone's desk, it was obvious – from the way the inspector immediately compared them – that he thought so, too.

'Which is which?' Blackstone asked.

'That one comes from the description given by the knife-maker,' Leighton said, pointing to one on the right, 'and the other is based on the telephone operator's impressions.'

'Splendid work, as always,' Blackstone said approvingly. 'We'll call you when we need you again.'

'Try not to make that too long,' Leighton replied. 'There's no shame in being a starving artist, but I'd rather avoid that fate myself, if at all possible.' He ran his eyes quickly up and down Patterson's frame. 'Speaking of starving, have you lost weight, Archie?'

Patterson positively beamed with pleasure. 'Nice of you to notice, old chap,' he said.

'I'm trained to notice,' Leighton said dryly. 'And you've still got a long way to go before *I'd* consider sculpting you in expensive marble.'

Blackstone and Patterson spent the next ten minutes examining the sketches from all angles.

'They're not exactly the same,' Patterson said finally.

'They never are,' Blackstone agreed. 'We all see what we *think* we see, or *expect* to see, or would *like* to see, so no two witnesses' descriptions will ever be a perfect match. But by and large, Marcus's sketches are usually a pretty good likeness of the man we eventually end up arresting.'

'We don't know that we actually *want* to arrest this bloke,' Patterson pointed out.

'True,' Blackstone agreed. 'But the fact that he's now popped up twice in the investigation is an indication that he has more than a casual connection with the murder.'

'I'm not sure I quite follow the logic of that, sir,' Patterson admitted. 'Would you mind explaining it to me?'

'I'd be glad to. My working theory up to now has been that the murderer didn't order the knife himself, because that would leave a trail leading right back to him. So, instead, he hires the little old man to do it. But why, when he needs to bribe the telephone operator, does he use the *same* little old man?'

'Because good help is hard to find?' Patterson suggested.

'I don't think so. Both tasks were fairly simple ones, after all. So what made the murderer expose himself to a potential witness – which is what the little old man is – more than he had to? Why give the old chap so many chances to study him? Why not use a second old man – or a young woman, for that matter – to bribe the telephone operator?'

'I don't know,' Patterson confessed.

'It can only be because the little old man isn't merely peripheral to our inquiry at all. It has to mean that he's a member of the team which planned the murder!'

'And how many people do you think there are on this team?' Patterson wondered.

'There may only be two of them – the old man himself, and his accomplice in the theatre.'

'But the old man must have some connection with the theatre, even if it's only in the dim and distant past,' Patterson said.

'That's just what I was thinking,' Blackstone agreed.

Granville Smith, the editor of the *London Evening Chronicle*, gazed down fondly at the letters' page of the paper's most recent edition.

What a fine thing the letters' page really was, he thought. It was both a haven and a forum for those members of the reading public who felt offended or insulted, cheated or lied to. And when a new outrage was exposed – and one was exposed nearly every week – letters would positively flood in from men and women who bared their souls and signed themselves 'A Loyal Subject', 'An Honest Rate-Payer' or 'A Seeker After Justice'.

Like most other editors, he recognized that some of his correspondents were undoubtedly being unreasonable, and that others were clearly verging on the insane, but – for reasons which were economic rather than journalistic – Smith would happily publish the letters anyway.

'We need something to fill up the space between the advertisements, and letters will do that just as well as articles could,' he would tell his assistant. 'The only difference between the two is that the people who write the articles expect to be paid, and the ones who write the letters don't.'

There were other advantages to publishing the letters, too. A man who has written one will invariably buy the newspaper to see if it has been printed. And even those readers who had *not* written to the paper themselves would enjoy the letters from those who had, since they tended to cater to one of the most characteristic of all English virtues: a strong sense of grievance. But best of all – though only very occasionally – the letters would even point him in the direction of a story which it *was* worth paying one of his reporters to write.

The latest controversy, concerning the penny sideshows, was just such a story. These shows had existed in London for as long as Smith could remember, and he himself had sometimes paid his penny to see the living skeleton, midget family, bearded lady or lion-jawed man. But lately, there seemed to have been a spate of them, and his correspondents were up in arms.

> My local undertaker has recently died, *one man had written*, and his establishment is currently up for sale. I have no objection to this.

The dead undertaker will be highly relieved about that, Granville Smith thought.

> But in the meantime, while a respectable buyer is being sought, the establishment has been rented out to one of those disgraceful businesses which calls itself a Penny Sideshow, *the writer continued*. Since this 'so-called' show opened, I have not known a minute's tranquillity. I will not comment on the quality of the exhibits on display (I have not seen them myself, though it seems to be me that in a God-fearing nation like this one, such things should not be allowed), nor on the fact that many of these entertainers appear to hail from foreign parts. But I feel I must complain about the noise. A barrel organ has been placed on the pavement outside the 'show', and from early evening until late into the night, it churns out hideous tunes. And even worse are the customers of this 'entertainment'. They are drawn from the lowest elements

110

of our society, as is only to be expected. They know no language but the language of the gutter, and, not content with uttering their filth, must scream it at the tops of their voices, regardless of the hour. My wife no longer feels safe, my children are now using words they have certainly not learned from me, and I think it is time that the so-called government did something about closing down these affronts to civilized behaviour.

Yours faithfully

A true and moral Englishman.

Granville Smith put the newspaper down on his desk and looked across at the man who was sitting opposite him, waiting for an assignment.

'Freak shows!' the editor said.

'Freak shows?' Talbot Hines repeated. 'What about them, sir?'

'They're a disgrace. An affront to civilized behaviour.'

'Are they? Since when?'

'Since our readers started getting hot under the collar about them. I want you to write an article which demonstrates that we can be just as moral – and just as disapproving – as the idiots who buy this paper.'

Talbot Hines did not look exactly overjoyed at the prospect – and indeed, he wasn't. Editors on crusades were dangerous editors, he thought, because when the crusade blew up in their faces – when the people they'd been crusading *against* started to fight back – it was usually the poor bloody reporter who had to take the blame for things going wrong.

'Is there any particular angle you'd like me to take on the story, sir?' he asked cautiously.

Smith sighed. 'For God's sake, why are you asking me that? You're supposed to be a *reporter*.'

'I'd still like some guidelines,' Hines persisted.

'I should have thought it was obvious. For openers, you could write about the hooligans who go to see these shows.'

'So you don't want anything me to actually say anything about the shows *themselves*?'

'I said that was just *for openers,* Cloth Ears. Most of the article will be about how wicked the shows are.'

'But what if they *aren't* wicked?'

Smith sighed again. 'I sometimes wonder why I ever bother employing you people at all,' he said. 'I could train a dog – and a very slow one, at that – to do what you do.'

'With respect, sir, that's not really an answer to my question,' Hines said, determined not leave the office until he had the editor's explicit permission to commit whatever outrage against the truth he would be required to commit in the interests of his story.

'A good journalist reports on all the news that there is to report,' Smith explained. 'But if other people aren't making any news to report on, then that same journalist will make it *for* them.'

'You're still not being very clear, sir,' Hines said stubbornly.

'If they're not acting wickedly when you get there, make sure they are by the time you leave.'

It was not the sweeping endorsement Hines had been looking for, but he supposed it would have to do.

'Got it, sir,' he said.

Lord Bixendale looked around Blackstone's office, then walked over to the window to admire the Thames. He did not seem entirely comfortable in these surroundings, the inspector thought.

'So this is what Scotland Yard looks like from the inside, eh?' Lord Bixendale said.

'You've never been here before, my lord?'

'No, I must admit that I haven't. Though I have served in most branches of Her Majesty's Government in my time, it has never been my lot to hold a position in the Home Office.'

The message behind that short speech was perfectly clear, Blackstone decided. I'm an important man, Inspector, Bixendale was saying indirectly, and even though I've done you the honour of coming here to see you – rather than summoning you to see me – you'd be wise not to forget exactly who you're dealing with.

'Is there anything *specific* I can do for you, now that you're here, my lord?' he wondered.

'Specific? No, I don't think so. But I'd be interested to know what progress you're making with the case.'

'It's early days yet,' Blackstone said, noncommittally.

'I worry about Miss Devaraux, you see,' Bixendale said awkwardly. 'She's almost like a daughter to me.'

'Yes, I noticed a certain amount of affection passing between you when I observed you standing together on the stage, yesterday morning,' Blackstone said, wishing, almost as soon as the words were out of his mouth, that he'd bitten off his own tongue.

Bixendale gave him a hard stare. 'You saw that, did you?' he asked quizzically. 'Did you, indeed?'

'I thought at first that it was no more than regard – yours for her as an artiste, hers for you as a patron of the arts,' Blackstone said, ladling on false sincerity with a trowel. 'But the more I saw of it, the more I realized that it was closer to the sort of affection that a father and daughter might have for one another.'

Bixendale nodded, as if he believed him – or at least was prepared to pretend that he did.

'What happened during that performance was a terrible shock to Miss Devaraux,' he said. 'Even when she does manage to fall asleep at night, it is a *troubled* sleep.' He paused. Then, perhaps afraid that he might have given the *right* impression, he continued, 'At any rate, that is what she told me, and I see no reason to disbelieve her.'

'She struck me immediately as a very truthful and candid lady,' Blackstone said.

'For that reason, and that reason alone, I am most concerned that the murderer should be apprehended as quickly as possible,' Bixendale continued. 'Only when he is safely dangling from the end of a rope in Pentonville Prison will Charlotte – will Miss Devaraux – feel at peace.'

'I can quite understand that is how she might feel,' Blackstone said sympathetically.

'And yet you still feel unable to tell me anything with which I can reassure her?'

He's about a minute away from demanding to see the file, Blackstone thought. And if he asks for it, I don't see how I can refuse him.

'As I said, there's very little to tell,' he replied, feeling his way as he went. 'But there may perhaps be a way in which you yourself could help to speed up the inquiry.'

'You have only to make your request,' Bixendale said. 'What

is it that you require? More policemen to be drafted into the investigation? That should be no problem at all. I will speak to Sir Roderick Todd – who is a close personal friend of mine – immediately.'

Everybody seems to be a close friend of Sir Roderick Todd's except me, Blackstone thought.

'At this stage of the inquiry, I'm not sure that having more men at my disposal would be of much use,' he said aloud. 'It was as a witness that I thought you might be able to help me.'

'As a witness? A witness to what?'

'Would you mind telling me how long you have been personally involved with the George Theatre, my lord?' Blackstone asked.

Bixendale looked pensive. 'My interest in it began when I first met Miss Devaraux,' he said. 'That would make it a little over two years ago, I think.'

'I see,' Blackstone said.

'Does this have anything at all to do with Kirkpatrick's murder?' Lord Bixendale asked, his voice hardening. 'Or is it merely that, like so many people of your class these days, you have developed a morbid curiosity about the affairs of your social superiors?'

Several appropriate responses came immediately to the forefront of Blackstone's mind, but he pushed them all away immediately.

'What my social superiors do with their time is no concern of mine,' he said. 'I was merely try to establish how likely it was that you might have come into contact with this man, who we believe may have visited the theatre on more than one occasion.'

He produced the two sketches that Marcus Leighton had made earlier that morning and laid them before Lord Bixendale.

Bixendale studied the sketches carefully. 'I can't be sure,' he said, 'but they both bear a remarkable resemblance to Thaddeus George.'

'Who?'

'Sebastian George's father.'

'Isn't he dead?'

'If he *has* died, I've certainly not been informed of the fact.'

114

'I haven't seen him around the theatre,' Blackstone said.

'No, you wouldn't have,' Bixendale agreed. 'Shortly after I began to develop an interest in this theatre myself, he quite lost his mind. And as far as I know, he has been locked away in a lunatic asylum ever since.'

As far as I know, Blackstone noted. He wondered whether Thaddeus George was still in the asylum, and if he was not, whether he had the temperament to become involved in a murder plot.

'What are your impressions of the man as a person?' he asked Lord Bixendale.

'Now that he's gone insane?' Bixendale responded. 'I couldn't possibly say – but I assume that he's not much like a *person* at all.'

You're just so full of the milk of human kindness, aren't you? Blackstone thought.

'But you knew him *before* he went insane,' he said. 'What kind of person was he then? Did you like him?'

'Well enough,' Bixendale said evasively.

'No more than that?'

'We had our differences. I'll openly admit that.'

'Differences? Over what?'

'They mainly concerned Miss Devaraux. As you know, she is now the company's leading actress, but that was not the case at the time.'

'Someone else held that position?'

'Yes, a Miss Sarah Tongue. I thought it was a shame that she should be given most of the leading roles, when it was perfectly obvious that she did not have half Charlotte's talent.'

'And you felt that you should do something about it?'

'I would not put it quite as crudely as that. Miss Devaraux asked me, as her friend and mentor, if I could use my influence to help her to secure the roles that we both knew she richly deserved, and I agreed to discuss the matter with Thaddeus George.'

'But without success?'

'I would prefer to say with only *limited* success. George was a very stubborn man.'

'And a ruthless one?' Blackstone asked, his mind very much still on the part that Thaddeus George might have played in the murder.

'I would not say he was ruthless, so much as obsessed,' Lord Bixendale said. 'The George Theatre was his life. He had sacrificed all else to it. So his refusal to grant my request was not born out of viciousness, but came from a belief that he knew what was best for the theatre.'

'But you think he was wrong?'

'I *know* he was wrong. Charlotte is a much better female lead than Sarah Tongue could ever have been. Nonetheless there was no doubting his sincerity, and I could see that however persuasive I might be, I would never succeed in changing his mind.'

'What eventually happened to Sarah Tongue?' Blackstone wondered.

'She left the company.'

'And Miss Devaraux took her place as leading actress?'

'She was the obvious choice.'

'Can you remember exactly when Miss Tongue left and Miss Devaraux was promoted, my lord?'

'I can't give you a precise date without first consulting my journal,' Lord Bixendale said, 'but I do know that Miss Tongue's departure occurred shortly after Thaddeus George went insane.'

Sixteen

Blackstone found Sebastian George in his office at the theatre. The impresario had his feet up on his desk, and his habitual large cigar planted firmly in his mouth. He looked to the inspector like a man who was more than well-pleased with the direction his life was taking.

'Had any luck with tracking down the murderer yet?' George asked, as casually as if he were inquiring about the likelihood of rain.

'You don't really care about it one way or the other, do you, Mr George?' Blackstone asked.

'It is certainly not my primary concern at this particular moment,' the impresario admitted.

'In fact, you'd probably prefer it if he wasn't caught *at all* – or at least, not caught in the near future,' Blackstone said.

Sebastian George smiled, but said nothing,

'Because as long as he remains at large, he's adding an air of mystery to the whole affair,' Blackstone continued, 'and it's that air of mystery which is selling tickets.'

'And what a *lot* of tickets it does seem to be selling,' Sebastian George said complacently.

'Doesn't it bother you at all that there might well be a homicidal maniac on the loose in your theatre?' Blackstone wondered.

'A homicidal maniac? I don't claim to be an expert on the subject of murderers and their motives, but I think – whoever he is – he can scarcely be described as that,' George replied easily.

'No?'

'No. A homicidal maniac, as far as I understood it, hates mankind in general. Isn't that true?'

'Normally, yes.'

'This murderer did not hate mankind in general. He hated William Kirkpatrick in particular – and now that Kirkpatrick is dead and buried, I can see no reason at all why he should wish to strike again.'

'So the hatred was reserved only for Kirkpatrick? And what do you think was behind this hatred of his?' Blackstone wondered.

'I have absolutely no idea.'

'But you're still convinced it was a *personal* hatred?'

'Yes.'

'Then would you mind explaining to me how you reached this interesting conclusion?'

Sebastian George took a puff on his cigar, and the area around his head was filled with blue smoke.

'I'll gladly explain,' he said. 'The murderer did not wish to kill William Kirkpatrick by his own hand, hence the highly elaborate business of switching the two knives around. Agreed?'

'Agreed,' Blackstone said.

'Yet at the same time, he wished to fully savour his moment of triumph. He wished, in other words, to be right there when

Kirkpatrick died. That is why he arranged for William to be killed on stage – so he could be in on the death, yet not conspicuously so.'

'Where was he, then? In the wings?'

'Possibly.'

'Or perhaps in the audience?'

'That's possible, too.'

Though he hated to admit it, Blackstone thought, George's theory made quite a lot of sense. But he knew from bitter experience that the obvious and logical answer was not always the correct one.

'Maybe Kirkpatrick wasn't his first victim,' the inspector suggested. 'Perhaps he's killed before.'

'Perhaps he has,' George agreed. '"But that was in another country, and besides, the wench is dead."'

'What?'

'I was quoting from *The Jew of Malta*.'

'Who's he, when he's at home?'

'It's not a "he" at all. *The Jew of Malta* is a play by Kit Marlowe, the great Elizabethan dramatist.'

'Why bring that up?'

'I was trying to indicate, by means of that particular quotation, that if our murderer *has* killed before – and I have no idea whether he has or not – it has nothing to do with the life of this theatre.'

Maybe that's what you *were* saying, Mr George, Blackstone thought. Or maybe you were just trying to show the thick bobby that you're well-educated and he's not.

'Perhaps his previous excursions into the gentle art of murder aren't so distant as you seem to think, Mr George,' he suggested. 'Perhaps he also killed Martin Swinburne.'

'Martin's death was nothing more than a tragic accident. If flying machines ever do become practicable, I'm sure they'll be responsible for many deaths in the future, but Martin's will have been the first. He would have liked that – he always enjoyed being first.'

'Was that meant to be humorous?' Blackstone asked.

'It was meant to be wryly ironical,' George told him.

'In other words, it was meant to be one of those jokes that's not really funny,' Blackstone said, unimpressed. 'You can't be sure it was an accident, you know. You really can't.'

'Perhaps you're right,' George agreed. 'But if Martin *was* murdered, he certainly wasn't murdered by the same man who arranged William Kirkpatrick's death.'

'And what do you base *that* theory on?'

George smiled, superciliously. 'You really shouldn't expect me to do *all* your work for you, Inspector,' he said.

'And you shouldn't automatically assume that because I ask for your opinion on the matter, I'll accept everything you might say as if it was the word of God,' Blackstone countered.

'But in this theatre, I *am* God,' George said seriously. 'I have absolute power over my company. If they please me, I reward them. If they do not please me, I punish them. And the vision of the world which is presented on that stage out there is *my* vision.'

'God doesn't have to play to an audience,' Blackstone said.

'I beg your pardon?'

'If God wants to put on a tragedy, rather than a melodrama, he can do it without worrying about what that might do to his box office receipts.'

George laughed. 'Were you trying to insult me, Inspector?'

Blackstone nodded. 'Yes, I was – and if I say so myself, I don't think I made a bad job of it.'

'No, in fact, it was rather fine,' George admitted. He took a long puff on his big cigar. 'You are both more spirited and more intelligent than I first took you to be, Inspector.'

'And you're not quite the self-obsessed dolt that I first took *you* to be,' Blackstone replied. 'But now we've exchanged compliments, I really think it's time we got back to discussing the case. So tell me, Mr George, why couldn't the same man have killed Martin Swinburne and William Kirkpatrick?'

'Because if it had been the same man, he would have wanted as much recognition for the first murder as he got for the second.'

'Recognition?'

'As far as actors are concerned – at least, all the actors I know – there is no point in putting on a fine performance without the public acclaim that follows it. A writer may write purely for his own satisfaction, a painter may paint because he driven by the urge to create a perfect vision of the world – but an actor never acts without an audience in mind.'

119

'So you're saying that Kirkpatrick was killed by an actor, and Swinburne was killed by someone who wasn't?'

'I am saying that Martin's Swinburne's death was an accident, and William Kirkpatrick was killed by someone who is either an actor or *wishes* he could be an actor.'

'Interesting,' Blackstone said. 'I'd like to ask you a few questions about your father now.'

'Isn't that something of a *non sequitur*?' Sebastian George asked.

'And that would be Latin, wouldn't it?' Blackstone replied.

'Yes.'

'Don't speak it myself. Never felt much of a need. Now, about your dad. Mr George—'

'Why would you wish to know anything about my father?' Sebastian George interrupted him. 'He's an old man, and extremely frail.'

'Physically frail – or mentally frail?' Blackstone wondered.

'That is neither here nor there. My father could have no possible bearing on your investigation, since he is . . . is . . .'

'Safely locked away behind the high walls of a lunatic asylum?' Blackstone provided.

'Since he is being cared for, in a secure institution, by those people who are best *able* to care for him.'

'In which particular lunatic asylum is he being cared for *securely*?' Blackstone asked.

'That is really not your business,' Sebastian George told him.

'Perhaps it isn't,' Blackstone admitted, 'but I'm still surprised you're so unwilling to supply me with the name of the institution. Is that because you have something to hide?'

'I have nothing to hide, and nothing to be ashamed of,' Sebastian George told him. 'If you really must know, my father is being taken care of in the Bethlehem Hospital.'

'Bedlam!' Blackstone exclaimed. 'That's where you can pay to go and look at the madmen running amok, isn't it?'

'That was certainly the case long ago,' George said, 'but we are at the dawn of a new century, and the treatment of lunatics is much more enlightened than it was formerly. The days of chaining up the poor madmen are now, I'm pleased to say, far behind us.'

'Is that right?' Blackstone asked.

'It most certainly is. Furthermore, Bethlehem Hospital is a great deal more selective in its admissions than it used to be, and *considerably* more selective than the county lunatic asylums which would have been the alternative for him. In Bethlehem, a man may rest assured that his former position in society will be both known and respected by the staff, and he may be confident that those with whom he engages in social intercourse will have a similar standing to his own.'

'In other words, he may be surrounded by stark staring madmen, but at least they'll be stark staring madmen of his own class,' Blackstone said.

'Well, exactly,' Sebastian George agreed. 'I couldn't have put it better myself.'

Seventeen

The sign over the door said:

R.H. Peabody
Undertaker's and Chapel of Rest
Mutes and Pure Black Geldings Provided
at Very Reasonable Prices

but even the most unobservant of passers-by would have realized that if Mr Peabody was still in the burial game, he certainly wasn't running his business from this particular establishment.

Talbot Hines – 'The Voice of the *London Evening Chronicle*, the Man whose Opinion **Matters**' – stood on the pavement opposite, taking in all the details of the scene for later use in his column.

'What a cacophony of noise these disgraceful shows are responsible for,' Hines wrote in his mental notebook. 'What a disturbance they create in the normally busy-yet-harmonious life of this great city of ours.'

The 'cacophony of noise' in question was being created by a barrel organ which had been placed directly in front of the former funeral emporium, and on which one of the showman's minions was grinding out a succession of relentlessly cheerful tunes.

To one side of the organ stood a young woman in a flesh-pink body-stocking. She was holding up a roughly-painted sign which proclaimed she was the strongest woman in world.

'Standing there, shamelessly, for all the world to see, she could very easily have been mistaken for a woman wearing absolutely nothing at all,' Hines composed in his head.

At the other side of the organ was a brown-skinned man, wearing only a loincloth. The sign *he* held up promised that, once inside, the customers would 'See Princess Tezel dice with death'.

'The heathen seemed even less aware of his near-naked-ness than the woman did of hers,' Hines wrote in his mental notebook. 'It was truly a sight to shame both those who were posing, and those watching them pose.'

Not quite right, he told himself, but he could polish it up once he was back at the office.

The queue which had formed at the door was made up of just the sort of people who might have been expected to attend this kind of vulgar entertainment. There were workmen, still covered with their day's grime, and men wearing patterned waistcoats who had never thought about doing an honest day's work in their entire lives. There were down-trodden flower sellers and washerwomen, domestic servants and prostitutes.

A few of the potential customers could – at a push – pass as being respectable, Hines supposed. Some were certainly dressed like junior clerks, ladies' personal maids or small shopkeepers. But, on the whole, it was not the kind of gathering which a man of some education would ever choose to attend willingly.

'Nor *do* I choose to attend it,' Hines said softly, as he willed himself to cross the street to the sideshow. 'The choice has been made for me.'

For while it was undoubtedly true that his opinion might 'matter' – as his by-line proudly proclaimed – it would only *continue* to matter for as long as the tyrant who paid his wages said that it did.

* * *

A group of five young men joined the back of the queue, just as Hines was about to reach it himself.

Even had they been as quiet and self-effacing as workhouse children at meal-time, the journalist would still have immediately identified them by their manner of dress – dirty neck-cloths instead of collars, heavy belts instead of braces – as being hooligans.

And, in point of fact, they were not being quiet at all!

They shouted.

They swaggered.

They slapped each other heavily on the back.

One of them had even brought a dog with him. It was a muscular creature, so battle-scarred that there was no doubt it had already made numerous appearances in the fighting pit, and its owner – showing no fear of its iron jaw and sharp teeth – was taking great delight in teasing it.

Hines hesitated, and almost determined to turn around and walk away. Then he reminded himself that his editor was not the most tolerant of men even at the best of times, and would be unlikely to greet his failure to deliver the story with anything akin to the kindly understanding it merited.

So there was nothing else for it, he decided – he would just have to force himself to join the queue.

Standing right by the door was a weedy man in a tattered overcoat. He had been assigned to collect the money, and as the hooligans drew level with him, he looked down at the dog with misgivings.

'Yer can't take that h'animal in there,' he said.

'But 'e wants ter see the show,' the hooligan protested. 'I promised I'd bring 'im to see it if 'e won 'is last fight – an' 'e did.'

'Tore the uvver dog's froat right out of 'im,' one his friends added, in support of the statement. 'Bit open 'is 'ead, an' gobbled down 'is eyes.'

'I can't 'elp wot you promised,' the money-collector told him. 'You can go in, but the dog 'as to stay outside.'

One of the other hooligans reached down to his belt, which was held together by a buckle far larger – and far sharper – than any buckle designed merely to hold a belt together ever needed to be. A second hooligan raised his arm high in the air, to show the money-collector just how stiff it had been made by the iron bar he had concealed up his sleeve.

'Tell yer wot,' said the dog-owner, 'why don't I pay yer for Butch's ticket, just like 'e was any uvver customer.'

The money-collector had been shown the stick of violence, and then offered the carrot of compromise. Wisely choosing to accept the carrot, he held out his hand, and the hooligan dropped two copper coins into it.

Hines, who had stepped as far back as the crush behind him would allow him to, found that he was experiencing emotions which were a mixture of disappointment and relief.

On the one hand, he told himself, if the hooligans had beaten up the collector it would have made good copy for his story.

On the other, it was undoubtedly true that that kind of brutality is always best observed from a very great distance.

Eighteen

'Admit it! This is not quite what you expected to find when you first decided to pay us a visit, now is it, Inspector?' asked the governor of Bethlehem Hospital as he glanced out of the window of his office at a number of the hospital's inmates, who were playing a spirited game of cricket in the grounds.

'No, indeed, it isn't what I expected to find at all,' Blackstone admitted freely.

From the road outside, the hospital, with its impressive central dome and tall Ionic pillars, had looked more like a library or a university college than a lunatic asylum. And inside, too, it had failed to live up to the conventional images of a madhouse. There were no screaming women tearing at their own hair and clothes, no demented men banging their heads against the walls until the blood ran. Instead, the lunatics were quiet, clean and well-dressed.

'It is our policy to admit only those lunatics who are

curable,' the governor explained, 'and if we are wrong in our assessment of them – if, after a year, they are still not cured – then it is our strict rule that they must be transferred to some other institution.'

'How can you tell if they've actually been cured or not?' Blackstone wondered.

'I should have thought that was obvious,' the governor said, slightly disdainfully.

'Not to me,' Blackstone said. 'But then, I'm not a doctor, you see. I'm only a simple bobby.'

The governor smiled condescendingly. 'Of course you are,' he agreed. 'I should have realized that. Let me explain it to you, then. Those inmates whom we decide to release into the world again have become demonstrably much calmer and more rational during the time they have spent at Bethlehem than they were when they were admitted. And what is that an indication of, I ask you, if it is not an indication that they are cured?'

It might be an indication that they've learned that if they play the game by your rules, you'll let them out, Blackstone thought.

'So you assumed that Thaddeus George was curable when he was admitted?' he asked.

'Of course.'

'But you were wrong?'

'Unfortunately, yes.'

'Then why is he still here? I thought you said that you discharged your failures after a year.'

'We do not consider it *our* failure that they are not cured, we consider it *theirs*,' the governor said severely. 'We give them every opportunity to regain their sanity, and if they fail to take advantage of it, it is either because they are too lazy, or because the madness has taken too firm a grip of them.'

'But whether it was Thaddeus George's failure or yours, he still hasn't been discharged,' Blackstone pointed out.

The governor had begun to look very slightly uncomfortable about the way the conversation was going.

'You are quite right,' he agreed. 'He has not been cured, yet neither has he been discharged. That is because it was decided to make a special exception in Mr George's case.'

'And why was that?'

'Because a great friend of this hospital – a great *patron* of this hospital – asked us to make that exception.'

'Who was he?'

The governor chuckled. 'I'm afraid that I cannot reveal his name to just anyone. Suffice it to say that he is an important man who has wielded considerable power for good.'

'So it was Lord Bixendale, was it?' Blackstone asked.

The governor blinked. 'I have already told you that I am not at liberty to reveal his name,' he said.

'Can I see Mr George now?' Blackstone said.

'I am still in two minds as to whether to allow the interview to proceed,' the governor said.

'Then you want to watch your step,' Blackstone warned him.

'I beg your pardon?'

'You want to watch your step – because if you're in *two* minds about it, you run a fair chance of getting locked up in here yourself.'

The governor smiled wanly. 'It might help if you were to give me a reason for seeking the interview.'

'And I would be more than willing to do so, if it were left up to me,' Blackstone lied.

He looked around, as if checking to see whether anyone was listening.

'But, you see,' he continued, in a much lower voice, 'I am not here merely as a policeman.'

'No?'

'No. I am also acting as agent for a man of considerable importance in the government.'

'Ah, then that is an entirely different matter, Inspector. Might I perhaps enquire who . . . ?'

Blackstone wagged his finger in front of him to cut the other man off.

'But unfortunately, I find myself trapped in a similar dilemma to your own,' he said.

'And what dilemma might that be?'

'That, for reasons I can't even begin to go into, I am not at liberty to reveal his name.'

In many ways, Thaddeus George bore a strong resemblance to the sketches that Marcus Leighton, the artist to the police, had drawn. The same nose, the same eyes, the same wrinkled skin. But the strength and determination hinted at in the sketches were both absent from the face of the man who was sitting opposite Blackstone now.

'When they first locked me up in this dreadful place, I raged and stormed throughout my every waking hour,' George said. 'But, in the end, I realized – as all condemned men must sooner or later realize – that such actions were pointless, and that my fate was sealed.'

'Do you know why they locked you up in here, Mr George?' Blackstone asked.

George smiled, showing a little of the spirit he must once have had. 'Of course I know why,' he said. 'They did it for the best of all possible reasons – because I am an incurable lunatic.'

'Or perhaps it was because you were in somebody else's way?' Blackstone suggested.

'Or perhaps it was because I was in somebody else's way,' George agreed. 'I was once a relatively rich man, you know.'

'No, I didn't know that,' Blackstone said.

'Oh yes. I took the modest fortune I had acquired in my business dealings and put it all into the theatre which now bears my name. But it took more than just my money to establish that theatre as a going concern, you know.'

'I'm sure it must have.'

'God, how I worked at it! While my podgy, spoiled son was whoring his way around the bars and brothels of Central London, I was devoting eighteen or nineteen hours a day to my theatre. And eventually, it paid off! In the eighties and the early nineties, the George was easily one of the most successful theatres in the whole of the West End.'

'So what went wrong?'

George shrugged. 'Every theatre, however well-run, always has its ups and downs. It's in the nature of the game. You put on a production which all your instinct and experience tells you will be a huge success, and – for reasons no one can ever satisfactorily explain – it's a complete flop. And that one flop can not only wipe out the gains from three or four previous successes, but it can also make the public wary of coming to see your next production, however good *that* might turn out to be.' He smiled again. 'It is much easier to roll a rock down a hill than it is to push it back up to the top again.'

'It must be very discouraging when that happens,' Blackstone said sympathetically.

Thaddeus George shrugged. 'As I said, it is in the nature of the game. The trick is to prepare for such an eventuality. And I had! There was plenty of cash in the reserve fund to see us through our hard times – or so I thought.'

'But when you really needed it, you discovered that it wasn't there any longer?'

'When I really needed it, I discovered that my worthless son had already frittered it away. And so I was faced with two alternatives. I could take on backers – but it was *my* theatre, and I was not prepared to compromise it – or we would have to learn to cut our cloth more sparingly for a while. The second of the two alternatives would not have been easy, but we would certainly have survived. Unfortunately, cutting the cloth sparingly is not my son's style at all, and he had other ideas.'

'He wanted you to take on the backers,' Blackstone said. 'And one backer in particular – Lord Bixendale.'

'Indeed. But Bixendale's assistance came with a price. He wished his paramour to be elevated to the position of leading actress.'

'And why did you object to that, Mr George? Is Charlotte Devaraux such a bad actress?'

'No. She is rather a good actress, as a matter of fact, and no doubt I would have promoted her myself, in time. But that is not the point.'

'Then what is?'

'As I've already told you, Inspector, it was *my* theatre. Mine! I was not about to take direction from a man whose artistic sensibilities were guided solely by the stirrings within his nether regions.'

'And so your son had you committed, in order that the deal could go through?'

'Judas Iscariot would have been a better son to me than Sebastian has turned out to be.'

'Have you ever thought of taking your revenge?'

'I have thought of little else.'

'Have you done anything about it?'

'What *could* I do, locked up in this place? As an incurable, I am not allowed to have visitors.'

'None at all?'

'You are the first man from outside Bedlam that I have spoken to since the day I was admitted. I am not permitted to write or receive letters either. It might, I suppose, be possible to smuggle letters out, but that would require paying a bribe, and I have no money.'

'Do you have a brother?' Blackstone asked. 'One who is of roughly the same age as you are, and might possibly be mistaken for you?'

'No, I come from a small family, and have no brothers. I had a sister, but she is long dead.'

'A cousin who might resemble you, perhaps?'

'None that I know of.'

There was the sound of heavy footfalls, advancing rapidly down the corridor outside.

Blackstone checked his pocket watch. 'They said I could only have ten minutes in your company, and they're obviously going to stick to it,' he said. 'I'm sorry.'

'Don't be,' Thaddeus George replied. 'I feel stronger for our ten minutes together than I have in the whole two years I have been in here, and memories of it may well give me the strength to struggle through another two years.'

'I hope that won't be necessary,' Blackstone said fiercely.

'What do you mean?'

'I don't think it will be very easy to get you out of here – in fact, it might turn out to be completely bloody impossible – but I'm certainly going to try my damnedest.'

A tear appeared in the old man's eye. 'Why would you do that for me?' he asked.

'Because injustice makes me angry,' Blackstone told him. 'And I'm very angry now!'

Waxwork figures were a common feature of many of the penny sideshows, and this one proved to be no exception to the rule. Once the customers had handed over their money to the man outside, they were ushered into a room where there were a dozen or more of them.

The effigies were crude representations at best, and that the viewers identified three of the figures as being the Prime Minister, Foreign Secretary and Home Secretary was due more to the names that had been pinned on them than it was to any actual physical resemblance.

'Waste 'o time, this,' said the hooligan with the dog. 'We don't want to see waxworks of old blokes like them. Why can't they make some of naked women wiv big nellies?'

'The wax figures in the vestibule were both a travesty of art, and an affront to the dignity of those eminent men whom they claimed to portray,' Talbot Hines composed in his head.

Huh! he thought. That might be true enough, but it wasn't a line to set the blood racing, now was it?

He hoped that once they were inside the second room, he would find something much more interesting – and preferably much more shocking – to write about. And if he did not, then perhaps he would be wise to follow his editor's veiled hint and *make* something shocking or interesting happen.

'Is there any way that Mr Thaddeus George could escape from here?' Blackstone asked the governor of Bethlehem Hospital, once he'd been escorted back to the man's office.

'Escape? From here? There is absolutely no possibility at all,' the governor replied with no hesitation.

'And you're quite sure about that, are you?' Blackstone pressed.

'Surely, the proof positive of my assertion is that Thaddeus George is still here.'

'But might it be possible for him to escape for a few hours, and then return without his absence being noticed?'

'Most definitely not. This asylum, as you will have noticed yourself, has high walls that even a fit young man would find difficult to scale. Besides, Mr George is locked up at night-time, and in the daytime we check up on him once every two hours, in accordance with Lord Bix . . . in accordance with the routine we have decided most appropriate to a lunatic like him.'

So there was simply no way that Thaddeus George could have commissioned the knife, nor bribed the telephone operator.

But Blackstone had pretty much dismissed both those things as possibilities within a couple of minutes of starting to talk to the old man. Thaddeus George was an honest, decent person. He would never have participated in a murder plot, however angry he had been.

'Is there any chance that Mr George will ever be released from here?' he asked.

'None at all, I'm afraid,' the governor said, without even a trace of regret discernible in his voice. 'This asylum will be his home until he dies.'

Some home! Blackstone thought.

'But surely, there must exist a procedure through which the cases of those committed can be re-examined,' he said.

'Well, yes, there is,' the governor admitted, somewhat reluctantly.

'And what does it involve?'

'The normal procedure is to petition the Lunacy Commission for a fresh hearing. If that hearing is granted – which is by no means always the case – then the alleged lunatic's friends and lawyers will have the opportunity to persuade the Commission that there is an argument to be made for his release.'

'So it doesn't have to be a life sentence after all?'

The governor frowned his displeasure. 'This is not a prison, and we do not think in terms of sentences.'

'Locked up for life is locked up for life, whatever way you care to describe it,' Blackstone said.

'Furthermore, if, in this general discussion, you are thinking specifically of Mr Thaddeus George's case, I must tell you that Mr *Sebastian* George, his closest living relative, has thus far shown no inclination to place an appeal. And even if he did . . .'

The governor pulled himself up short, and began to take a sudden interest in fiddling with his watch-chain.

'Even if he did?' Blackstone prompted.

'Nothing. Since Sebastian George will place no appeal, that is the end of the matter.'

'But *even if he did*, Lord Bixendale – who no doubt has many friends on the Lunacy Commission – would ensure that the appeal had no chance of being successful?' Blackstone suggested.

The governor stopped playing with his watch-chain, and made an ostentatious show of consulting the pocket watch itself.

'You would not tell me which government minister you are representing,' the governor said, 'but whoever he is, I feel he

131

can have no complaint about the amount of my time I have made available to you, Inspector Blackstone. And now, if you will excuse me, I must return to my normal duties.'

'You may think Lord Bixendale has influence, but he's got about as much as a babe in arms when compared to the influence my principal wields,' Blackstone said stonily. 'And I feel it only fair to warn you that he will be greatly displeased by the way in which you have handled this whole affair.'

'I have behaved with the utmost propriety!' the governor said.

'And I can only hope that you have a private income, and are not dependent on your salary here to keep a roof over your head and food on your table,' Blackstone concluded.

It was an empty threat, but if it managed to cause the governor even *one* sleepless night, then Blackstone considered it had been well worth making.

Nineteen

Having been given more time than they would ever have wished for to study the crude wax figures in the ante-room, the paying customers of the penny sideshow were now ushered through into a second room of the ex-undertaking establishment, where the main event was due to take place.

In its former days of glory, the room had probably been used for display purposes. There would have been a range of coffins – the more expensive ones placed in the most favourable light, the cheaper ones crammed into the corner – rolls of black crêpe, and all the other paraphernalia of a funeral which the undertaker would have attempted to sell to his less-than-usually-resistant clients. Now that was all gone. A crude and hastily erected wooden stage filled one corner of the room, and the rest of the floor space had been given over to the eager spectators, who were being squeezed into it like sausage meat into a skin.

The smell of sweat, cheap perfume and poverty was already almost unbearable, Talbot Hines thought, and he determined that if he must endure this humiliation, he would at least emerge from the sideshow with a story which would make headlines.

Though they had been in the room for little more than a minute, the audience in general – and the gang of hooligans in particular – were already starting to become restive.

'Where's the Princess What's-it?' the hooligan with the dog demanded loudly. 'I want ter take a butcher's at 'er.'

'Why's that, Rollo?' one of his friends asked.

'I want ter see if she's worth me slippin' a length to 'er!' the hooligan with the dog replied.

The other hooligans laughed, but a man in a good second-hand suit, who was standing next to them, said, 'Hush!'

'You tell me to 'ush again, mate, an' I'll fill yer face in for you,' Rollo threatened.

'But there are ladies present,' the man protested.

'Ladies?' Rollo repeated. 'I don't see no ladies. All I see is a bunch of prozzies an' scrubbers.'

The youth had an exceptionally foul mouth on him, Talbot Hines thought, but it would have been difficult to disagree with his analysis of the social composition of the audience.

A middle-aged man stepped on to the stage. He was wearing a long, faded red coat of the kind normally worn by ring-masters in circuses. As he looked out at his audience, the expression on his face seemed to suggest that he wished that, like a real ringmaster, he had brought a whip with him.

'Welcome, ladies and gentlemen, to the most exciting sideshow in London, if not in the entire world,' he said in a voice which was loud enough, yet somewhat lacking in convic-tion. 'I will be your master of ceremonies for this perform-ance, and it will be my pleasure to bring wonders to you that, hitherto, you will only have read about.'

''Oo sez we can read at all?' Rollo called out.

Around him, his mates laughed, as if they had suddenly discovered the new Oscar Wilde standing in their midst.

The master of ceremonies wisely decided to ignore the comment.

'Later in the programme, you will be astounded by the feats of strength performed by Miss Emily Judd, the strongest woman in the world,' he said. 'But first may I present an artiste who has travelled all the way from Columbia, in South America, to be with us. She is the only daughter of Mantinus, the paramount chief of the Choco tribe.'

'The *chocolate* tribe?' Rollo shouted.

'Will you please welcome Princess Tezel and her troupe!' the master of ceremonies said, now apparently deaf to any comment that might emanate from the hooligan.

The Indian, who had been standing out on the street next to the barrel organ, now climbed on to the stage. He was followed by another man, and a woman. The second man was dressed, as he was, in only a loincloth, but the woman was wearing an elaborate gown which seemed to be composed mainly of brightly-coloured bird feathers.

The most striking thing about all three of them was their faces. They were dark, sharp and lacking subtlety – as if they had been hastily carved from a piece of teak or mahogany – and as expressionless as if they really *were* made out of wood.

The men squatted down on the floor. One of them picked up a hand-drum, the other a crude set of pipes. They started to play a tune, though it was not one the audience knew. Indeed, some of those standing watching them began to question whether it was a tune at all.

The woman did not move for the first half minute or so, then she began to dance as stiffly as a statue caught in an earthquake.

'This is a swizz!' Rollo called out. 'She's the ugliest woman wot I've ever seen in my life, an' I want my money back!'

His friends needed little encouragement to join in with his criticism.

'Revoltin' old bag.'

'She's so ugly that she shouldn't be allowed out of the 'ouse 'till after it's gone dark.'

Princess Tezel stopped dancing, and looked at the hooligans with utter loathing. Though she had not understood a word of what they had said, it was perfectly plain that she had caught the tone of their comments easily enough.

'Now she ain't even shakin' her nellies for us no more,' Rollo complained. 'Not that they're much to talk about, even when she does.'

The master of ceremonies, deciding somewhat reluctantly

134

that the time had come to intervene, stepped back on to the stage again.

'Please be patient,' he implored the audience in general, and the hooligans in particular. 'Once she has finished her dance, Princess Tezel will show you one of the most amazing sights you have ever seen in your life – a sight so dangerous that it will chill you to your marrow.'

'Why don't she show it to us now, 'stead of borin' the pants off us wiv this dance of 'ers?' Rollo demanded.

'The dance is all a part of the necessary ritual,' the master of ceremonies explained. 'Princess Tezel needs to cultivate the proper state of mind before embarking on her dangerous exploit.'

'Yer wot?' Rollo asked.

'It's like when you know yer goin' to 'ave a fight,' one of his friends explained to him. 'Yer 'ave to get yerself good an' mad even before it starts, don't yer?'

'Oh, I see what yer gettin' at,' Rollo said. He turned his attention back to Princess Tezel. 'You just carry on then, darlin'.'

The dance continued for another two minutes. When it had finished, one of the male attendants left the stage, and returned a moment later carrying a wicker basket in his hands.

'In this simple container lurks one of the most dangerous creatures alive,' the master of ceremonies said dramatically.

'Is that right?' Rollo called out. 'Looks too small to me to be 'oldin' a man-eatin' lion.'

'What you are about to see is the poison arrow frog,' the master of ceremonies said. 'This frog excretes a poison which can kill a man in seconds. In Princess Tezel's tribe, the warriors run their arrows across its back before they go into battle.'

'Let's see it, then,' Rollo said.

'The process is not to be rushed,' the master of ceremonies told him. 'Anyone who does not handle the poison arrow frogs with the greatest of care is almost certain to die.'

Princess Tezel's face was even less animated than it had been earlier, Talbot Hines thought. It was almost as if the woman had fallen into some kind of trance.

The princess lifted the lid off the basket, and carefully reached inside. She withdrew her hand slowly again, and, with extreme gentleness, placed what she was holding on to her arm. She repeated the whole operation twice more, then held out the arm for the audience to see. Clinging to it were three very small, brilliantly yellow frogs.

'Them's just ordinary frogs like yer might find in any pond,' Rollo said scornfully. 'They ain't poisonous.'

'I can assure you that they most certainly are,' the master of ceremonies said. 'They are deadly poisonous.'

'Prove it!' Rollo challenged.

'And how do you suggest I do that?'

'Let my dog, Butch 'ere, eat one of the frogs. Let's see just what it does to 'im.'

'We can't do that.'

'Told yer they wasn't poisonous,' Rollo told his cronies. He turned back to the master of ceremonies. 'The 'ole fing's nuffink but a swizz, an' I want my money back.'

'I don't think you quite understand just how rare and expensive these frogs are,' the master of ceremonies protested.

''Ow much are they worth. Thruppence? A tanner?'

'Much more than that.'

'*The* London Evening Chronicle *exposes the true shame of the fake princess*,' Talbot Hines composed in headlines in his mind's eye. '*Top reporter* Talbot Hines *of the* London Evening Chronicle *exposed the true shame of the fake princess*,' he amended.

'*I'll* buy one of these so-called rare and expensive frogs for the dog,' Hines shouted out. 'Will a gold guinea cover it?'

'Good for you, mate!' one of the hooligans said.

'The bloke may look like a bit of a tosser, but 'e's a real sportsman,' another chipped in.

The master of ceremonies spoke in a soft aside to one of the princess's retainers. The retainer, in turn, spoke to Princess Tezel. The princess hesitated for a moment before replying, but when she had, her translator conveyed her message to the master of ceremonies.

'You offered a gold guinea for one of the frogs, sir,' the master of ceremonies said to Talbot Hines. 'Do you happen to have the money on your person, by any chance?'

'Certainly I have the money on me,' the journalist replied.

He reached into his watch pocket, extracted the coin, and then flicked it through the air in the direction of the stage.

The master of ceremonies caught it with alacrity, then took a bite at it to establish whether or not it was genuine.

'That seems to be in order,' he said.

He handed the coin to one of the Indians, as if it had nothing to do with him. Later, of course, when there were no witnesses around, he would probably demand a substantial share of it back, Talbot Hines thought.

'The transaction is completed,' the master of ceremonies said. 'The frog is now your property, sir, to do with as you wish.'

'There is just one thing I'd like to know before we go any further,' Talbot Hines said.

'And what might that be?'

'I'd like to know exactly what it was that the princess said to her attendant just now.'

'That is surely neither here nor there,' the master of ceremonies replied.

'Perhaps not,' Hines agreed. 'But I've just handed over a considerable amount of money, and I'd like an answer.'

'The princess said that we all have to make our own choices in life, and if your friend wishes feed the frog to his dog, then it's his funeral. Or rather, to be more accurate, it's his dog's funeral.'

'My dog ain't scared of no little frogs,' Rollo said. 'My dog ain't scared of nuffink.'

'Then, by all means, bring him up on to stage,' the master of ceremonies invited.

'Be glad to.'

Princess Tezel returned two of the small yellow frogs to their basket, as slowly and carefully as she had taken them out. While the hooligan and his dog were climbing up the rickety steps on to the stage, she placed the third frog on the floor. And then, totally unexpectedly, her lips curled upwards and her face lost a little of its immobility.

Dear God, she's smiling! Hines realized, with shock. The woman's bloody smiling!

And suddenly, he found himself wondering if all this had been such a good idea after all.

'There is your one-guinea frog, sir,' the master of ceremonies told the hooligan. 'Do what you will with it.'

'Go on, Butch, eat it up,' the hooligan said jovially. 'That'll do for your supper, that will.'

The dog could see the small frog, but showed absolutely no interest in it. Then the frog made the tactical error of taking a small leap, and the dog swooped down on it, swallowing it in a single gulp.

Rollo looked at his friends in the audience. 'Told yer it wasn't poisoned,' he said triumphantly.

But the expressions forming on the faces of his fellow hooligans, as they watched the dog, were already beginning to suggest that he was wrong.

For perhaps fifteen seconds, Butch shook violently. Then he opened his mouth to bark, but no sound came out. Finally he froze – for perhaps two more seconds – before his legs buckled under him, and he fell to the floor.

Twenty

The piles of books balanced precariously on Ellie Carr's desk were even taller than they'd been the last time Jed Trent had visited her office, but from the expression of exhausted disappointment on her face, it did not look to Trent as if she had had any more luck consulting the additional volumes than she'd had with the previous ones.

'It was a good idea of yours to say I should consider the possibility of spiders and snakes as a source of the poison, Jed,' Ellie told Trent. 'But even good ideas don't always come to fruition, and I'm afraid this one certainly doesn't seem to be leading anywhere.'

'There's an article—' Trent began.

'I've tried,' Ellie said wearily. 'Goodness knows, I've tried. I really don't know how many species of spiders and snakes there are in the world. Nobody does with any degree of certainty. But I must have read about hundreds of specimens of both, and not one of them – not a single bloody one – can cause the kind of reaction through its poison that I saw on the stage of the George Theatre.'

'Maybe you'll find the answer that you're looking for in here,' Trent suggested, holding up a copy of the *London Evening Chronicle* for her to see. 'As I started to say before, there's an article on—'

'For God's sake, Jed, do try and talk a little sense,' Ellie interrupted. 'If I can't find the solution to the problem in dozens of books written by distinguished toxicologists – and I can't – then what chance is there that I'll find it in the evening newspaper, conveniently located somewhere between the court circular and the classified advertisements?'

'I thought you scientists claimed never to rule out anything,' Trent said mildly.

'That's true. We don't. But we do make a point of looking in the most obvious places first.'

'This is obvious,' Jed Trent said.

'Really, Jed, I haven't got time to—'

'Read it!' Trent said firmly.

Ellie sighed. 'All right, if it will make you happy,' she agreed. 'Is this what you want me to read? "Terrible Happening in London"?'

'That's what I want you to read.'

Terrible Happening in London
By Talbot Hines
The Voice of the Evening Chronicle
The Man whose Opinion *Matters*

In the interest of truth and enlightenment, towards which we journalists always strive, I today attended a penny sideshow on the Mile End Road. I had not anticipated enjoying the 'entertainment', but felt it my duty to my readers to attend it. I fully expected to be disgusted, but had not expected the horror which turned the stomach of even this seasoned reporter.

The spectacle commenced with a barely-clad woman who performed a dance clearly designed to ignite the passions of the baser element of the audience. But worse was to follow. The woman then produced a number of slimy poisonous frogs, which she proceeded to allow to crawl up and down the naked flesh of her arm. One of the rougher members of the audience,

who had brought his sweet little doggie with him, called
out that he did not think the frogs were poisonous at
all. A *lady* would have let this comment pass, but the
woman then insisted that he feed one of the frogs to
his doggie to demonstrate just how poisonous it was.
This he did, and the poor dog quickly died in a manner
that I will not assault my readers' sensibilities by
describing, save to say that it was horrific indeed.

The woman is clearly guilty of great cruelty, but
she is not alone in this. They say that a dog is a man's
best friend, but this man was certainly not this
dog's best friend, or he would never have allowed the
doggie to run the risk of being poisoned. I am a man
of moderate views, as my regular readers know, but
I feel that no injustice would be committed if both the
man and the woman were whipped through the streets.

'Well?' Jed Trent asked.

'That might be it, you know, Jed,' Ellie said excitedly. 'That
just might be it.'

'I thought you'd say that.'

'We have to get our hands on one of these frogs. We must
go down to the Mile End Road immediately.'

'I thought you'd say that as well,' Jed Trent told her. 'That's
why I've got a cab waiting right outside.'

Blackstone found Charlotte Devaraux sitting in her dressing
room, staring into the mirror.

'I do this every day,' she told him, when she saw the reflection of him standing in the open doorway. 'I search for signs
of ageing, as if they might have sneaked up on me overnight.
So far, I haven't found anything that I should become seriously worried about.'

'I'm delighted for you,' Blackstone said, with no trace of
delight in his voice at all. 'But what will happen, do you think,
when you do find the signs, Miss Devaraux?'

'I'll be devastated for a day or two – perhaps even longer
than that – but I imagine I'll get over it eventually. Stage make-
up can hide a multitude of sins, you know. And when even
that fails to mask the ravages of time, the Scottish play will
still need its Weird Sisters, and Juliet must always have a nurse.'

'You're very philosophical about it,' Blackstone said, with grudging admiration.

'I'm a realist, Inspector,' Charlotte Devaraux replied. 'Do you think I would ever have taken a rich lover, so much older than myself, if I wasn't?'

'And you're also very honest,' Blackstone said.

'I try to be. We thespians live in a world of illusion, but we should never mistake that for the world which lies just beyond the stage door.' Charlotte checked the mirror once more, then swung round on her stool to face Blackstone. 'Still no real signs of the inevitable decline quite yet, so what can I do for you, Inspector?'

'I'd like you to look at these,' Blackstone replied, stepping into the dressing room and laying the police artist's two sketches of the old man on the dressing table. 'Does he look familiar to you?'

'Do you know, he looks like he might almost be old Mr George,' the actress said.

'He may look like it, but he isn't,' Blackstone replied. 'Thaddeus George has been safely locked away in Bethlehem Hospital for the last two years, and this man was very much at liberty only two days ago. So is there anyone else you know who he might remind you of?'

Charlotte Devaraux laughed. 'I'm afraid not. The social circle in which I move is a *young* social circle, Inspector, and all my friends and acquaintances are my own age or even younger.'

Except for Lord Bixendale, of course, Blackstone thought – but he kept the comment to himself.

'It was such a shame about what happened to Mr George,' Charlotte Devaraux said. 'I liked him a great deal, you know. I was most terribly upset when he was committed.'

What a hypocrite, Blackstone thought.

'Most terribly upset, but not upset *enough* to stop the committal,' he said aloud.

Charlotte Devaraux seemed surprised by the statement. 'How could *I* have stopped it?' she asked. 'And why *would* I have stopped it, even if I had been able to? Surely, once poor Mr George had gone mad, the lunatic asylum was the best place for him.'

'He didn't go mad,' Blackstone said.

'But if he was—'

'He wasn't mad when they committed him, and – by some miracle, considering all he's been through since then – he's not mad now. And I should know. I was talking to the old man less than two hours ago, and I can assure you that he's easily as sane as we are.'

'But that's . . . that's too horrible!' Charlotte Devaraux said, looking truly aghast. 'If he's not mad, then he should not be in the asylum.'

She was an actress, Blackstone reminded himself, yet her shock really did seem to be genuine.

'I'd assumed that you knew,' he said, 'but now I'm beginning to have my doubts.'

'Knew what?'

'The truth about what happened to Thaddeus George. What exactly were you told?'

'Why, that old Mr George had begun to act strangely, and though, at first, Sebastian thought he could care for him at home, he soon came to realize that the old man was in need of professional care.'

'What actually occurred was that Thaddeus George was foolish enough to cross your "friend" Lord Bixendale,' Blackstone said.

'What do you mean?'

'You asked Bixendale to use his influence to get you bigger roles in the productions, didn't you?'

'No, I . . . I may have said that I *wished* I had bigger roles, but I never expected him to—'

'He went to see Thaddeus George, and said that he was willing to invest money in the theatre if you were made the leading lady. Thaddeus wouldn't agree to that, but Sebastian was willing enough to go along with it. The only problem was that it was Thaddeus, not Sebastian, who was in charge.'

'Are you saying that Sebastian George . . . that Sebastian George . . .'

'I'm saying that Sebastian George *and* Lord Bixendale conspired with two crooked doctors to have him locked away.'

'I don't believe you!' Charlotte Devaraux said angrily. 'I simply *won't* believe you!'

'Don't take just my word for it, then,' Blackstone said. 'If you need confirmation, all you have to do is ask Lord Bixendale.'

'No, that wouldn't do any good,' Charlotte Devaraux said, calmer and sadder now. 'He tries to shield me from all the unpleasantness of life, and so he would only deny it.'

'But you sound like you're at least *starting* to believe I'm telling the truth,' Blackstone said.

'I am,' Charlotte Devaraux admitted. 'Now I've had time to get used to the idea, it all makes sense. I never expected Sarah Tongue to leave the company – or, at least, not quite in the way that she did.'

'And what way was that?' Blackstone wondered.

'Suddenly. Out of the blue. One day she was there, the next day she was gone. I assumed she'd been poached by one of the other theatre companies. That kind of thing does happen, now and again. I kept expecting to see her name up on the marquee of the Theatre Royal or the Criterion, but that never happened.'

'It didn't occur to you she'd been given the push?'

'No, why should it have done? She was a very good actress, and the audiences loved her. Theatre managers always tend to stick with what's tried and tested, and there would have been no point in Sebastian George getting rid of someone as well-established as Sarah was.'

'Unless Lord Bixendale had told him to,' Blackstone pointed out.

'Yes, unless that happened,' Charlotte Devaraux agreed. She looked up at Blackstone. Her eyes were wide with innocent confusion, and there were tears in them. 'I didn't know what had happened to old Mr George,' she continued. 'You must believe me, *I didn't know.*'

'I think I do believe you,' Blackstone said. 'But now you know, what are you going to do about it? Is it your intention to right the terrible wrong that's been committed?'

'Of course.'

'So you'll tell Lord Bixendale that you've finally learned the truth, and you'll insist on Thaddeus George being set free.'

Charlotte Devaraux shook her head. 'No. If I went about things in the manner you suggest, I'd *never* get the poor old man released.'

'Why not?'

'Because Lord Bixendale is the kind of man who always has to be right, and by giving in to a demand like that, he would almost be admitting that he had been wrong.'

'So what will you do?'

'I'll begin by telling Robert just how much I miss old Mr George – how I used to value his guidance, and how Sebastian is no more than a rather poor substitute for him. Then I'll let matters rest for a while.'

'How long is "a while"?'

'A few days. Perhaps a week. It will depend when Robert next takes me to his bed, and how he performs once we are there.'

'How well *he* performs?' Blackstone asked. 'Or do you mean how well *you* perform?'

Charlotte Devaraux laughed. 'You don't know much about old men – and how they react – do you?' she asked. 'But then, why should you? You are a long way from being an old man yourself.'

'Tell me about the way old men react,' Blackstone suggested.

'If they perform badly, they feel the shadow of death hovering over them, and fall into a depression. If they perform well, it is almost as if they have recaptured their youth. After a good performance, they see the world as a golden place, and want to make others as happy as they are themselves. That is the time you should ask them for favours.'

'And what favour will you ask him for?'

'I won't ask him for any, directly,' Charlotte Devaraux said. 'Or, rather, I won't *call* it a favour. I'll say that while it is beyond dispute that old Mr George was mad when he was committed to the asylum, isn't there a possibility that he has since regained his sanity? I will suggest that it might be a good idea to have him re-examined. And Lord Bixendale will agree, because, at that moment, he would agree that black was white, if he thought it would please me.'

'So you're confident you'll be able to get Thaddeus George released?' Blackstone asked.

'Oh, yes,' Charlotte Devaraux replied. 'It may take a month or so – it might be even longer than that, but eventually the gates of the asylum will swing open, and he will walk out a free man.'

'You do you realize, don't you, that if you succeed, you'll probably be cutting your own throat?' Blackstone cautioned.

'By which you mean that once old Mr George takes control of the theatre again, he may well decide that, though I

144

eventually helped him, I am still as responsible for his two years of hell as Lord Bixendale and Sebastian are – and I might be out of a job?'

'That's right.'

Charlotte Devaraux shrugged. 'As with the knowledge that one day I'll lose my looks, it's something I'll just have to learn to come to terms with it. And I'm a good actress – possibly even a great one – so there'll be other companies which will want to employ me.'

'I'm sure there will,' Blackstone said.

'But should they all turn me down, I can always persuade Lord Bixendale to buy a theatre of his own, and install me in it as its brightest star.'

'That would be good.'

'Yes, it would be – at least, until he grew tired of me.'

A long, excited queue had already formed outside the ex-undertaking establishment on the Mile End Road, but Ellie Carr and Jed Trent ignored it and walked right up to the door.

The weedy-looking money collector was no longer alone, but now had an assistant – a big East End bruiser – and it was the assistant, not the money collector, who stepped out to block Ellie and Jed's passage.

'If yer want ter see the show, it starts in fifteen minutes,' he told Ellie. 'It'll cost you a tanner each to get in, an' you'll 'ave to join the queue just like everybody else.'

'A tanner!' Ellie said. 'Sixpence!'

'That's right.'

'But I thought this was a *penny* sideshow.'

'Yes, that's exac'ly what it was,' the tough agreed. 'But then it got itself into the papers, didn't it?'

'There was a time when you'd have killed for a tanner, Lew,' Jed Trent said. 'What's the going rate these days?'

The tough stopped looking at Ellie, and turned his attention on to her companion.

'Mr Trent!' he exclaimed. 'I ain't seen you in years. I 'eard you'd left the Force.'

'And so I have,' Trent agreed. 'But I'm still a hard man, and I can still take you – if I have to.'

'There's no need for that kinda talk, Mr Trent,' the tough said. 'If yer want to stand right 'ere at the front o' the queue, that's perfec'ly all right wiv me. An' if yer want to go in wivout payin' – you an' your lady-friend both – well that's all right wiv me as well.'

'What if we don't want to see the show at all?' Trent asked. 'What if we just want to talk to the princess?'

'Then you shall,' the tough said magnanimously. 'You always played fair wiv me when you were on the Force, Mr Trent, an'—'

'Always played fair with you, did he?' Ellie interrupted, with an amused expression coming to her face.

'He did, Miss. Fair as fair could be. He never once – an' yer goin' to 'ave to pardon my French 'ere, Miss – he never once beat the shit outta me when I didn't deserve it beaten out. So if I can't do 'im a little favour now, what kind of bloke would I be?'

'Appreciate it, Lew,' Trent said.

'But there is just one fing I'd like to clear up before you go in, Mr Trent,' the bruiser said.

'And what might that be?'

'I never killed nobody for no tanner piece, like what you just suggested I done.'

'You're quite right,' Trent agreed amiably. 'It was an insulting thing to say, and I apologize wholeheartedly for it.'

'S'all right, Mr Trent,' the tough said, mollified.

'As if you'd kill a man for sixpence!' Trent scoffed. 'Whatever could I have been thinking of? A gold guinea was your usual rate, wasn't it?'

'It depended on the circum—' the tough began. Then he stopped, and pointed a jocular – though accusatory – finger at Trent. 'Nearly caught me out there, Mr Trent. Good fing yer not still on the Force, ain't it?'

'A very good thing,' Trent agreed.

Princess Tezel was wearing a faded floral dress which even a scullery maid would have thought twice about before putting on in public. She was sitting in a cane chair which had only three legs and owed its dubious stability to a house brick which had been jammed under the fourth corner. She showed no interest at all in the fact that the master of ceremonies had led Ellie and Trent into the room, and nor did her two attendants – both still wearing only their loincloths – who were flanking her.

'This lady is a scientist,' the master of ceremonies explained to the princess. 'She wants to buy some of your frogs.'

Not a muscle moved in the princess's carved face, but one of her attendants said, 'What is siretist?'

The master of ceremonies looked helplessly around the room as he searched for the right word.

'Scientist? I'm not sure I can explain it exactly,' he said finally. 'She's . . . she's a kind of witch doctor.'

'He's not far off the mark with that one,' Jed Trent said, in a whispered aside to Ellie.

The Indian spoke to his mistress in a guttural whisper, and she answered with a few equally unintelligible words of her own.

'Frogs not for sale,' the Indian said.

'Well, there you have it, the frogs are not for sale,' the master of ceremonies said. 'Shall I show you the way out?' he continued, hopefully.

'Ask her why she was willing to sell one earlier, but she won't sell any now,' Ellie said, speaking directly to the Indian.

The Indian consulted his mistress. 'Not do for money,' he said. 'Do it for make enemy feel bad.'

'When she talks about an enemy, I think she means the hooligan in the audience who was causing her some grief during the performance,' the master of ceremonies explained. 'It was *his* dog that ate the frog.'

'Tell her I will not harm the frogs, and she can have them back when I've finished with them,' Ellie said to the Indian. 'Tell her I need them because I have enemies, too.'

After this message was conveyed, the princess studied Ellie for a full minute before she spoke again.

'You want poison enemy?' the interpreter asked.

'No, I want to use the frogs to help me catch him. And when I have caught him, I will hang him by the neck until he is dead.'

'You've missed out a few steps in the judicial process, but I suppose that's accurate enough, in its own way,' Jed Trent whispered.

'Quiet, Jed!' Ellie hissed.

'Come to princess,' the interpreter said. 'You must kneel at feet.'

'All right,' Ellie agreed.

147

'You're never going to kneel before a heathen, are you?' Jed Trent asked, outraged.

'This is no time for you to be showing your prejudices, Jed,' Ellie said sharply. 'The woman *is* a princess, whatever her religion'

'So *she* claims!'

'I see no reason not believe her. You shouldn't be so narrow-minded as to expect all royalty to be a carbon copy of our own, Jed. And you can't even be sure she's a heathen. For all you know, she could be solidly Church of England, with her own private pew in her local church.'

Ellie Carr crossed the room, and knelt down at the princess's feet.

The Indian woman put her hands flat on Ellie's head, and appeared to be massaging her skull. Then the hands moved on to her face, and gently glided over her features. Apparently satisfied, she removed her hands, and said a few more words to her interpreter.

'Princess say go back,' the Indian told her.

Ellie climbed to her feet again, and rejoined Jed Trent.

'Never seen anything so disgusting in my life,' Trent whispered. 'You're probably covered with lice now.'

'I don't think so. She was very clean – if a little strange-smelling,' Ellie whispered back.

'Princess say you are sister,' the Indian told her. 'She say your enemy her enemy. Take frogs.'

'How much money do you think I should give her?' Ellie asked the master of ceremonies.

'The man who bought one earlier paid a gold guinea, and that was for only one frog,' the master of ceremonies replied. 'If you are taking more than one, I think it would more than reasonable to ask for at least—'

'No money,' the Indian said. 'Not from sister. But when you kill enemy, you bring her present.'

'What kind of present?' Ellie asked.

The Indian shrugged. 'Not matter. Not big, like head. Enemy finger. Enemy toe. Something small.'

'What!' Jed Trent exploded.

'I'll see what I can do,' Ellie promised.

Twenty-One

The balloon was hovering high above the stage – though, thanks to the illusion created by the sinking tent and bushes, not as high as it appeared to be – and Pittstock was clinging desperately on to the basket.

Lady Wilton produced the sheath from her handbag, pulled the dagger from it, and held the blade above her head, so that the whole audience could see the cruel, naked blade.

'With this knife, I will have my revenge for the evil you have visited on me,' her ladyship said.

There was not a sound from the auditorium – not a cough, not a shuffling of feet.

The whole audience knew the knife was probably a clever fake. But they also knew that just once – for one performance only – it had been real, and it had killed. And tonight, perhaps, if they were lucky, it would kill again.

Lady Wilton swung the dagger.

There had to be a point, somewhere in the arc of that swing, at which the blade retracted, thought Blackstone as he watched the performance from the wings. But he was damned if he could spot exactly when that point was.

Pittstock fell from the balloon, and the audience gasped. He hit the padding on the stage, and was perfectly still. Lady Wilton held the knife high again, and once more its blade was glinting for all to see.

Beside him, Patterson whistled softly. 'How *does* she do that?' the sergeant asked, in awe.

'She's a true professional,' Blackstone replied. 'You should know that by now. Let's go and have a drink.'

'But the performance isn't over yet,' Patterson pointed out.

'It is for me,' Blackstone told him. 'I've had about as much as I can take of the theatre – and of theatre folk – for one day.'

* * *

149

The small yellow frogs sat placidly in a glass tank on one laboratory bench, a dozen large rats squeaked and squirmed in cages on another.

'Ideally, I'd like to see how the poison works on human beings, but since there seems to be a marked shortage of volunteers for the job, the rats will have to do,' Ellie Carr said.

'Are you going to poison *all* of them?' Jed Trent asked.

'Of course,' Ellie replied. 'But not all at once. I need to use different doses, under different conditions, to get a really clear picture.'

'I must admit, it all seems rather cold-blooded to me,' Jed Trent said dubiously.

'They're rats,' Ellie reminded him.

'I know that, but—'

'They carry diseases. The Black Death was one of their major successes. And they show no consideration for us humans, you know. There've been cases of them eating the faces off sleeping infants.'

'Even so—'

'Have you ever used a rat-trap, or laid down poison for rats, Jed?' Ellie asked.

'Well, of course.'

'Have you ever used a dog for hunting rats?'

'Once or twice.'

'So what's the difference?'

'Like I said, it just seems a bit cold-blooded, the way that you're going to do it.'

'It's not cold-blooded at all – it's called *science*, Jed,' Ellie said exasperatedly. 'And you'd better get used to it, because the further we advance into this new century of ours, the more of it there'll be about.'

'Maybe so, but—'

'It's because of people like me "cold-bloodedly" killing rats instead of having dogs tear them apart, that great advances will be made – advances that will be to the benefit of all humanity.'

'Like what?'

'Well, I wouldn't be surprised if, by the start of the *next* century, for example, we can even transplant organs from one person to another.'

'Now you *are* talking stupid, even by your standards,' Jed Trent said dismissively.

Patterson came back from the bar of the King's Head Tavern with two pints of bitter held firmly in his beefy hands.

'What happened to the soda water?' Blackstone wondered.

'Soda water's very gaseous stuff,' Patterson said.

'Is it now?' Blackstone asked.

'That's why it's got all those bubbles. And the bubbles create pockets of air inside the stomach, which make you look even fatter than if you'd been drinking best bitter.'

'You don't say,' Blackstone said, a smile creeping slowly to his lips.

'I *do* say,' Patterson retorted. 'I read it.'

'In a book?'

'Yes.'

'And what was this book called?'

'All right, so I didn't read it at all,' Patterson admitted, sitting down and taking a more-than-healthy swig of his beer. 'But it makes sense, when you think about it.'

'Which is more than this case does,' Blackstone said. 'Was there one murder or two? If there were two, were they both committed by the same person? And who the bloody hell is the little old man working for?'

'That last one's easy to answer,' Patterson told him. 'The little old man is working for the murderer.'

'And the name of the murderer is . . . ?'

'Ah, that's a bit more difficult,' Patterson admitted.

'Meaning, we have no bloody idea?'

'It has to be someone who's part of the company – or connected to the theatre in some other way,' Patterson suggested helpfully. 'We've already pretty much agreed on that.'

'Well, that certainly narrows it down,' Blackstone replied sarcastically. 'The problem, as I see it, Sergeant, is that there's dozens of people with the means and opportunity.'

'Then maybe we should concentrate on the motive,' Patterson suggested. 'Who have we got so far?'

'Three possible suspects,' Blackstone said, beginning to count them off on his fingers. 'One, Sebastian George – because he's been making a fortune from increased ticket sales since the murder. Two, Lord Bixendale – because he might have thought, mistakenly, that the shock would make Charlotte Devaraux give up acting forever. And three, Richmond Clay – because now he's the leading actor instead of William Kirkpatrick.'

'We had those three yesterday,' Patterson said. 'We haven't advanced much since then, have we?'

'We haven't advanced at bloody all,' Blackstone said.

The street door swung open, and Tamara Simmons stepped through it. She paused on the threshold, and glanced around the bar.

'She's looking for somebody,' Patterson said.

Then Tamara Simmons began to walk towards their table, and it became obvious who that 'somebody' was.

Sebastian George turned the handle on the door of Charlotte Devaraux's dressing room and stepped inside.

Charlotte was sitting at her dressing table, removing her make-up. 'Don't you ever knock?' she asked.

'Why *should* I knock?' Sebastian George asked. 'When all's said and done, it is my theatre.'

'It's your *father's* theatre,' Charlotte corrected him.

'Technically, perhaps, but it won't be even *that* for very much longer. My lawyer is already working on transferring the deeds over to my name.' George strode across the room and sat down. 'Tamara Simmons came to see me yesterday.'

'Oh yes?'

'She doesn't think she's getting big enough roles in the plays we're putting on. She suggested that she share the Lady Wilton part with you.' George paused. 'The reason she believed she could get away with making an outrageous demand like that is that she thinks she holds all the cards.' He paused again. 'You know what I'm talking about, don't you?'

'Yes, I know.'

'I sent her away with a flea in her ear. I don't think she'll be bothering either of us again.'

'Good,' Charlotte said.

'Is that it?' Sebastian George demanded. 'Is that all you have to say to me? "Good"?'

'What else is there that you would *like* me to say?' Charlotte Devaraux wondered.

152

'You could have said "thank you". You could perhaps have shown just a little gratitude.'

Charlotte spun round on her stool to look at him. Her face was ablaze with anger.

'I will not be lectured to on the subject of gratitude by a man like you,' she exploded.

'A man like me?'

'Is it true that your father is not insane at all? Is it true that you had him locked away merely so you could take charge of the theatre?'

'Who told you that? Was it Blackstone?'

'It doesn't matter who told me! Is it true?'

'I am not the only one who has benefited from my father's incarceration,' George pointed out reasonably. 'You yourself haven't exactly done *too* badly out of it, now have you?'

'I have talent! In time, I would have risen to eminence anyway,' Charlotte said. 'But not you! Without your dirty tricks, you would still be nothing more than a glorified props boy.'

'We'll gain nothing by fighting amongst ourselves,' George said in a conciliatory manner.

'I'm not intending to fight you,' Charlotte told him. 'I intend to go to Lord Bixendale and persuade him that the wrong you two have committed together must be put right.'

'That would not be a wise move,' George warned. 'You are no more than his concubine – his "bit of fun". I, on the other hand, am his business partner. When I speak, I have his ear.'

Charlotte laughed. 'Do you really believe that?'

'He took me shooting on his estate in Scotland. He said that for a man who had never shot before, I did outstandingly well. He said I was a natural. And I have bought my own gun now, and I have been practising. The next time he invites me, he will be even more impressed.'

'There will not be a next time,' Charlotte said.

'Of course there will. You know how to please a man in bed, but you have no understanding of the kind of hearty – but deep – relationship that one man can have with another.'

Charlotte looked amused. 'And that is what you have with him, is it? A hearty – but deep – relationship?'

'Yes, it is.'

'You poor fool,' Charlotte said, almost pityingly. 'The only reason you were ever asked to join the shooting party is because *I* requested it.'

'You?'

'I wanted to find some way of paying you back for giving me the leading role. But Robert wasn't keen on the idea at all. He said it would be almost like taking a *tradesman* out shooting with him. He said his ghillies would laugh at you behind your back. I had to use all my wiles to get him to finally agree.'

'I don't believe you,' Sebastian George said, his lip quivering like that of a small, disappointed child.

'I don't care whether you believe me or not,' Charlotte said. 'But please believe this: if you try to interfere, in any way, with my plans to get your father released from the lunatic asylum, then I will tell Robbie Bixendale *why* an inexperienced actress like Tamara Simmons has suddenly been given the opportunity to stand centre-stage. And if I once do that, you'll be ruined.'

'And what about you?' Sebastian George demanded. 'Do you think you'll escape Bixendale's wrath yourself? Because I can assure you, you will not! You'll be ruined, too!'

'I am more than willing to run that risk,' Charlotte said coldly. 'And now, Mr George, I would like you to leave my dressing room.'

'I was hoping to find you here alone, Archie,' Tamara Simmons said disappointedly, looking down at the seated Patterson.

'Does this have something to do with the investigation, Miss Simmons?' Blackstone asked.

Tamara Simmons appeared confused, both by the question and by the fact that it was Blackstone who had put it.

'Yes, it does,' she said. 'Well, no, I suppose it doesn't really.' She paused for a second, in an attempt to re-order her thoughts. 'I just wanted to talk to Sergeant Patterson about . . . about things in general, if you know what I mean. But if you're too busy to talk me now, Archie, then I suppose we could leave it until another time.'

'Well, as you can see for yourself, I am somewhat occupied in having a discussion with my superior, Inspector Blackstone,' Patterson said, almost as confused as the woman was.

'That's no real problem, because I was on the point of leaving for home anyway,' Blackstone said.

'You were?' Patterson gasped, giving him a look which accused him of the blackest kind of betrayal.

'I was,' Blackstone confirmed, ignoring the look. He turned back to the woman. 'Can you just give us a couple of minutes to finish off our business, Miss Simmons?'

'All right,' Tamara Simmons agreed, though she showed no signs of moving away.

'I meant, *in private*,' Blackstone said gently.

Tamara Simmons blushed. 'Oh, of course,' she said, backing away towards the bar.

'What's going on?' Patterson asked, as soon as Tamara Simmons was out of earshot.

'What's going on is that a woman who very well might turn out to be a very important witness in this case has come to talk to you of her own free will,' Blackstone explained. 'And – think about it, Archie – just how often does that happen?'

'But she doesn't want to talk about *the case* at all,' Patterson said, sounding increasingly panicked. 'You heard her! She said that she wanted to talk about things in general.'

'And you don't think that will possibly include the murder – the most dramatic event she's ever witnessed in her entire life?'

'Maybe it will,' Patterson agreed reluctantly. 'But I still don't like the idea at all, sir.'

'Why not?'

'I don't know how to handle women on my own.'

'Don't know how to handle women on your own? You're engaged to be married, for God's sake!'

'Yes, I am – and I'm no longer certain how much that was actually my own idea,' Patterson said. 'The bloody dieting part of it wasn't – that much I *do* know for sure!'

'I'm not asking you to sleep with her,' Blackstone said.

'Good!'

'In fact, since I like Rose so much, I'd much rather you *didn't* take Tamara to bed. But I can't see any harm in you just talking to her, for half an hour or so. After all, if you start to feel uncomfortable—'

'I'm uncomfortable now!'

'—if you start to feel *excessively* uncomfortable, you can always make your excuses and leave.'

'Are you *asking* me to stay, sir, or is it more in the nature of an order?' Patterson asked miserably.

'It's an order – if that's what it takes.'

'And you wouldn't rather stay yourself?'

'What would be the point of that? She doesn't want to talk to *me*, she wants to talk to *you*.'

'I'd rather face a gang of heavily-armed toughs down at the East India docks than stay here and talk to her,' Patterson said.

Blackstone grinned. 'So would I,' he said. 'So would anybody. But life can't be *all* fun and games, you know.'

Twenty-Two

Blackstone noticed the woman the second he had left the pub and stepped out on to the street. She was standing on the corner, her head bowed. For a moment, he suspected she was intoxicated. But drunks have a tendency to sway from side to side, and the only part of this woman that was moving was her shoulders, which rose and fell in an almost rhythmical manner.

He set off up the street towards her. The large, wide-brimmed hat she was wearing prevented him from seeing her face, but from her build and stance, he guessed that she was a youngish woman.

As he got closer, he could hear that she was crying. They were not, his policeman's brain told him immediately, the tears of the victim of a crime – loud, disbelieving, verging on the hysterical. No, these were softer, yet deeper – the expression of some inner unhappiness. And since he was a bobby, rather than a priest, they had absolutely nothing to do with him.

He was almost level with her now. He could come to a stop, or walk on.

He stopped.

'Is there anything I can do to help?' he asked.

The woman lifted her head, and he saw the face below the wide-brimmed hat for the first time. 'Hello, Inspector Blackstone,' she said.

'Miss Devaraux!' Blackstone replied. 'What's the matter?'

Charlotte Devaraux forced a smile to her lips. 'Nothing,' she said. 'Nothing at all.' She paused. 'Well, not *quite* nothing, if I'm to be entirely honest. Two nights ago, I accidentally killed another actor in front of an audience of over two thousand people, you know.'

Blackstone smiled back. 'I remember. I was there.'

'Then, just today, I learned that in order for me to become the leading lady of the George Theatre Company, a perfectly sweet old gentleman has been unfairly locked up in a dreadful lunatic asylum.'

'That wasn't your fault.'

'And finally, as the bloody cherry on top of the bloody cake, I've had a blazing row with Sebastian George, as a result of which he will now feel he has no choice but to try to drive a wedge between Lord Bixendale and myself. So, as you can imagine, I feel as if my cup runneth over. The problem is that the sodding cup runneth over with bloody bitter liquid.'

'You need a drink,' Blackstone said. 'Come with me to the King's Head, and I'll buy you one.'

'I need *several* drinks,' Charlotte Devaraux corrected him. 'But, if you don't mind, I'd rather have them somewhere I'm less well-known.'

Tamara Simmons and Sergeant Patterson sat opposite each other at the small round table in the saloon bar of the King's Head. Though the actress had indicated that she desperately needed to talk, she hadn't shown much inclination to say anything at all since Blackstone had left.

Patterson shifted uncomfortably in his seat.

'I've only had the one pint,' he thought miserably, 'and already my arse seems to have gained a couple of pounds in weight.'

'Do you think that I'm a wicked person, Archie?' Tamara Simmons asked suddenly.

'Wicked? No!'

'Thank you for that, at least. But I can tell from your tone that you don't think I'm a very nice one, either.'

Patterson felt himself starting to sweat. Maybe that would melt a little of the fat which the single pint of best bitter had added to his frame.

The woman was clearly expecting him to say something.

'I don't really know you, Miss Simmons,' he began, 'but—'

'Please call me Tamara.'

'—but I can't see that there's anything about you that I would have to call *not* nice.'

'It's so difficult to know anything for sure when the only people you ever get to talk to are *theatre* people,' Tamara Simmons continued, 'because, you see, theatre people aren't *real* people at all.'

'Is that so?' Patterson asked, wondering how soon he dared leave without incurring Blackstone's ire.

'It *is* so,' Tamara Simmons said. 'They only care about themselves, and they're so used to acting all the time that even when they're not supposed to be, they just can't help themselves.'

'I suppose that could be a problem,' Patterson said.

Could he go in another ten minutes, he wondered. Or would he be wiser to endure this for another *fifteen* minutes, just to be on the safe side?

'That's why it's so refreshing to talk to somebody *ordinary*, like you are, Archie,' Tamara Simmons said.

'Do you have any theories of your own about Mr Kirkpatrick's death?' Patterson asked.

'Oh, I don't want to talk about the murder,' Tamara Simmons replied. 'I really don't.'

You see, Patterson said silently to the empty chair that Blackstone had only recently vacated. You see! I was right! She doesn't want to talk about the murder at all!

'Is it wrong to keep a secret, if revealing it would make a lot of people very unhappy?' Tamara wondered.

'I suppose that would depend on whether or not *keeping* the secret would make a lot of *other* people very unhappy,' Patterson said, starting to understand what a drowning man must feel like.

'Keeping it wouldn't make anyone unhappy.'

158

'Then I don't see what your problem is.'

'But say that in order to keep the secret, I would have to tell a great many lies. Is that wrong?'

'I don't know,' Patterson said helplessly. 'I couldn't possibly judge, unless you were prepared to tell me more about it.'

'Do you think that anyone will ever love me?' Tamara Simmons asked plaintively. 'Do you think that if something bad was about to happen to me – if, say, I was about to be falsely imprisoned – that anyone would love me enough to try and prevent that happening? Or am I too stupid – and too dull – to be loved?'

'Of course, you're not too stupid or too dull,' Patterson said, feeling a sudden – and totally unexpected – burst of sympathy, which somehow caused him to reach across and take her hand. 'I'm sure someone will love you. After all, someone already has.'

'Have they?' Tamara Simmons asked, looking perplexed.

'Yes! Of course!'

'Who?'

'Martin Swinburne, you silly little goose!' Patterson said. 'And even if William Kirkpatrick didn't actually *love* you, he did at least care enough to *fight* over you.'

'Oh yes,' Tamara Simmons said. 'I'd forgotten about them.' She pulled her hand free of his. 'If you'll excuse me, Sergeant Patterson, I think that I'd better go now.'

Patterson knew he should feel relieved, but the only emotion he was experiencing at that moment was frustration.

What game was the woman playing? he wondered. He had sat there and patiently listened as she poured out her troubles. He had been sympathetic to her in her moment of self-doubt. And now she had to go!

'Was it something I said?' he asked.

'No,' Tamara Simmons replied. 'You've been very nice – very understanding.'

'Then I'm entitled to an explanation for your sudden departure, don't you think?'

Tamara Simmons hesitated. 'It wasn't something *you* said,' she told him. 'It was something *I* shouldn't have said.'

The South American Indians poisoned their arrow heads by simply pressing them down on the backs of the little yellow frogs, and that was what Ellie Carr had done with the flat edge of her knife.

The frog had been distressed by the experience, but not physically harmed. The rat had not fared quite so well. Only a few seconds after Ellie had made the insertion in its neck, it had begun to show signs of panic, and within a minute, it was dead.

'Now you must admit, this poison is a lot more humane than any you might have used on rats yourself,' Ellie said to Jed Trent.

'But is it the same poison as the one that killed William Kirkpatrick?' Trent asked.

'I won't know that until I've taken this rat – and several of his little friends – and cut them open, so I can look at their brains.'

Trent shook his head. 'Whatever you might say, this is no job for a woman,' he told her.

Ellie laughed. 'You're so old-fashioned, Jed,' she said. 'You really do believe that a woman's place is in the home, don't you?'

'Yes, I do,' Trent said seriously. 'At least, it is when she's your age, Dr Carr.'

'But it's at my age that scientists do their best work.'

'It's at your age that women have kids. And you should start planning to do just that – before you get too old.'

'And to hell with medical research?'

'And to hell with medical research!'

'Now that is an interesting idea,' Ellie said.

'It is,' Jed Trent affirmed. 'And I think you should give it some serious thought.'

'Let's see what happens when we poison the second rat, shall we?' Ellie suggested.

The pub was called the Maid of Kent. Charlotte Devaraux had chosen it because it wasn't one of her normal watering holes, but, even so, a number of the customers recognized her the instant she walked through the door, and though none of them approached her, they continued to look at her with deep fascination even after she had sat down.

'Being recognized wherever you go is the price of fame, I suppose,' Blackstone said.

'Yes, fame does have to be paid for,' Charlotte Devaraux

agreed. 'I'm sorry about my moment of weakness earlier. Breaking down on the street isn't like me at all.'

'There's no need to apologize,' Blackstone told her. 'None of us are ever as strong as we sometimes like to think that we are.'

'I won't pretend that I burn for Lord Bixendale with a passion which almost consumes me,' Charlotte said, out of the blue, 'but I really do care about him, you know.'

'Now why did you suddenly feel the need to tell me that?' Blackstone wondered.

'I'm not sure. Perhaps it's because I like you, and I'd rather you didn't despise me in return.'

'And you think I do?'

'And I want to make sure that you *don't*. There are a great many men in your position who would see me as little more than a whore, you know.'

'There are a great many men in my position who would see absolutely no distinction *at all* between you and a whore,' Blackstone said. 'But I'm not one of them.'

'So what elevates me in your eyes?' Charlotte Devaraux asked, with just a hint of bitterness in her voice.

'I've been thinking about that, ever since I saw you with Bixendale yesterday morning,' Blackstone admitted. 'And I've come to the conclusion that while, in order to get what we want, we all have to do things we don't always enjoy, what's really important is how we go about doing them.'

'Go on,' Charlotte Devaraux said.

'Some people don't care who they hurt – or what they have to do. But others have taken the decision that's there a line they simply will not cross – and I think you're one of those who's drawn that line.'

'That's not really much of a compliment, now is it?' Charlotte Devaraux said.

'Oh, I'm sorry, I wasn't aware that you were fishing for compliments,' Blackstone countered. 'But if that's what you're after, I'll do my best to provide you with a few.'

'You're right,' Charlotte Devaraux said. 'I *wasn't* fishing for compliments. I was looking for an honest answer – and that's what you gave me. Have you ever been in love, Sam?'

Both the question itself, and the use of his Christian name, jolted him, but he answered anyway.

'Yes, I have. Twice.'

'And what happened to these two loves of yours?'

'The first one was a revolutionary. She'd always intended to lay down her life for her cause, but when the time came for her to do so, it took her completely by surprise. Still, at least it was quick.'

'You're being very enigmatic,' Charlotte Devaraux said.

'Yes, I am, aren't I?' Blackstone agreed.

'Which is as good a way of telling me to mind my own business as any,' Charlotte Devaraux said. 'What about your second love?'

'She was a government agent – though it wasn't *our* government she was working for.'

'And did she die as well?'

'No, she didn't. As far as I know, she's still working for that same government.'

'So what went wrong between you?'

'She used me,' Blackstone said.

'Used you?'

'She loved me, but she loved her work more, and so she turned me into a tool for advancing its aims.' Blackstone took a deep sip of his beer, in an effort to wash away the taste of his sorrow. 'And what about you?' he asked. 'Have you ever been in love?'

'Once,' Charlotte said. 'He was an actor, and, like your first love, he died. Now I don't think I shall ever love again. I'm not even sure that I want to.' Her face had grown quite serious as she was speaking, but now she smiled again. 'Will you escort me home when we've finished our drinks?'

'Of course,' Blackstone agreed.

'And what does that mean, exactly?' Charlotte wondered.

'I'm sorry?'

'Will you take care of me only to my door, or will you take care of me beyond it?'

'I rather think that my protection has to come to an end at the door,' Blackstone said.

Charlotte laughed. 'Don't take everything so seriously, Sam,' she said. 'You do know just what I mean when I talk about taking care of me beyond the door, don't you?'

'Yes, I know.'

'And you do understand that I'm not offering you a lifetime of love, don't you?'

'Yes, I understand that, too.'

'Never mind love, I'm not even offering you *companion-ship* – at least, not beyond one single night. But if companionship for that single night would suit you, then it's there for the taking.'

Blackstone stood up. 'Do you happen to know where the nearest phone box is?' he asked.

'I think I noticed there was one on the corner.'

'Then if you'll excuse me for a short while, there's a call that I have to make.'

Charlotte Devaraux nodded – perhaps sagely, perhaps sadly. 'Of course there is,' she said.

Ellie Carr had just killed the third of her rats when the phone started to ring. At first, she tried to ignore it, but after a minute or two – when it became perfectly plain that the caller was not about to give up – she grabbed at the phone and said, 'I think you probably have the wrong number.'

'It's me,' said the voice on the other end of the line.

Ellie sighed. 'Listen, Sam, I think I may just have found the source of the poison, but it's far too early for me to be able to give you any definite results, so don't even bother to ask.'

'I wasn't *going* to ask,' Blackstone replied. 'The reason I called you was that I was wondering—'

'In fact, from the amount of work that I've been able to do so far, I can't even say, with any certainty, that this is even the same poison as the one that killed William Kirkpatrick.'

'Forget work,' Blackstone said.

'I beg your pardon?'

'Forget work. Give it a rest for tonight. It's still a couple of hours until the pubs close. I could meet you outside the hospital, and we could go and have a drink somewhere.'

'The kind of work that I'm involved in at the moment can't just be dropped whenever I feel the inclination,' Ellie said severely.

'What does that actually mean?' Blackstone wondered. 'That you *can't* stop? Or that you *won't* stop?'

'A little of both, I suppose,' Ellie Carr admitted. 'I think I may be breaking completely new ground here, and it's very difficult to tear yourself away from something like that.'

'Is it? Even if I ask you to? Even if I say that I'm feeling low, and would *really* appreciate your company tonight?'

'For heaven's sake, Sam, stop being so difficult,' Ellie said irritably. 'If you want company, why don't you give Archie Patterson a call?'

'It wouldn't be the same.'

'No, since he's a man and I'm a woman, it would obviously be somewhat different,' Ellie said, with maddening scientific logic. 'But Archie can keep you amused tonight, and, once my investigation's over, I'll find some way to make it up to you.'

'You really *don't* understand, do you?' Blackstone asked sadly.

'Understand what?' Ellie asked impatiently. 'I understand that you want the results of my tests. You *do* still want them, don't you?'

'Yes, but—'

'So I'm doing my level best to get them for you as soon as possible. And I promise you this, Sam – in the morning, you'll be glad that at least one of us has shown some self-discipline.'

'Who *knows* how I'll feel in the morning?' Blackstone said. 'Goodnight, Ellie.'

There was something in his tone which made Ellie Carr suddenly start to feel very uneasy.

'Listen, Sam . . .' she said.

But Blackstone had already hung up.

Charlotte Devaraux was sitting tranquilly at the table where Blackstone had left her, seemingly oblivious to the several sets of eyes which transfixed her as if she were an exhibit in a museum.

She looked beautiful, Blackstone thought. Hell, she didn't just look it – she *was* beautiful.

She gazed up at him. 'You have all the appearance of a man who's just heard some bad news,' she said.

'Appearances can sometimes be deceptive,' Blackstone told her. 'If you're ready to leave, I'll take you home now.'

Charlotte Devaraux smiled. 'Just to my door?' she asked quizzically. 'Or beyond it?'

'Beyond it,' Blackstone said. '*Well* beyond it.'

Twenty-Three

It was the telephone, ringing insistently and incessantly, which eventually woke Charlotte Devaraux up.

'Could you be an angel and answer that for me?' she pleaded, pulling the two ends of the pillow tightly over her ears.

There was no response.

'You *must* be awake,' Charlotte groaned. 'Nobody could possibly sleep through this.'

Keeping her eyes closed, she reached her arm across to the other side of the bed, in an effort to prod the man lying there into some kind of action – and found nothing to prod but a feather mattress.

He had gone. The ship of passion, which had carried the two of them on their uninhibitedly erotic journey throughout most of the night, was now deserted, save for herself alone.

And still the bloody telephone would not stop ringing.

'Buggeration!' she said, climbing out of bed and stumbling into the living room.

She picked up the phone. 'Sam?' she said. 'Is that you, Sam? What time did you leave?'

'Who's Sam?' asked the voice at the other end of the line.

'Oh, it's only you, Sebastian,' Charlotte said disappointedly. 'What do you want?'

'I thought you'd like to know that I've arranged for you to go up in a balloon,' Sebastian George said.

'You've done what?'

'I've arranged for a short balloon flight for you.'

'When?'

'Today. On Hampstead Heath.'

'But why?'

'Because, in case you've forgotten, my dear, that's just what Lady Wilton does in the play.'

Charlotte shook her head, in an effort to clear her mind.

'It's a little early in the morning for me, Sebastian,' she said. 'I'm afraid you'll have to explain things more slowly.'

Sebastian George snorted contemptuously. 'It's really very simple, Charlotte,' he said. 'We need to sell more tickets.'

'But I thought we were booked up solid.'

'We are – for this month and the next. But for the month after that, advance sales aren't going half as well as they might. So, unless you intend to kill someone else on stage—'

'That's not kind, Sebastian.'

'—we need to do something else to keep our name in the papers. Hence, the balloon trip.'

'Did I dream our conversation in my dressing room last night?' Charlotte asked, wonderingly.

'No. It was real enough – and unpleasant enough – to remain in both our minds for quite a long time.'

'And yet, from the way you're talking, it's as if it had never happened. You do remember that I said I'll do all I can to get your father released from the lunatic asylum, don't you?'

'Yes.'

'And you do appreciate that if he *is* released, the first thing he'll want is to take his theatre back?'

'Of course.'

'But yet you're still carrying on your business as if none of that is ever likely to happen?'

'And who's to say it will?' George replied. 'There's many a slip twixt the cup and the lip, you know.'

'What are you talking about?'

'The Lunacy Commissioners are not mere marionettes who will meekly dance to his lordship's tune, you know. They will want to listen to the counter-arguments, which will be put to them by the finest legal brain I can find. I am confident I will prevail, should that prove necessary. But, of course, it *won't* be necessary.'

'No?'

'Absolutely not! To put it plainly, you are convinced Lord Bixendale will listen to your pathetic pleas to intercede on my father's behalf—'

'Yes, I am, and then—'

'—whilst I am equally convinced he'll be more inclined to take the advice of a man he's done business with than a woman who's merely shared his bed whenever he clicked his fingers at her.'

'You're so unspeakably arrogant!' Charlotte said.

'Besides, however matters are resolved, I *care* about the future of the company, even if you don't,' Sebastian George continued, cuttingly. 'I want it to go from strength to strength, even if I am no longer at the helm. And do you know why, Charlotte?'

'Why?'

'Because *I'm* a professional.'

'And so am I.'

'Well, I must say, you don't always show it.'

'What time do you want me on the Heath?' Charlotte asked, through gritted teeth.

'Two o'clock, if that's not too inconvenient for someone with a busy social life like yours.'

'I'll be there.'

'Of course, if your friend Sam – whoever he is – finds that he can't spare you for a couple of hours—'

'I said I'll be there!' Charlotte screamed, before hanging up the phone.

She listened carefully for the sound of anyone moving around, and then decided that she was quite as alone in the whole apartment as she'd found herself to be in her bed.

She had told Sam Blackstone that all she could offer him was one night of companionship, she thought.

And this was the result! He'd gone without waiting for her to wake up. He didn't seem to have even left a note.

Well, you laid out the rules, she told herself, so you can't blame him when he follows them to the letter.

Patterson stood at the window of the office, looking out over the Embankment. There were a few clouds in the sky that morning, he observed, but a betting man – which he had ceased to be the moment he got engaged – would have put his money on it turning out to be an almost perfect day.

He turned around to look at his boss, who was sitting at his desk with the telephone to his ear. There was something very strange about the inspector that morning, he thought – something he couldn't quite put his finger on, however much he tried.

'That was Dr Carr who was just on the phone,' Blackstone said, hanging up the ear-piece.

Dr Carr? Patterson thought. Not *Ellie*, but *Dr* Carr?

'She's up early this morning, isn't she?' he said.

'Not exactly,' Blackstone replied. 'She told me she'd never actually been to bed.'

'Now that's what I call real dedication to her work,' Patterson said admiringly.

Blackstone frowned. 'Yes, I suppose that is what you *would* call it,' he agreed.

What the hell was wrong with him? Patterson wondered. It was almost as if Ellie had done something to really *hurt* Blackstone. But how was that possible when she'd spent the entire night in her laboratory?

'Did Ellie – Dr Carr, I mean – have anything interesting to tell you?' he asked.

'Yes, she did. Which is only what you'd expect from someone as *dedicated* as she is,' Blackstone said. 'But before we get on to that, why don't you tell me about your evening with Miss Simmons?'

'Didn't turn out to be much of an evening after all. Ten minutes after you left, she was gone herself.'

'Which is very strange, considering how eager she seemed to be to talk to you – and how little she seemed to want me there when she did,' Blackstone mused. 'Did she give any reason for her abrupt departure?'

'Yes. She told me it was because she'd said something she shouldn't have said.'

'And what did she mean by that?'

'I don't honestly know,' Patterson admitted. 'I've spent most of the night puzzling over it, and still couldn't come up with an answer. But I think I have managed to work out what it was that *I* said which seemed to disturb *her*.'

'And what was it?'

'I reminded her that Martin Swinburne had been in love with her. And I use the word *reminded* deliberately – because Tamara seemed to have forgotten all about it.'

'Well, maybe he wasn't ever in love with her,' Blackstone said disdainfully. 'You know what these theatrical people are like. Sex has very little at all to do with emotion, and they sleep with each other – or anyone else, for that matter – at the drop of a hat.'

'I wouldn't know about that,' said Patterson, who'd never

168

slept with anyone at the drop of an anything – in fact, had never slept with anyone *at all*. 'But even if there was no love involved, it was still an affair, wasn't it?'

'Yes.'

'And she seemed to have forgotten even that.'

'That's women for you,' Blackstone said.

What *was* the matter with him? Patterson wondered.

'You were going to tell me what Ellie has found out,' he said aloud.

'Ah, so I was,' Blackstone agreed. 'She's now almost certain that William Kirkpatrick was killed by a toxin obtained from a poison arrow frog. Furthermore, she's had her assistant, who's called Severn or Mersey, or some other peculiar name of that nature—'

'Trent,' Patterson supplied. 'Jed Trent.'

'Just so,' Blackstone agreed. 'She's had Trent checking around to see if he can find out where the murderer might have laid his hands on the poison. And as far as he's been able to establish so far, the only specimens of that particular deadly frog in London – and possibly in the whole of Europe – are to be found at a penny sideshow on the Mile End Road, where they're part of the act of a woman calling herself Princess Tezel.'

'So we go and see this princess, do we?' Patterson guessed.

'So we go and see this princess,' Blackstone agreed.

At some point in the middle of the night, Jed Trent had finally decided he'd had enough of playing the faithful assistant for a while, and had gone off in search of a bed in one of the empty isolation wards. Now, after a couple of hours sleep – and with two cups of hot black coffee inside him – he felt strong enough to return the lab and make one last attempt to persuade Ellie Carr that sleep was a good thing for clever young doctors, too.

He found Ellie Carr standing over one of the cages with a pocket watch in her hand.

'Victim Number Seven?' he asked, making a quick count of the cages that were already empty.

'No, it's *Specimen* Number Seven, Jed,' Ellie Carr corrected him automatically.

'You look completed exhausted,' Jed said. 'Do you want help in dosing this one?'

'I thought policemen were supposed to be observant,' Ellie replied, somewhat waspishly.

'Sorry?'

'Or are your powers of observation something you have to hand in at the desk along with your truncheon and your whistle when you retire?'

'Now don't you go taking your tiredness out on me, Dr Carr,' Trent chided her.

To her credit, Ellie looked a little ashamed.

'Have a look at the rat's neck, Jed,' she suggested.

Trent did as he'd been instructed. There was a small red spot clearly visible on the neck.

'So you've *already* poisoned him?'

'That's right.'

Trent took a closer look at the rat. It seemed to be in some discomfort, but it was clearly far from dead.

'So what's gone wrong?' he asked.

'I'm not sure yet. Perhaps the frog which I used to extract the toxin from wasn't as poisonous as the others. Or perhaps this particular rat has an immunity to the poison which the rest of them simply didn't. But I'm rather hoping there's a third explanation.'

'And what might that be?'

'I introduced the poison into the other specimens shortly after I'd drawn it from the frog. This time, I let the poison dry first.'

'So maybe when it's dried out, it's not poisonous any more?' Trent suggested.

'That's certainly a possibility,' Ellie Carr admitted, 'but it's not the only one. It's also possible that when the poison has dried, it simply takes longer to have an effect.'

The rat had begun to quiver as they were speaking, and now its legs gave way, and it collapsed.

Ellie looked at her pocket watch. 'Twenty-five minutes,' she said. 'And it's not even dead yet. This is a major breakthrough, Jed.'

'Is it?'

'But of course. We now know that in different states, the poison has different degrees of toxicity.'

'But will that be of any help to your pal Inspector Blackstone?' Trent wondered.

Ellie looked puzzled. 'I'm sorry?'

'The whole point of you doing these experiments was to help the police to solve their murder, wasn't it?'

'You're right,' Ellie admitted. 'I do seem to have lost sight of that, don't I? It must be the tiredness.'

'Or it could be that you're like a kid in a toyshop – so wrapped up in your own little world that nothing else exists.'

Ellie grinned. 'Guilty as charged,' she said.

'So, to repeat my question, Dr Carr, will what you've just found out about the poison be of assistance to Inspector Blackstone when it comes to solving his murder?'

'Most certainly it will. Which reminds me, once Sam's arrested his murderer, I must ask him if it's possible to obtain a souvenir for the admirable Princess Tezel. I don't think a finger or toe is really practicable, but perhaps he might manage a lock of the killer's hair.'

Trent sighed. 'Getting a straight answer out of you is harder than pulling teeth,' he said.

'But I gave you a straight answer,' Ellie replied innocently. 'You asked me if what I've found out will be of any help to the investigation, and I've told you it will.'

'But *how*?' Trent asked in an exasperated voice.

Ellie's grin widened. 'If you think about it, Jed, I'm sure you'll be able to work that out for yourself,' she said.

The penny sideshow – in common with all the others operating in London – did not normally open its doors to its customers until the late afternoon. But the article in the *London Evening Chronicle* had changed all the rules, and when the Hansom cab containing Blackstone and Patterson pulled up outside the door of the ex-undertaker's establishment, there was already a large queue building up for a hastily-scheduled morning performance.

'Death sells tickets,' Patterson said.

'It certainly does,' Blackstone agreed. 'It worked for the George Theatre, and it's working here.'

The two detectives were shown into the ante-room where the princess held her audiences. This morning, she was draped in an old grey coat which had been out of style for at least twenty years, and when she looked at her visitors from her broken cane chair, her blank face told them nothing at all about whether she welcomed their visit or merely resented it.

* * *

171

'We have some important questions that we need to put to the princess,' Blackstone told the Indian who acted as her interpreter. 'Please make it clear to her that as long as she answers those questions as truthfully as she is able, she will not be in any trouble.'

The interpreter translated, and then listened to the reply from the blank-faced princess.

'What did she say?' Blackstone asked.

'Princess say that head-hunters in jungle trouble,' the interpreter replied. 'Cannibals trouble, and hungry jaguars trouble. You not trouble. Don't have spears. Don't have blow pipes. Don't have claws. She answer questions if she want, she don't answer if she don't want.'

'We could lock her up in prison if she refuses to help us, you know,' Patterson said.

'Shut up, Sergeant,' Blackstone said. 'Can't you see that kind of talk simply isn't going to work with her?'

But what would work, he wondered.

Ellie Carr had managed to get the princess to co-operate without threatening her with gaol. Ellie Carr had come away with everything she wanted.

'Does she remember the woman who came to see her yesterday?' he asked the interpreter.

'She say she not stupid,' the interpreter replied, after another exchange with the princess. 'She say, yes, she remember.'

'Then tell her that the honour of that woman is at stake.'

'Honour?'

'Tell the princess that if she doesn't help us, the woman will almost certainly lose face.'

The princess digested the information, and nodded to her retainer.

'The woman is princess's chosen sister,' the Indian said. 'What you want know?'

'I need to know if she's sold any of her poisonous frogs while she's been in London.'

'Sell one yesterday, to man who work for newspaper,' the Indian said evasively.

'But did she sell any *before* that,' Blackstone insisted.

The Indian conferred with his mistress again. 'Sell one other frog,' he admitted. 'Five, six day past.'

'I need to know who she sold it to,' Blackstone said, though he suspected he already knew the answer.

'Sell to small old man,' the Indian said.

Twenty-Four

Charlotte Devaraux stepped down from the cab and walked towards the stage door of the theatre.

She had not expected to be there at that time of the morning. Since there was no matinée that day – since even *Sebastian George* had seen the need to give the cast a *little* rest – she had been planning to spend the day quietly in her apartments.

George's phone call had changed all that.

'I'm a professional,' the bloody little man had said to her – had *dared* to say to her!

As if – by implication – she was not!

She had been an actress for nearly fifteen years. She had started at the very bottom of the ladder, taking parts that even Tamara Simmons would have considered beneath her. She had studied the performances of other actresses, and worked hard to polish and perfect her own skills. She had given her all to productions which she personally despised – in roles she hated – because she knew that particular play would be popular, and hence good for the company.

Yet after all that, Sebastian-bloody-George – the dilettante, the dabbler, the sideshow-manager-posing-as-impresario – had had the nerve to suggest that he was the true professional, not she.

Well, she would show him what professionalism *really* meant! She would put on a performance on Hampstead Heath to match any she had ever given in the theatre.

The reporters and photographers gathered there would be so entranced by the way she played her part that they would forget for the moment that she was Charlotte Devaraux, the actress, and see only Lady Wilton, the dramatic heroine.

And she would forget it, too, of course. As long as she was Lady Wilton she could brush aside the miseries and frustrations of her life – as long as she was Lady Wilton it wouldn't matter that Sam Blackstone had gone without even leaving her a note.

She knocked on the stage door, and was admitted by the porter. She had never liked the spotty little man, but – perhaps out of compassion for his affliction – she had always forced herself to be nice to him.

'Do you happen to know if the wardrobe mistress is here at the moment, Mr Wilberforce?' she asked.

'Do I *happen* to know, Miss Devaraux?' the porter repeated, as if she'd just insulted him. 'If she was here, I'd *definitely* know. I know *everything* that goes on in this theatre. It's my *job* to know.'

There were some people it just didn't pay to be nice to, Charlotte Devaraux thought sadly.

'When I ask a direct question, Wilberforce, I expect a direct answer,' she said, using the same thrilling voice she had employed to play Lady Bracknell in *The Importance of Being Earnest*.

Wilberforce actually cowered under the assault. 'Of c . . . course, Miss Devaraux,' he stammered.

'Well, then?' Charlotte demanded, in much the same way as her Lady Bracknell had said, 'A handbag?'

'The wardrobe mistress isn't here, Miss Devaraux. Neither is her assistant. It's a bit early in the day for either of them.'

'Then who *is* here?'

'Only me. And young Horace, of course – he's always here.'

'But not Mr George?'

'No, he left half an hour ago.'

So much for dedication! Charlotte Devaraux thought. So much for professionalism!

'But you have keys to all the doors in the theatre, don't you, Wilberforce?' she asked.

'Indeed I do,' the porter said proudly. 'Mr George knows a man he can trust when he sees him.'

'Then you can let me into my dressing room?'

Wilberforce looked troubled. She had scared him a few moments earlier, but there were other bullies – bullies he saw much more often – who also had to be considered.

'I said, you can let me into my dressing room, can't you, Wilberforce?' Charlotte repeated.

'Well, I'm not sure I know about that, Miss Devaraux,' the porter said doubtfully. 'Mr George didn't leave me any instructions about—'

'It is *my* dressing room, and I am the *leading lady* of the company,' Charlotte pointed out.

'So it is, and so you are,' Wilberforce agreed.

'Well, then?'

'I suppose it will be all right – but if there's any trouble, you will tell Mr George that you insisted, won't you?'

It would have been easier to put on her costume if her dresser had been there to assist her, but she managed well enough alone. She would have appreciated the advice of the make-up artist, too – what looked effective on stage would not necessarily have the same impact in the open air on Hampstead Heath – but she had applied enough of her own make-up in her time to have a fair idea of what would work, and what wouldn't. So it was that, less than half an hour after she had entered her dressing room, she was looking in the mirror at a perfect image of Lady Wilton.

'With this knife, I will have my revenge for the evil you have visited on me,' she told her reflection.

And then, because it seemed ridiculous to be uttering the line when she *didn't* have a knife in her hand, she giggled.

She slipped on a light cloak over her Lady Wilton costume, and was ready to leave.

This would show Sebastian George what she was made of, she thought, as she walked down the corridor towards the stage door. She *looked* like Lady Wilton, and though – unlike her character – she was afraid of heights, she would *act* like Lady Wilton.

She left the theatre, and hailed a passing cab. It had only just pulled away when the one bringing Blackstone and Patterson from the penny sideshow arrived at the theatre door.

'When will someone in authority be here?' Blackstone asked his old 'friend', Spotty Wilberforce.

'Somebody in authority's *already* here,' the porter said, prodding his own chest with his thumb.

Blackstone sighed. 'I'm sure you *do* have a great deal of authority, Sp . . . Thomas,' he conceded, 'but, even so, you probably don't have the information that I require.'

'Oh, do you think so? And what information might that be?' Wilberforce asked.

'A list of the members of the company who went on the tour of South America.'

The porter opened the drawer of his desk, and riffled through the thick sheaf of papers it contained.

'As a matter of fact, I do have such a list,' he said. 'I wrote it out myself, personal.'

'And why would you have gone to the trouble of doing that?' Blackstone wondered.

'For the same reason I make out all my lists. Because it's important information, and one day somebody might need it.'

Spotty Wilberforce insisted that the two detectives should examine the list in his office ('Don't want valuable pieces of paper like that leaving here. You never know where they might end up!'), but he did agree, with some show of reluctance, to remove himself from the scene while they discussed it.

The list contained a number of names already familiar to Blackstone and Patterson, as well as many they had never seen before. Wilberforce – driven, no doubt, by both an obsession for detail and an almost insane belief in his importance as chronicler – had added extra information to most of the names when he considered it appropriate.

> Martin Swinburne (actor, dead)
>   William Kirkpatrick (actor, murdered)
> Tamara Simmons (actress)
>   Piers Dalaway (dresser, left the company)
> Samuel Horton (stage manager, fired for drunkenness) . . .

'There must be around fifty names here,' Blackstone said, studying the list. 'And most of them still work for Sebastian George.'

'And we can't even say that the murderer is definitely one of the people who went on the company's tour of South America,' Patterson pointed out. 'He could just have easily have overheard those who were on the tour talking about poison frogs once they'd returned to England.'

Blackstone nodded despondently. He'd been half-hoping – in one of those uncharacteristic bouts of optimism which afflicted him occasionally – that one of the names on the list would jump out at him.

And indeed, one of the names had!

Charlotte Devaraux's name had not only leapt from the page, but had practically flown around the room, singing sweetly and seductively as it went.

But that had little – or nothing – to do with any theatrical tour of distant parts, and a great deal – or *everything* – to do with the events of the previous evening, Blackstone thought.

What a night they had spent together! What things they had said to each other – and done to each other!

It was one of the hardest decisions he had ever made, to leave her apartment that morning – and though he could come up with at least half a dozen explanations for his actions, he was still not entirely sure which one of them was the truth.

The phone rang.

Blackstone reached out for it automatically. But before his hand had even made contact with it, Spotty Wilberforce – who must have been hovering outside – had flung the door open, and grabbed it.

'It's *my* telephone that's ringing,' he said, by way of explanation. 'In *my* office.'

'*You'd* better answer it, then,' Blackstone suggested.

'Just what I was thinking,' Wilberforce replied. He lifted the ear-piece, and seemed quite disappointed at what he heard come through it.

'Well?' Blackstone asked.

'It's for you,' the porter replied. 'Some woman.'

Blackstone took the phone from him. 'If you wouldn't mind excusing us again, Mr Wilberforce . . .' he said.

'Bloody liberty, that's what it is,' Wilberforce muttered, stepping out into the corridor.

'It's Ellie,' said the caller.

'I thought it might be,' Blackstone replied.

'I was a little abrupt with you, when you called me last night, wasn't I, Sam?' Ellie asked, and giggled uncomfortably. 'I'm sorry about that.'

'I'm sorry, too,' Blackstone said.

'You're sorry? Why? What have *you* got to be apologetic about?' Ellie wondered.

'Nothing that I'd want to talk about over the phone.'

'Oh, we are being mysterious all of a sudden, aren't we?' Ellie said, her nervous giggle transforming itself into a genuinely-amused chuckle. 'But I really *am* sorry, Sam,' she added, growing more serious again. 'I get so wrapped up in my work sometimes that I can become really objectionable.'

She paused for a moment to give him a chance to respond to her, but he said nothing.

'Speaking of work,' Ellie continued, awkwardly, 'would you like to hear my preliminary findings?'

'If you wouldn't mind.'

'Well, they are *very* preliminary at the moment, but as far as I can tell from my experiments, the longer the gap between harvesting the toxin and using it, the slower the poison works.'

'What do you mean by that?'

'Well, for example, I kept the last batch exposed for a full two hours before I used it, and forty minutes after it was introduced into the rat's bloodstream, the little bugger's still very much alive.'

'Dear God!' Blackstone groaned.

'Is something wrong, Sam?' Ellie Carr asked, alarmed.

'Yes,' Blackstone said. 'I'm afraid that something is very *very* wrong.'

'The last time I talked to you, you told me that all kinds of strange creatures somehow managed find their way into this theatre,' Blackstone said to Horace, the general factotum.

'It's like the London Zoo in here sometimes,' the boy agreed.

'And one of those strange creatures was a frog?'

'That's right. I don't know where he was, exactly, 'cos I never saw him for myself, but he was croaking away like billy-o.'

'Could you say *roughly* where you think he was?'

'My best guess is that 'e was somewhere near the dressing rooms.'

'Or actually *in* one of the dressing rooms?'

'Might 'ave been, I suppose. But you'd 'ave thought 'ooever

was in that room would have noticed for themselves.'

'Yes, you would,' Blackstone agreed. 'Now I want you to think carefully about the next question I ask you. All right?'

The boy nodded. 'All right.'

'Was it on the night that William Kirkpatrick was murdered that you heard the frog?'

'No,' the boy said, without a moment's hesitation.

'Then when was it?'

'I think it was a couple of nights – or maybe three – before the murder.'

'And you definitely *didn't* hear it on the night that William Kirkpatrick was killed?'

'Definitely.'

That didn't make any sense at all, Blackstone thought, especially after what Ellie had told him about the toxin growing less effective the drier it became.

And then – suddenly – it did make sense!

Perfect sense!

What he was dealing with here was actors, Blackstone reminded himself. And before the first performance before an audience – before the first *real* performance – actors always had dress rehearsals.

In order to spot any faults!

So they could iron out any difficulties they might encounter!

And that was just what had happened here. A couple of nights before the murder, the killer had brought the frog into the theatre, and soon realized that it made a noise which other people might easily hear. On the *actual* night of the murder, therefore – the night of the live *performance* – the frog had been kept somewhere enclosed, where its croak would be muffled.

There were just a couple more pieces of the jigsaw puzzle to be slotted into place before he would have the whole picture. And Patterson had already been dispatched to collect one of those pieces.

'My sergeant's just nipped off to Scotland Yard, but he should be back within the half-hour,' Blackstone told the boy. 'And when he *does* get back, there's just one more little thing I'd like you to do for me.'

'What is it?' Horace asked.

'I'd like you go though exactly the same routine that you

179

went through in the last hour before the murder. Do you think you'll be able to manage that?'

Horace grinned. 'No problem at all,' he said confidently. 'It'll be good training for when I'm an actor.'

Sebastian George had taken elaborate and careful pains over the planning for his morning's work.

His own appearance had been his very first consideration. The flamboyant style of dress he normally adopted might look well enough in the glamour of the theatre, but it would make him stand out like a sore thumb on mundane Hampstead Heath – and the last thing he wanted, once it was all over, was for anyone to remember seeing *him* there.

So the flowery waistcoats and heavy cotton jackets had had to be temporarily abandoned, and instead he was dressed in a second-hand frock coat and a felt hat with a curled brim, both of which blended in perfectly with what the other men out on the Heath that morning were wearing.

His cloth holdall, too, was an integral part of what he thought of as his cunning disguise. It was highly improbable than anyone would even notice it, but if they did, they would be more than likely to assume that he was some sort of craftsman – a master plumber, for example – and that the bag contained the tools of his trade. Or perhaps they would take him to be a door-to-door salesman – cutting across the Heath as he moved from one part of his sales territory to another – and assume that the bag housed his samples.

Both assumptions would, of course, be very far from the truth. What the bag *actually* held was something altogether more deadly.

The final touch to his disguise had been to exchange the long, fat cigars he habitually smoked for a packet of cheap cigarettes. It had not been an easy decision – a man under stress instinctively reaches for those things which bring him comfort – but it had certainly been a wise one. With his cigars sitting safely on his desk back at the theatre, he had completely eliminated the risk of absent-mindedly leaving a butt behind – and so providing a valuable clue for the legion of policemen who would undoubtedly be swarming all over the area in an hour or so. Besides, cigarettes were the right prop for this role, far more in keeping with the persona he had temporarily assumed than even *small* cigars would have been.

George glanced across the Heath, up to Parliament Hill. As yet, the event he had planned – the *disaster* he had planned – was still in its early stages.

He watched as the ground crew from the hot air balloon company began to inflate the silk envelope which would lift the wicker gondola high into the air. He noted the arrival of several of the reporters and photographers who were to cover the flight.

There was still no sign of Charlotte Devaraux, but that did not overly concern him: after the way he had deliberated goaded her that morning, he was certain that she *would* be there.

George licked his index finger and held it up in the air.

There was a stiff breeze blowing from the east, which meant that the hot air balloon would inevitably move in a westerly direction.

Excellent!

The clump of trees he had already picked out would provide the perfect cover for him, when the time came to do what he had to do.

But even if the wind should suddenly decide to change direction, there would be no cause for panic, because he had already scouted out several other locations – on other parts of the Heath – which would serve his purpose just as well.

The kind of careful advanced planning he had been involved in that morning was all-important if a successful outcome was to be achieved, he told himself, with just a hint of self-congratulation. Soldiers knew that, grouse-shooting parties knew that – and assassins *certainly* knew that.

Twenty-Five

The props were laid out on the prop table, as they always were before a performance, but the trick knife which Charlotte Devaraux had used – on every occasion but one –

181

had been removed from its leather sheath and replaced by the knife that Patterson had brought back with him from Scotland Yard.

Blackstone stood close to the prop table. From somewhere up the corridor, he heard the sound of whistling.

Horace was on the way. And probably whistling exactly the same tune now as he had been whistling on the night of William Kirkpatrick's murder, if Blackstone knew anything about him.

Horace knocked on the door, opened it, and said a cheery, 'Good evenin', Mr Foster. 'Ow are yer doin' tonight?'

Patterson, who was standing in for the props master, said nothing.

'He's talking to *you*,' Blackstone told his sergeant.

'Oh, right!'

'Answer him, then.'

'Good evening, Horace,' Patterson said, woodenly. 'I'm doing fine, thank you.'

Despite the serious purpose behind the exercise, Blackstone could not help grinning. Horace might well make an actor of himself yet, he thought, but Patterson had been very wise to choose a career in the Met instead.

'I'll take the knife to Miss Devaraux now, shall I, Mr Foster?' young Horace asked.

'Yes, you take it,' Patterson said, even less convincingly like the props master than he had been earlier.

Horace went over to the table, and carefully picked up the sheathed dagger by the handle.

Blackstone held his breath as the boy, seemingly unaware that there had been any substitution made, walked towards the door.

'Could I be wrong?' the inspector asked himself silently. 'Given the way the evidence was pointing, could I really have got it *so* wrong?'

Horace suddenly stopped in his tracks and looked suspiciously down at the dagger.

No, Blackstone told himself, he hadn't been wrong at all!

The boy held the dagger up, and examined it thoughtfully. Next, he balanced it on the palm of his hand, and bounced it up and down.

'Is this some kind of test yer puttin' me through, Inspector?' he asked worriedly.

'Now what would make you think that?' Blackstone wondered.

'You *must* be testin' me,' the boy said. 'Uvverwise you wouldn't 'ave given me a different knife.'

'A different knife?' Blackstone said non-committally.

'It ain't the knife wot I normally take to Miss Devaraux,' Horace told him. 'It looks almost the same . . .'

'Almost?'

'It don't quite fit in the sheath as well as the uvver one did.' He held it up for Blackstone to examine. 'Yer can see just a tiny bit of blade stickin' out above the leather. Yer don't get that wiv the real one . . . I mean . . . wiv the *fake* one.'

'I know what you mean,' Blackstone assured him. 'Is there any other way that it's different?'

'The weight an' the balance. Some'ow, it just don't feel quite *right*.'

'Clever of you to spot all that,' Patterson said approvingly. 'You're quite right that that's not the knife you normally take to Miss Devaraux. But it *is* the one you took to her on the night of the murder, isn't it?'

'No, it ain't,' the boy said firmly.

'You're sure?'

'If it 'ad 'ave been, I'd 'ave noticed it then, just like I'm noticin' it now.'

Of course he would, Blackstone thought, because however skilful the knife-maker had been, he'd never have produced a perfect copy when he was only working from a photograph.

'Do you know what time Miss Devaraux is due to arrive at the theatre?' he asked.

'She's already bin 'ere,' the boy told him. 'Come in earlier to pick up 'er costume, didn't she?'

'Why would she do that?'

'So she'd look the part for the balloon ride.'

'What balloon ride?'

'The one on 'Ampstead 'Eath. The one that Mr George fixed up for 'er. It's like, an advertisement for the play.'

How could she have been so stupid? Blackstone wondered.

How could she have told Sebastian George that she was determined to pursue a course of action which was bound to ruin him, and then been so *bloody* stupid as to agree to take a balloon ride that *he'd* arranged?

'We have to get to Hampstead Heath as quickly as we can,' he told Patterson urgently. 'We could *already* be too late!'

Quite a crowd – spectators as well as newsmen – had gathered at the top of Parliament Hill by the time Charlotte Devaraux arrived, and their enthusiastic applause did just a little to help settle her queasy stomach.

The aëronaut, however, was not so reassuring. He was a big, bluff fellow – the sort of man who had never known fear himself, and found it almost inconceivable that anyone else could.

'The best time for a flight like this is either the early morning or the early evening,' he explained to her.

'Is it? Why?'

'The air temperature's cooler then, so it's easier to get the lift. And you avoid having to deal with all those awkward thermal currents we'll probably come across once we're up. Still, Mr George did insist it had to be now. I suppose he thought we'd get a bigger crowd if we took off in the afternoon.'

'Just what exactly *are* thermal currents?' Charlotte Devaraux enquired, apprehensively.

'Don't worry your pretty little head about that,' the aëronaut said. 'That's what I'm here for.'

'But I *do* worry,' Charlotte insisted. 'How high up will we be going in that dangerous thing?'

'A hundred feet. Maybe a bit more.'

'But we'll still be safely moored to the ground, won't we?'

'Those are my instructions,' the aëronaut said, looking away from her.

The envelope was now fully inflated, and the gondola had been attached to the webbing which covered it.

'Ready when you are,' the aëronaut said.

He helped Charlotte into the gondola. It was about the same size as the one she was used to in the theatre, Charlotte noted. But the one in the theatre didn't have a gas burner in the centre of it. And the one in the theatre never rose more than twelve or fourteen feet off the ground.

'Off we go,' the aëronaut said, turning up the power of the burner.

Charlotte looked out of the basket, first at her expectant public, then at the spot on the edge of the basket where Pittstock had clung, during so many performances.

'With this knife, I will have my revenge for the evil you have visited on me,' she said, swinging an imaginary knife at the imaginary man.

Her public cheered her – and the balloon began to rise.

Hidden in a clump of trees, some distance from Parliament Hill, Sebastian George watched the balloon rise. He was quite alone on this part of the Heath, and that was no accident. He had anticipated, when planning all this, that any people out walking would automatically gravitate towards the balloon and the famous actress – and he had been proved right.

It was ironic, he thought, that Lord Bixendale – of all people – had been the man who'd made what was about to happen possible. But it was undoubtedly true that he had. If Bixendale hadn't invited him up to the estate in Scotland . . .

The only reason you were ever asked to join the shooting party is because I requested it,' Charlotte had said. Well, she would pay for that.

. . . hadn't invited him up to the estate in Scotland, he would never have learned just what a 'natural' he was with a rifle – and how much he enjoyed being in on the kill!

The balloon was now clear of the ground – well above the height from which the evil Pittstock fell nightly – and was already beginning to respond to the prevailing air currents. Though Sebastian George had no personal experience of ballooning, he did not think it would take long for the craft to drift into a position which would suit him perfectly.

He hoisted the rifle carefully to his shoulder and squinted down the telescopic sight.

The difference between balloons and stags, he thought, was that balloons moved slower – and were much bigger.

Charlotte Devaraux looked down at the ground – so very far below the balloon – and began to feel sick.

'How high up are we now?' she asked.

'No more than seventy or seventy-five feet,' the aëronaut told her.

Charlotte found that hard to believe. Already, the people below were looking like matchstick men. Already, she was wishing that she had not allowed Sebastian George to talk her into going up in this bloody balloon.

It was then that she noticed the two police vans – or Black Marias, as they had become popularly known – arriving on the Heath. The two vans came to a halt, and at least a dozen men in blue uniforms were disgorged from them.

'What's going on down there?' she asked.

'I don't know, and I don't care,' the aëronaut said, indifferently. 'When I'm up here with the birds, I have no interest in what's going on down there with the worms.'

'At what point will the mooring ropes stop us from going any higher?' Charlotte asked.

'Mooring ropes?'

'The ones that are holding us down?'

'Oh, the *restraining* ropes. They were cast off while you were making your pretty little speech to the crowd. Can't inhibit the movement of the balloon once it's airborne. That would be very dangerous.'

'But you said . . . you told me . . .'

'I told you a little white lie. Mr George said I'd have to do that, in order to get you up here in the first place.'

'I want you to land this thing immediately,' Charlotte said, verging on hysteria.

'Can't do that, I'm afraid,' the aëronaut said. 'Mr George is paying me more than double my normal daily rate for this balloon, but only if we stay in the air for at least an hour.'

Charlotte looked down again – and immediately wished that she hadn't. The matchstick men walking about below had now become little more than ants, she saw with horror, and the balloon in which she had become a prisoner had already drifted some distance away from Parliament Hill.

Sebastian George felt his stomach lurch as he saw the uniformed policemen advancing across the Heath in the distance.

It was the *way* they were moving which disturbed him most – each policeman separated from the next policeman by several yards, but moving at exactly the same speed. It was as though they were all individual points on a fisherman's net, which was being dragged slowly through the water, he thought – and that was *exactly* what they were.

How did they know? he wondered. Who had told them?

It could only be Blackstone!

He considered abandoning his plan altogether. If he dropped the rifle now and simply walked away, he would be in the clear. Of course, Blackstone would know what he had been trying to do – Blackstone knew *already* – but he would never be able to prove it!

But if he did abandon his plan, where would that leave him?

Poor and discredited!

A figure of ridicule and pity!

He was not sure he could stand that. And, unless he was caught in the act, the inspector would be no more able to prove the rifle belonged to him *after* he had fired the shot than he would have been *before*.

He looked up into the sky. The balloon was clearly heading in his direction. All he had to do was stay concealed for a couple more minutes, and he could finish the job and then escape.

He had read somewhere that searchers rarely look above eye-level for their quarry. Well, he was about to put that to the test. It had been a long time since he had climbed a tree, but he would climb one now.

Blackstone looked up at the balloon, making its way serenely across the Heath. His first fear had been a bomb – and there might still be one, ticking away in that basket. If that were the case, there was nothing he could do about it.

But if George had decided to bring the balloon *down*, instead of blowing it *up*, then there might still just be time to stop him.

He glanced at the balloon, calculated its likely flight path, and then tried to work out exactly where he would have positioned himself if he had been in George's shoes.

Lady Wilton wouldn't behave like this, Charlotte Devaraux told herself. Lady Wilton would remain calm throughout.

Lady Wilton's a bloody character in a bloody play! a voice at the back of her mind screamed. She's *made-up*! Her balloon's never going to go hurtling to the ground, because she doesn't bloody exist!

'I think I'm going to be sick,' she said, holding tightly on to the side of the gondola.

'Everybody thinks that, at some point or another,' the aëronaut replied cheerfully.

'Maybe they do. But not like this. I *know* I'm going to be sick!'

'Well, in that case, you'd better do it over the side of the basket. And not into the wind – or it'll fly straight back in your face.'

'Take me down,' Charlotte pleaded.

'Stick it out for another hour or so, and you'll be wishing you could stay up here forever,' the aëronaut told her.

The police sweep had passed through the immediate area – a couple of the officers had even entered the copse, though they hadn't looked up – and was now receding into the distance.

The constables would probably still hear the shot, Sebastian George thought, but they might not recognize it as gunfire. And even if they did identify it for what it was, they would have only a vague idea of where it had emanated from.

Besides, once the balloon crashed down on to the Heath, the resulting pandemonium would command all their attention.

He was going to get away with it, he told himself.

Blackstone would suspect the truth, but what did that matter? He would have no proof – and *he* was not a personal friend of Sir Roderick Todd.

The balloon was easily in range now, and one shot was all it would take. He raised the rifle to his shoulder, and placed his eye against the telescopic sight. Satisfied that everything was as it should be, he began to gently squeeze the trigger.

The pain in his leg was as sudden as it was instantly unbearable. It felt as if he were on fire – from the tips of his toes right up to his hip.

The sound of the rifle exploded in his ear, but he knew that his shot had gone wild of the mark. Knew, too, this was the *second* explosion he had heard, and that the *first* was the source of all the agony he was now experiencing.

188

He lost his grip on the rifle, then his hold on the tree, and then he was falling ... falling.

He hit the ground with as heavy a thud as a fat man should expect. The impact knocked the wind right out of him, but the pain which followed was strangely reassuring, since, as long as he was hurting so much all over, he couldn't possibly be dead.

He was lying on his back, and when he turned his head to the side, all he could see was the base of a couple of trees and a pair of boots.

'Rather unfortunately for you, I've had dealings with a few snipers in the past,' said a voice that he recognized as belonging to Blackstone. 'It was when I was serving in India. They hid in all sorts of places, those buggers, but trees were always one of their favourites.'

It was a hospital bed in a hospital ward, but there were thick bars on the windows and his right wrist was manacled to the bedpost. So it didn't take a brilliant intellect to work out that this particular bed and ward were in a prison, Sebastian George thought sourly.

He became aware that someone was standing next to the bed, and turned to find it was Blackstone.

'Come to gloat, Inspector?' he asked, with some bitterness.

'No, I haven't, as a matter of fact,' Blackstone said.

'Then why are you here?'

'To charge with you with the attempted murders of Miss Charlotte Devaraux and Mr Charles Whitney.'

'Charles Whitney? Who the hell's he?'

'He was the pilot of the hot air balloon you hired. If you'd succeeded in shooting it down, he'd have died too, you know.'

'My leg hurts,' George complained.

'I'd be surprised if it didn't,' Blackstone said indifferently. 'But, for all the pain it's causing, it's still not much more than a flesh wound, and you'll survive it well enough.' He paused for a moment. 'I take it Charlotte Devaraux is heavily insured, is she?'

'It's a foolish theatre manager who doesn't take out heavy insurance on his leading actress,' George said.

'So her death would have achieved two objectives, as far

as you were concerned. It would have prevented her from persuading Lord Bixendale to get your father released from the lunatic asylum, and it would have made you rich enough not to need Bixendale's money any more.'

Sebastian George grinned ironically. 'I did whatever I did in the cause of my art,' he said.

'Balls! You did it because you liked the life you were leading, and you wanted to keep on leading it,' Blackstone contradicted him. 'You've done all kinds of things to ensure that – including giving Tamara Simmons roles in your plays that she had neither the experience nor the talent to handle.'

'She'd earned those roles,' George said.

'Indeed she had,' Blackstone agreed. 'If she hadn't pretended to be Martin Swinburne's mistress, the company would have been in deep trouble long before now.'

'Are the attempted murders the only thing you're charging me with?' George asked.

Blackstone thought about it. 'I suppose I could throw in "disturbing the peace", if I was of a mind to, but given the heavy sentence you'll be facing anyway, there really doesn't seem to be much point in that.'

'I'm surprised you're not also charging me with the Swinburne and Kirkpatrick murders,' Sebastian George said. 'That's what I would do, if I were in your position.'

'I'm sure you would – but don't judge everybody else by your own miserable standards,' Blackstone said mildly. 'Besides, we don't know if Martin Swinburne *was* murdered. We'll probably *never* know now, since the only person who could have cleared that up, one way or the other, is also dead. And as for William Kirkpatrick's murder, well, frankly, Mr George, I really don't think you're clever enough to have planned it.'

'I resent that!' Sebastian George said angrily.

'Do you?' Blackstone asked. 'You've no grounds for resentment, you know. Kirkpatrick's murder was so much more subtle than yours. It had a finesse about it which your crude effort was totally lacking in.'

'Perhaps if I'd had more time to think about how to kill Charlotte—' Sebastian George began.

'You're not nearly as bright as you think you are, Mr George,' Blackstone interrupted him. 'If you had have been, you'd have made your own way in the world, instead of climbing to where you are – or rather, where you *were* – on the backs of better men than you are.'

'You *know* who killed William Kirkpatrick, don't you, Blackstone?' Sebastian George asked.

'Yes, as a matter of fact, I do.'

'Then who was it?'

Blackstone smiled. 'You're looking very tired, Mr George,' he said. 'I don't want to weigh you down with any more details.'

'Tell me who it was, you bastard!' George screamed, as Blackstone walked towards the door.

'When you're feeling better, you can read all about it in the papers,' Blackstone promised. Then a look of mock-regret came to his face. 'Oh, I forgot,' he said, 'they don't allow you newspapers in prison, do they?'

Twenty-Six

The queue outside the George Theatre stretched right down the street. And it would have been even longer, Blackstone thought as he climbed out of the Hansom cab, if the news had already broken that Sebastian George had been arrested. For while Charlotte Devaraux had been a terrific draw when she was only known as the actress who had killed a man on stage, how many more people would be clamouring to see her when they learned that her own boss had attempted to murder her – in a most spectacular way – on Hampstead Heath?

Yes, on the face of it, the production had a golden future, with the public clamouring to buy tickets and backers falling over each other in their efforts to invest. But such a golden future was no more than an illusion. The final performance had already been given. The play had thrilled for the last time.

'I never liked that Sebastian George,' Spotty Wilberforce said as he let Blackstone in through the stage door. 'When Miss

Devaraux told me he'd been arrested, I wasn't the least bit surprised.'

'Weren't you?' Blackstone asked.

'I was not. Well, that's only natural, isn't it? I know everything that goes on in this theatre. I *see* everything that goes on is this theatre. And I had him marked down as a wrong 'un from the start.'

'Why didn't you tell me that the first time we talked about him?' Blackstone asked, barely managing to hide his smile. 'It would have saved me a great deal of time.'

For a moment, Wilberforce looked lost for an answer. Then he rallied. 'Ah well, you see, Sam, I thought it would be much better if you found out for yourself,' he said.

'And why didn't you tell me that Martin Swinburne's death was no accident?' Blackstone wondered.

'No accident?' Wilberforce asked.

'No accident,' Blackstone repeated.

'Well, to tell you the truth, I wasn't completely sure about that,' Wilberforce said. 'And I didn't want to go spreading suspicions without absolute proof, now did I?'

'Of course you didn't,' Blackstone agreed. 'You said you'd spoken to Miss Devaraux, didn't you, Thomas?'

'That's right. She never passes my office without stopping to have a word. She relies on me, you see.'

'As do we all,' Blackstone said. 'Is she still in the theatre?'

'Yes, she most certainly is. Matter of fact, she's in her dressing room, making herself beautiful.'

'Not that she needs any artificial help,' Blackstone said.

'She certainly doesn't,' Wilberforce agreed. A leer came to his blotched face. 'I've fancied bedding her for years. I expect that you've had similar thoughts yourself, Sam – not that either of us would have much of a chance.'

'I think you'd have more of a chance than I would,' Blackstone said.

'Oh, I don't know about that,' Wilberforce contradicted him. 'I think you might well give me a fair run for my money.'

The door to Charlotte Devaraux's dressing room was slightly ajar, and from the corridor Blackstone could see that she was sitting in front of her mirror, going through the daily ritual of examining her face for signs of the march of time.

She need not have bothered to do that, he thought. Even after the horrendous ordeal she had undergone, she was still one of the most ravishing creatures he had ever seen.

As he stepped through the door, Charlotte saw his reflection in the mirror. She stood up – so quickly that her stool fell over – then she rushed across the room, and flung her arms around him.

'Thank you, Sam,' she said, before burying her face in his chest. 'Thank you for saving my life.'

He gently untangled her. 'I'd like you to sit down again, please, Charlotte,' he said.

'Sit down again? Why should I do that, when all I really want is to hug you so tightly it will almost squeeze the life out of you?'

'There's something we need to talk about, and it will be easier if you're sitting down,' Blackstone said.

Charlotte smiled. 'How serious you can sound when you want to,' she said, looking up into his eyes. 'Just like a real policeman.'

'I am a real policeman,' he reminded her. 'And it's a serious matter that we have to discuss.'

She nodded, as if she understood completely.

'You're frightened, aren't you?' she asked. 'You're terrified by the passion we aroused in each other last night, and you're using your job as a shield to protect you from it happening again.'

'Charlotte . . .' Blackstone said.

'If you wish to pretend that it meant nothing, then that's your right, and I won't complain,' Charlotte told him. 'But if you feel as I do – that you finally discovered love again, and are willing to embrace it, rather than run from it – then you'll make me the happiest woman in the world.'

'There really are things we need to talk about, Charlotte,' Blackstone said quietly.

'And I know what they are. You want to tell me that a man like you is not willing to share me with Lord Bixendale. I understand that, Sam. Did you think that I wouldn't? Well, I couldn't bear it either. So I promise you, here and now, that I will see no more of him.'

'I'm not here to talk about what happened between us in your apartment last night, and I'm not here to talk about whether or not we have a future together,' Blackstone said firmly.

'Then why are you here?'

'To discuss the murder of William Kirkpatrick.'

Charlotte raised her hand, and smoothed down her hair.

'I see,' she said, a little coldly and a little disappointedly. 'Then perhaps you're right, and I *had* better sit down.'

'You told me you'd only ever loved one man,' Blackstone said, when she had returned to her stool. 'What was his name?'

'I thought you said that wanted to discuss William Kirkpatrick's murder,' Charlotte said evasively.

'His name, Charlotte!'

'I can't see what his name has to do with you – or with anyone else, for that matter.'

'It was Martin Swinburne, wasn't it?'

Charlotte looked down at the floor. 'Yes, it was Martin,' she admitted in a whisper.

'You were the woman who he and William Kirkpatrick fought over, not Tamara Simmons. But that had to be kept secret – because if Lord Bixendale had learned you had another lover apart from him, he would have stopped funding the theatre immediately. So Tamara Simmons pretended that Swinburne had been *her* lover, and was rewarded for it by being given bigger roles to play than she'd ever had before.'

'That's quite true, but—'

'When Martin Swinburne was killed, you probably told yourself it was an accident, but there must have been a small part of you, at least, which suspected that William Kirkpatrick had arranged it.'

'I couldn't see that God would be so unjust as to take from me the love of my life in such a terrible way,' Charlotte confessed.

'I'm guessing the next bit,' Blackstone admitted, 'but it's the only explanation that fits the facts.' He paused for a moment. 'Once Swinburne was out of the way, Kirkpatrick thought you would fall into *his* arms.'

Charlotte Devaraux nodded. 'I think he really did love me, you know. Perhaps even more than Martin did.'

'But you didn't fall into his arms. In fact, you wanted nothing

194

at all to do with him. And then, one night, he said something he shouldn't have.'

William Kirkpatrick is clearly intoxicated when he accosts Charlotte at the stage door after the evening's performance.
'Come home with me, Charlotte,' he begs.
'What would be the point of that?' Charlotte asks disgustedly. 'Do you want to make love to me?'
'Yes. It's all I've ever wanted.'
'Even if I'd agree, you're too drunk to take advantage of it.'
'Why are you so cruel?' Kirkpatrick asks plaintively.
'Why are you so persistent?' Charlotte counters.
'It's months since Martin died.'
'And I'm still mourning *him.'*
'He didn't care for you as much as I do. He wouldn't have killed for you, would he?'
'Of course he wouldn't. And neither would you.'
'I did *kill for you.'*

'I'm guessing all this, you understand, but I think it's pretty close to the truth, isn't it?' Blackstone asked.

Charlotte Devaraux said nothing.

'Of course,' Blackstone continued, 'in the morning, when he'd had time to calm down – or sober up – he denied he'd ever meant it. He probably claimed it had been no more than a joke, which he now realized was in very bad taste. But you knew that he'd been speaking no more than the truth, didn't you, Charlotte? And that's why you decided to kill him.'

'Why *I* decided to kill him?' Charlotte asked, horrified. 'Why I decided to *kill* him?'

Blackstone shook his head sadly. 'You're a good actress, Charlotte,' he said, 'but even *you* are not that good.'

'It's preposterous!' Charlotte said.

'You might even have got away with it, if you'd known a little more about the poison you were using. But all you *did* know – all you'd learned on the George Theatre Company's tour of South America – was that the toxin from the poison arrow frog was both quick-acting and lethal.'

'I don't know what you're talking about,' Charlotte said.

'Creating the little old man was a touch of brilliance,'

Blackstone told her. 'From the moment I'd talked to Thaddeus George – and seen the resemblance between him and the suspect – I began to think that the man I was looking for was wearing a disguise, and must have modelled his disguise on Thaddeus. But it never occurred to me – at least, not until everything else had fallen into place – that he might not be a *man* at all.'

'Lunacy,' Charlotte said.

'But the touch I admire almost *more* than I admire the disguise is what you did with the knife,' Blackstone continued. 'A lesser woman than you would have taken the knife she'd commissioned, and substituted it for the fake one on the prop table. But there was always a risk you'd be seen doing that, and that people would begin to wonder why the principal actress would bother to go to the props room at all, when she had a boy to do all her running around for her. Then you suddenly realized there was no need to take such a risk at all.'

'You make me seem very clever,' Charlotte said.

'You were very clever,' Blackstone replied. 'You see, you understood that all you actually needed to do was create the circumstances in which the knife *could have* been substituted. And that's exactly what you did. The props master was called away to answer the phone call which you'd paid the operator to make, so the knives could easily have been swapped then. But they weren't. The knife that young Horace brought to you was the *fake* one that you normally used on stage. The real one, the one you'd commissioned, was in your dressing room all along.'

'You couldn't possibly prove that,' Charlotte told him.

'Maybe not,' Blackstone agreed, 'but I think I'd have more than a fighting chance at it. You see, now he's had both knives in his hands for the first time, Horace *knows* it was the fake one that he handled on the night of the murder, and a smart lad like him would make a very credible witness at your trial. But I don't actually need to prove anything about the knife, only about the poison. And that's where Dr Carr comes in.'

'Dr Carr?'

'You've never met her, of course – and I don't think you'd like her if you did. But she's a very clever woman – perhaps even cleverer than you – and she's established just how long the poison takes to act under all kinds of different conditions.'

196

'Am I supposed to be impressed by that?'

'Yes, I think you should be, because it's that particular finding which points the finger of guilt conclusively at you.'

'Go on,' Charlotte Devaraux said, and there was now a hint of foreboding in her voice.

'To have the effect that the toxin did have on William Kirkpatrick – to kill him almost immediately – it must have been smeared on the blade only shortly before he was stabbed. In other words, the blade had to have been poisoned in your dressing room, just before the third act. Only three people could have done it – Horace, your dresser, or you. Would you like me to arrest one of the others?'

Charlotte shook her head. 'No, of course I wouldn't. That boy's had enough trouble in his life already without having to go through that. And nobody would believe poor little Madge could be a killer, even if she said she was.'

'So you'll confess?'

Charlotte nodded. 'There doesn't seem to be much point in doing anything else now, does there?'

'Why did you decide to kill Kirkpatrick in the theatre, with an audience watching?' Blackstone asked.

'Oh, there were any number of reasons for that decision,' Charlotte said, almost airily.

'Why don't you tell me what they were?' Blackstone suggested.

Charlotte raised her hand in the air, as if she were holding the dagger.

'With this knife, I will have my revenge for the evil you have visited on me,' she said in her Lady Wilton voice. She paused, and smiled. 'I wanted William Kirkpatrick to die on stage, just as his victim, poor Martin, had. And I wanted to be there when he died – so that I could see the look of fear in his eyes; so I could tell him, with the look in *my* eyes, that he was dying by my hand.'

'And you think that he really did understand that, do you?' Blackstone wondered.

'Oh yes,' Charlotte replied. 'A good actress can convey a thousand words with just one flash of her eyes, and, as you've admitted yourself, I am a *very* good actress.'

'What were your other reasons for choosing to kill him in that way?' Blackstone asked.

'I thought it would put me above suspicion. I thought the police would devote all their efforts to finding out who duped me into killing Kirkpatrick, rather than wondering if I had been duped at all.'

'And it nearly worked,' Blackstone admitted. 'In fact, for quite a while, it *did* work.'

'There is one more reason I chose that particular method,' Charlotte said, after a moment's hesitation. 'It is perhaps less laudable and more selfish than the others, but I still cannot deny that it exists.'

'And that reason is that you *enjoyed* it!' Blackstone guessed.

'I don't think "enjoy" is quite the right word, Sam,' Charlotte told him seriously. 'I have never enjoyed my work *as a process*. A potter may get great pleasure out of creating a pot, but I have never experienced that same pleasure in creating a role. Nor did I experience it in planning the murder.'

'It's the effect, once the work is finished, that you care about,' Blackstone said, with a sudden flash of insight.

'I knew you'd understand,' Charlotte told him. 'I live to see my audiences react. And my audience back stage that night – actors all – were completely taken in by the way I played the role of the innocent woman who had been tricked into killing. Which must mean, when you think about it, that it was the finest performance of my life.'

'Let's hope you can put up one that's just as good in front of a judge and jury,' Blackstone said.

'You still mean to arrest me?' Charlotte asked, shocked.

'I do.'

'Even though you know that I killed for love?'

'Yes.'

'And that the man I killed was nothing but a murderer himself?'

'I don't have any choice *but* to arrest you,' Blackstone said.

'Of course you do,' Charlotte said dismissively. 'We all have choices, if only we have the courage to cast aside the rules and conventions which this bourgeois little queen and her bourgeois little parliament have decided to impose on this bourgeois little society.'

'And which are enforced by bourgeois policemen and bourgeois courts,' Blackstone added.

'Exactly! But we could rise above all that. You and I could

leave this theatre – and this country – forever. Think about it, Sam! We could live on a tropical island – just the two of us. I would cook for you, and care for you, and do whatever you wanted me to do. I would do it all gladly, sacrificing my life to your pleasure. Because I do love you, Sam. You know that, don't you?'

Blackstone said nothing.

'You do know I love you, don't you?' Charlotte Devaraux repeated.

'I certainly believe you when you say it,' Blackstone admitted. 'But you're such a good actress that how would I *ever* know when you're telling the truth?'

Twenty-Seven

The morning after Charlotte Devaraux's arrest was the second time that Lord Bixendale had chosen to come to Blackstone's office – and on this occasion he looked no less resolved to get his own way than he had on his previous visit.

'I am told, Inspector Blackstone, that you have great concerns over the condition of Mr Thaddeus George, who is currently incarcerated in Bethlehem Hospital,' Bixendale said.

'That's right, I have,' Blackstone agreed. 'I'm always concerned when people are punished for things they didn't do.'

'These are concerns that I share,' Bixendale said. 'And you are quite right in your assessment of the situation – by all accounts, great wrongs have been done to the poor man.'

'Great wrongs in which you yourself played a major part,' Blackstone reminded him.

'I admit to having made certain mistakes in the past,' Lord Bixendale replied.

'You do?' Blackstone asked, glancing out of the window to see if, by any chance, the sky was falling down.

'I do. And I am more than willing to correct them. That is

199

why I have come to see you today – to assure you that I will do all within my power to have Mr George released from the asylum as soon as possible. Not only that, but, until he manages to get the theatre back on a sound financial footing by his own efforts, I am prepared to continue subsidizing him.'

'That's very generous of you,' Blackstone said, sounding far from impressed. 'Now let's see the other side of the coin.'

'The other side of the coin? I'm afraid I don't know what you're talking about.'

'Of course you do,' Blackstone said. 'You've offered me the bribe – and very smoothly, too. Now tell me what you want in return.'

'I think you're forgetting your place, my good man!' Bixendale said, clearly outraged.

'And I think you're forgetting that we're standing on the threshold of the twentieth century, and that it's getting much harder than it used to be for people like you to have people like me horsewhipped for what you consider to be their insolence,' Blackstone countered.

Lord Bixendale took a very deep breath. 'I didn't come here to fight with you, Inspector Blackstone,' he said. 'I did not even come here to ask for your active co-operation.'

'No?'

'Emphatically not. All I need from you is a simple guarantee of your compliance.'

'In what?'

'I require an undertaking from you that you are willing to stand to one side – and do or say nothing – while the necessary procedures are enacted. In truth, I do not even really *need* your assurances at all – though it will make things somewhat easier if you willing to give them.'

'What procedures are we talking about?' Blackstone wondered.

'Charlotte Devaraux will not stand trial for the murder of William Kirkpatrick. Instead she is to be released from prison, and confined to an institution for the criminally insane.'

'But she *isn't* insane,' Blackstone pointed out.

'Her doctors would, I think, disagree with you.'

'And are they the same two doctors who decided Thaddeus George *was* insane?'

'I will not dignify that question with an answer,' Lord Bixendale said haughtily.

'I'll bet you bloody won't,' Blackstone said.

'Even if she were not insane, should she really be punished for what she did?' Bixendale asked reasonably. 'The man she killed was a murderer, when all's said and done. If he'd been arrested and found guilty of his crime, he'd have been executed. Does it make a difference whether he was hanged or poisoned? It might be argued that poison is swifter and more merciful.'

'It might be argued that he wasn't a murderer at all – that he only said that he was in order to impress Charlotte with the depths of his love. But we'll never know now, will we, Lord Bixendale? Because Charlotte decided to take the law into her own hands.'

'I may not still be able to have you horsewhipped, but if you raise any objections to Charlotte's transfer, I will certainly see to it that your career is destroyed,' Bixendale said, with a harder edge entering his voice.

'I'll raise no objections,' Blackstone said. 'What would be the point? You have powerful friends and influence on your side, and all I have on mine is a belief that justice should apply to all equally. It would be no contest, would it?'

'None at all.' Lord Bixendale smiled. 'That being the case – and taking you at your word – I believe we have no more to say to each other.'

He stood up. For a moment it looked as if he might offer Blackstone his hand, then he simply turned and walked to the door.

'Might I be permitted to ask you a question before you leave?' the inspector said.

Bixendale turned again. 'I can see no harm in that, providing you can curb your customary insolence,' he said.

'I'll do my very best,' Blackstone promised. 'Where is Charlotte Devaraux going to be confined? In Bethlehem Hospital? Or is it to be the county lunatic asylum?'

'Bethlehem Hospital, as I believe you already know, does not cater for long-term illnesses of the kind she is suffering from,' Bixendale said. 'And as for the county lunatic asylum, that is certainly no place for a lady like Charlotte.'

'Then where . . . ?'

'She is to be entrusted to the care of the Bixendale Foundation for the Mentally Ill.'

'And where is this foundation located?'

'On my estate in Scotland. Charlotte's doctors think the fresh country air there will do her good.'

'Is it doing the other lunatics good?' Blackstone wondered. 'As a matter of interest, how many other lunatics are there?'

'The foundation is still in the very early stages of its development,' Bixendale said.

'How early?'

'It was only established as a legal entity this morning.'

'So it has no inmates at all?'

Bixendale smiled. 'Not as yet,' he admitted. 'But by tomorrow morning, it will certainly have at least one.'